WHEN
GRANDMA
CHASED THE
SPIRITS

Novels by Helen Gumienny Glowacki

When God Broke Grandma's Heart
When God Took Grandma Home
When Grandma Chased the Spirits
The Granddaughter and the Monkey Swing
Grandma's Little Book of Poetry: The Story of God's Plan of
Salvation
Abiding Faith, Hidden Treasure
And Then They Asked God

Why God Why Series by Helen Glowacki

To What Purpose?
Why God Why?
Why Trust Scripture?
What Should I Know About Life after Death And The
Coming Tribulation?
What Does God Want Me To Do *RIGHT NOW*?
Do The Little Sins REALLY Count?

Other non-fiction Books by Helen Glowacki

Politically Incorrect: The Get Some Gumption Bible Study
When Enough is Enough
What No One Is Telling You about Addictions
The Many Faces of Depression: How to be Happy
****

Authors Website: www.Helenglowacki.com

Face book: http://www.facebook.com/pages/The-
Grandmother-Series/155300907853909?ref=ts

WHEN GRANDMA CHASED THE SPIRITS

A NOVEL

HELEN GUMIENNY GLOWACKI

To order additional copies of this book:

Visit the author's website at:
www.helenglowacki.com

For wholesale or multiple copy information:

Send inquiry to helen@helenglowacki.com

Contents

Dedication

The books of The Grandma Series are dedicated to those who
lived their life in a way that allowed them to be a role model to others, to
shape lives and demonstrate how the word of God teaches us how much
God loves us, how to love Him back, and that through this love we
can even bridge the chasm of death.

For Lillian

BOOK REVIEWS

THE GRANDMA SERIES

From Dallas, Texas:

I have just read one of the most inspiring books I have read in a long time! The story and characters reveal real-life situations in a remarkable and inviting form. I am certain that such a riveting story can also serve as an effective supportive tool for pastoral and mental health counselors. Ms. Glowacki described the stages of grief and God's comforting plan in an extraordinary way and through characters that really grab the heart. She is an author I expect to see on the bestseller lists very soon and for many years to come. I look forward to the next books in her wonderful, inspiring series. A pleasure to read, a masterful idea, *When God Took Grandma Home* by Helen Gumienny Glowacki is filled with the most beautiful insight into God's plan for us!

> —Reverend Fred Krueger,
> retired Lutheran minister of twelve years and
> clinical social worker for twenty-six years

From Sea Cliff, New York:

Helen Gumienny Glowacki is a magnificent writer, who is truly able to weave a story that will make the reader become emotionally involved in the character's lives. It was a joy to read this book, and the reader will appreciate the strong Christian values portrayed therein. This book will certainly whet the appetite for the other books in the series. *When God Broke Grandma's Heart* by Helen Gumienny Glowacki is a certain bet to be a best seller.

> —Reverend Richard C. Freund, president,
> New Apostolic Church USA

Once again, Helen Gumienny Glowacki enthusiastically presents a scenario, which will delight readers and bring comfort to anyone who is grieving. This book, *When God Took Grandma Home*, will inspire all readers and give them a deeper insight into the afterlife. This book is a masterful portrayal of young people searching for the truth. It is sure to be a great success.

—Reverend Richard C. Freund, president,
New Apostolic Church USA

From Odenton, Maryland:

As a counselor to many who struggle with challenging circumstances in their lives, I found *When God Broke Grandma's Heart* an inspirational story of hope. Despite cruelty and betrayal from those she trusted, and the multiple adversities Grandma endured, she was able to find strength and understanding through her faith in and love of God. Helen Gumienny Glowacki beautifully portrays the phases that individuals move through and the transformation that can occur when one is able to let go of negative events in their past and strive towards the understanding that regardless of how unjust, none of the pain was for naught.

—Tammera L. Shelton, MS in psychology

From Clifton, New Jersey:

I am the wife of a retired minister. Many times during my husband's ministry I was aware that a parishioner was living through a difficult circumstance, but because of my husband's responsibilities to provide assistance and counseling, I was not always able to help in the matter. Helen Gumienny Glowacki's The Grandma Series are a wonderful way to provide help and support to someone in need when other avenues of communication are closed. These books are inspiring, uplifting, educational, and heartwarming. The characters are loving and believable and every story ends with a beautiful example of how God explains our pain, renews our hope, shows us the way out of our situation and creates a miracle for our lives. I love this series.

—Edith Stier, wife of a minister for forty-two years

From Brookfield, Wisconsin

"Wow! I've just finished reading the third book in this series of great novels and can't find words great enough to describe them. At a time when there are so many troubles in the world and so many people who suffer, these books are a real eye opener about God's plan of salvation and why bad things happen to good people. They remind me of Jim LaHaye and Jerry B. Jenkins "Left Behind Series". These books are a MUST READ!"

Ben Lodwick, Avid Reader

From Online Bookstore Websites: Reader Reviews

5 star rating: When God Broke Grandma's Heart: "This is a book written from the heart with such thoughtfulness and grace. The author provides the reader with a meaningful experience. The messages are gentle yet powerful to the soul even through experiencing grandma's struggles and grief throughout the novel. The author shares the ideas of strong belief in ourselves, carries our faith, and shelters us in times of need and guides us home. Transformation and courage are profound themes of this novel to find truth and faith within all of us. The reader will be captivated at the books end and will want to read what comes next. Thank you Grandma."

Debra Forman

5 star rating: When God Broke Grandma's Heart: "Fantastic! A must read for all generations."

A Reader

5 star rating: When God Broke Grandma's Heart: "Heartwarming! This book touched my heart. It is both heartwarming and very spiritual."

Debbie Espeland

5 star rating: When God Broke Grandma's Heart: "Remarkable for someone looking for answers! Found it

extremely inspirational and deeply moving. A fascinating storyteller with a real message."

5 star rating: When God Broke Grandma's Heart: "Wonderful, Inspirational! I enjoyed reading this book. It is well written . . . ."

5 star rating: When God Took Grandma Home: "A very captivating book, keeps you moved from the beginning".

Acknowledgments

To my husband, Wally, who lost me to computer, Bible, and concordance for long periods, made my computer behave, and painstakingly read and edited the manuscript;

To my children, Julie, Joe and daughter-in-law Deb; and grandchildren, David, Michelle, Scott and Samantha;

To Richard Levinson, whose kindness can never be repaid;

To new friends and old friends who prayed for me, made me keep trying, never doubted, and in so many wonderful ways gave me the greatest support: Barbara, Bob and Edith; Dina and Ferdie; Anna Mae and Fred; Jeanne and Duke; Lisa, Becky, Sue, Ruth, Debbie, Pat, Nancy, Mary, Janet, Bill, Dr. Jimmie Colson Jackson and Jackie and Ed; and to Ouida Schall and Pat Gerlipp for reading the first manuscript. Thank you.

To John Feldcamp and his staff, Lynnel Landerito, Tiffany Arranguez, Sweetie Guzman, Liana Smith, Kevin Desabelle, Sherry Elliot, Jackie Ford, Vanessa Marzo and John Sign and the many others who helped make the series a success.

To the ministers and deacons of the New Apostolic Church who diligently pray for me;

And most of all, to my Heavenly Father who guides my life, gives so much, loves so much, and made all this possible!

My Heartfelt And Humble Thanks

Note to the Reader

The King James Version (KJV) of the Bible, which is public domain in the United States, is used throughout the books of The Grandma Series. However, for further study, the author recommends the New King James Version (NKJV) of the Bible for easier reading and less usage of the old-world language while remaining true to the original text.

The books in The Grandma Series are works of fiction. References to real people, events, organizations, or locales are intended only to provide a sense of authenticity, and are used fictitiously. All other characters and all incidents and dialogue are drawn from the author's imagination and are not to be construed as real. Any resemblance to actual persons, living or dead, is entirely coincidental. No part of these books may be used or reproduced in any manner whatsoever without written permission except in the case of brief quotations embodied in critical articles and reviews.

This book contains a scriptural index. Instead of assembling this index according to the *Chicago Manual of Style*, I have put it together in a format I believe might be more useful to the reader. I have chosen key words that may highlight the readers' specific concern or interest, and under those words I have listed the scriptures that address those concerns. I believe that this index style may also better support a teaching program based on this book. I would love to hear your suggestions for making these scriptures easy to find and understand.

Message From The Author

When there seems no solution to our daily challenges nor a refuge from the worries they bring, fear and anxiety can become destructive to our lives. Sadly, this is not limited to adults. Children also suffer from fear and anxiety and often from a depression that robs them of a happy childhood and a productive life. This also inhibits their ability to learn and transition from child to adult with a good education and healthy self-esteem. This is so prevalent in our society that physicians now treat these conditions as a matter of course, usually with medications.

Because panic attacks, bouts of anxiety, and depression often begin with insecurities initiated by a failure in our relationships, even as children we may unconsciously learn to employ withdrawal, denial, aggression, or an almost manic activity to help us cope or feel safe. Our efforts to alleviate the suffering brought about by these conditions creates a vulnerability to the promise of the quick fix, the all-purpose Band-Aid that claims to put us back on track or take away the pain.

TV ads bombard us with the promise of a magical duct tape that will fix all troubles, all fears, and repair our sometimes irrevocably damaged relationships and sense of self. We spend millions of dollars on quick fixes and find our hopes dashed time and time again, increasing our mania and our anxiety.

With certain lifestyles and highly competitive jobs creating even more anxiety, we slowly begin to realize that we are no longer in control of our lives. Our challenges demand more time and energy than we have and many of our challenges impel us to look for shortcuts while we continue to set unrealistic and unimportant goals. Our true quest, however, is to overcome the fear and feel good again, but often, we don't know how to accomplish this.

Amazingly, scripture makes reference after reference to fear. God speaks to us through scripture about the pitfalls we will encounter in this world. He tells us we needn't be afraid if we follow a few simple guidelines. Thankfully, scripture also gives specific guarantees for our joy and protection. The guarantees God provides are exquisite. Yet few of us know this and fewer teach this to their children.

> *God is our refuge and strength, a very present help in trouble.*
> *Therefore will we not fear, though the earth be removed,*
> *and though the mountains be carried into the midst of the sea.*
>
> —Psalm 46:1

> *Blessed is the man that walketh not in the counsel of the ungodly,*
> *nor standeth in the way of sinners, nor sitteth in the seat of the scornful.*
> *But his delight is in the law of the LORD; and in*
> *his law doth he meditate day and night.*
> *And he shall be like a tree planted by the rivers of water,*
> *that bringeth forth his fruit in his season; his leaf also shall not wither;*
> *and whatsoever he doeth shall prosper.*
>
> —Psalm 1:1-3

In the first verse, God tells us not to fear for He is our refuge. And in the second verse, He says that if we seek His word and strive to do what He asks of us, He will prosper us. He wants us to know that within His words are found the warnings, directions, and promises necessary for us to survive in today's world. He wants to show us why our fear exists and how to rid ourselves of it. His desire is that we attain happiness here on earth as well as in the incredible future He has planned for us.

The word of God, as expressed in scripture, is a constant source of wonder in that it continues to address all areas of life, all situations, and all times. God's word has never and will never change, yet can be applied to new concerns that arise as times and circumstances change. When we encounter roadblocks to our endeavors, we experience anxiety, but God tells us He can alleviate our anxiety and provide for our safety and well-being. He also demonstrates that we can trust His help. All He asks is that we strive to learn His words and incorporate them into our lives. He wants to teach us; He wants to help us.

Further, to augment our understanding, God gives us insight into His nature and provision, not only through scripture, but also through what we observe every day in our environment. As we experience what He has created throughout nature and our universe, we learn that He takes great interest in form and balance, color and harmony. From every flower, every tree, and every unique snowflake, from the majesty of mountain and sea, we see a hand that knows and desires harmony, balance, design, beauty, and peace.

God provides us with a glimpse into the perfection He can create by allowing us to witness the interaction between the various elements surrounding us. In nature, He shows us how miraculously the sand of the beach and the water of the ocean work together to allow a mutually beneficial interaction, how the weather and our crops work in mutual harmony to create their bounty, how our bodies respond to a proper balance of nutrients for good health, even how there is a perfect harmony between an insect and the pollination of plants. We learn through these observations that a certain balance is required that only God can control. The book of Job asks question after question about who ultimately controls the earth, the atmosphere, and all things in the earth.

Dost thou know the balancings of the clouds, the wondrous works of him which is perfect in knowledge?

—Job 37:16

Who hath divided a watercourse for the overflowing of waters, or a way for the lightning of thunder?

—Job 38:25

Interestingly, scripture provides us with many passages where God clearly states the number of cubits and type of wood to be used for various structures. He designates what design He wants carved into that wood and addresses color, fabric, even curtains, further demonstrating His interest in design, harmony, proportion, and adornment. One of the most striking confirmations of this interest is recounted when God commissions King David to gather the supplies for and King Solomon to build the temple. All through the Bible, wherever God commissions a structure, we find these incredible details of design.

And the cedar . . . was carved with knops and open flowers.
—1 Kings 6:18

He made two cherubims of olive tree.
—1 Kings 6:23

And he overlaid the cherubims with gold.
—1 Kings 6:28

With a network and pomegranates all around . . . all of bronze.
—Jeremiah 52:22

And thou shalt make a covering for the tent of rams' skins dyed red . . .
thou shalt make boards . . . of shittim wood.
—Exodus 26:14, 15

And thou shalt make a candlestick of pure gold . . .
beaten work . . . his shaft, and his branches, his bowls,
his knops, and his flowers shall be of the same.
—Exodus 25:31

God also uses the word *peace* throughout scripture. This demonstrates that He is fully aware of our desire for peace and happiness. Since peace is a condition we subconsciously seek, this too is a perfect venue where our enemy can capture our attention while circumventing our natural caution. God explains that when we truly know Him by learning of Him through His words, we strengthen both our belief in Him and ultimately our complete trust in Him. When we do this we learn how to protect ourselves from our enemy and avoid the fear attached to his attacks.

Studying the word of God is fascinating. The more we seek to learn, the more God reveals to us. An amazing part of the miracle of the Bible is that what was written in scripture two thousand years ago applies to the problems we encounter today. It is the only real way to find peace and safety. God not only shows us what dangers we should watch for, but He also shows us how to live together, how to set the right example, and how to instruct our children. He gives us the armor with which to fight fear. He clearly and unequivocally promises wonderful rewards for doing this and promises us His protection. He gives the ultimate guarantees about our life and our home. This doesn't mean we won't have problems, but it does mean we will be brought through those problems, will be refined in the process, and will not need to fear the outcome when we do go through these difficulties.

When we know God, we can trust Him and let go of our fear. But in doing so, we must be aware of the dangers God so graciously warns us about which includes the spirits that serve our enemy, the ease with which we can be led astray, how fear can be used against us, and the incredible subtlety of our enemy. Our enemy is as subtle, tempting, and dangerous as He was when he presented the apple in the Garden of Eden. It is easy for us to forget that this powerful enemy still lurks today, more dangerous than ever, still the sly and enticing stalker who revels in the chaos of our daily lives. Armed with the knowledge that this enemy will seek to trap us in such a way, we need to look carefully at what dangers might exist in today's world.

God's first words of direction to us in the Ten Commandments warns us not to put any other gods before Him. The words of the First Commandment found in Exodus 20:2-3 tell us, *"I am the Lord thy God . . . Thou shalt have no other gods before Me."* As the first commandment given to Moses, it is clear that God placed this commandment first, above all the others on His list. Therefore, we can assume that it should reign in importance.

While I felt I understood the first six words of this commandment, the last eight words left me wishing for a list of what these "other gods" were. I felt that there must be more to these words than I could see on the surface because most of us believe that we have no others gods in our lives. However, when pressed, some might admit to spending an inordinate amount of time and energy, even occasionally sacrificing standards of integrity, in the quest to be financially secure. We may also understand how lust, power, fame, or beauty could become a powerful motivator in some lives. But these gods are easily recognized, and my heart told me that there was something more, something hidden, less easily defined. Satan rarely takes the obvious path.

When I began to consider various forms of idolatry, I was actively searching for one with a specific, subtle influence, one that promised to alleviate our fear and anxiety. Perhaps because of my background in interior design, I began to notice newspaper and magazine ads that had never caught my attention before. These ads promised harmony, peace, and well-being to whoever followed the practices of this "new" technique. These ads came from hair salons, gyms, housing developments, furniture stores, and even hotels. I also noticed that more and more decorating books and magazine articles featured this technique, espousing its incredibly practical and psychologically sound aspects and its promises for a foolproof method to attain a peaceful, harmonious environment. Its benefits were beginning to be touted by various newspaper columnists. This "new" technique was in fact the ancient art of Feng Shui, a strict form of interior design purported to bring peace, harmony and good fortune into the lives of its practitioners.

As I delved deeper into my research, I was fascinated by the subtlety of the enemy's hook and how simple, innocent, and practical another god can appear. Through this study of Feng Shui, I was again reminded that our enemy is a magnificent liar, making what he presents incredibly appealing and, on the surface, amazingly beneficial to our lives. He begins by providing us with an innocent resource that promises to help us solve our most difficult problems and which initially appears perfectly safe, helpful, practical, and logical.

Initially, I had understood and accepted many of the premises put forth in these ads and articles because they addressed simple, commonsense, practical and psychologically sound ideas. But as I studied, and the world of Feng Shui opened to me and fascinated me, by God's grace I also saw its terrible danger, its hidden tenets, its subtle temptation, and the power behind it.

Harmony, peace, and tranquility were words that suddenly stood out and I recognized how fitting they were for our present lifestyle, our level of stress, our fear, and our desire to create a private Bethany for ourselves. Through these simple words I found that even the innocent desire to decorate our homes or choose an environment for conducting our daily business allows the enemy access to us through his promises to provide us with peace and harmony. The ads told me that if I obtained a haircut, exercised, bought new furniture, selected a housing development, even purchased landscape supplies while in an environment where Feng Shui was practiced, I would obtain harmony, tranquility, peace, and good fortune, words which seem to have become a great enticement.

However, seeking harmony and good luck by decorating according to the tenets of Feng Shui or Vastu are dangers that scripture warns against. Innocent in premise, practical in application, touting common sense in thought, and a lack of clutter in presentation, Feng Shui and Vastu appear a perfect decorating choice for creating the refuge we need to calm our fears in today's world. But God warns of the power that lurks behind these practices and how they can move our trust away from Him and be used as tools to destroy our future with Him.

It is hoped that this novel will not only touch the hearts of those who currently seek more harmony in their lives or believe in good luck, or use Feng Shui or astrology to find their answers, but that this will also help those who have suffered in life and have developed an inordinate fear of the future. This is not a book that negates ancient studies and discoveries. Many of these studies and discoveries were and are today filled with information about nature and mathematics and certainly contain points of merit. This is why they can become an instrument that works so well for Satan. My hope is that this book can show you how the valuable work of ancient scholars has evolved to become an attractive playing field for those spirits that the Bible warns about. My hope is to highlight the dangers that God wants us to avoid and to show that almost everything good can be perverted into something that can harm us if we do not listen to what God tells us. God's word is our most potent protection.

The first novel in The Grandma Series, *When God Broke Grandma's Heart*, is the story of Grandma, depicting the various joys, difficulties, and traumas of her life and her spiritual growth as she turns more and more to God to lead her through the bad times. Through the injustices and betrayals she experiences, she learns to forgive. Eventually trusting God completely, she finally finds the peace she had always sought. The second novel of the series, *When God Took Grandma Home*, describes God's incredible plan for those who are burdened in life and seem to us to die too young or under unfair circumstances. It is a beautiful story that explains why some die young and the very important role God wants us to take when this occurs.

This third book of The Grandma Series, *When Grandma Chased the Spirits*, is a novel that addresses the subtlety of idolatry and how it can be the unseen and dangerous force hidden in many quick fixes offered in today's world that are purported to help us with our harried, time-restricted lives. This book also shows us why we are unable to see many of these seemingly marvelous options as a form of idolatry and how the word of God clearly warns us of the subtle and dangerous power that drives them. For many of the quick fixes so popular today and many that rely on ancient discoveries or commonsense practicality to support their premise, scripture tells us how our enemy so cleverly uses them to trap us. Interestingly, scripture never says that these practices do not work. If we understood this, we would be far more careful.

It is hoped that through this single subject, we can appreciate the importance of learning what God says so we can avoid many of the pitfalls (forms of idolatry) that our enemy creates for us. It is hoped that those who suffer the agony of fear, panic attacks, and anxiety can find the true peace God offers when we overcome that fear by trusting God.

As in all the books of The Grandma Series, woven into the story itself, the characters find ways to gain God's blessing and protection for their lives. Also, this book addresses not only many practical applications of Feng Shui but also the dangers of Feng Shui and its relationship to astrology, numerology, divination, symbolism, and good luck. Interspersed throughout are the scriptural verses that inform, inspire, and direct us in regard to discerning those spirits driving most of the quick fixes offered to us.

In this book, we embark on a wonderful journey where amazing promises and guarantees abound, where God is the ultimate interior designer and Noah and King Solomon His design apprentices. The story of Grandma's continued legacy begins with the new home that her granddaughter and the granddaughter's fiancé have recently purchased. We meet their new neighbors and walk a path of pain and discovery with them. We become familiar with the tenets of Feng Shui, Vastu, and various discoveries of the ancients and point out what is practical and what is dangerous. We will examine how certain objects gained the reputation of bringing us good luck.

As we continue, our path moves through a dark valley where we begin to see that there are powerful spirits that drive the practices of Feng Shui, Vastu, astrology, numerology, tarot, and other divination tools. Here we will examine the warnings scripture provides and what God says about these spirits. We then begin to leave the darkness of this valley to reach the beautiful light of God's word where we learn the amazing guarantees and promises that God gives. These promises are far better than the quick fixes and fads we would fall prey to if we did not understand that our enemy uses them to pervert and misplace our trust.

The journey continues as we learn what God asks of us in return for those gifts He wants to give us. Finally, our journey culminates with the ultimate quick fix: a guarantee from God that we can create our own Bethany, a place of replenishment to which we can escape the cares and concerns that we find in the world. I truly hope that this book can help you gain the knowledge that God's promises never fail, that His warnings are important to know and understand, and that He has the most gentle, loving, and beautiful heart we can ever imagine.

THE QUEST FOR HAPPINESS

I long to find my happiness yet seem to always turn
To futile quests not ending the pain with which I burn.
I work and labor daily with turmoil in my soul,
Aware so much is lacking in my life and in my goal.
I search for peace and harmony, looking for the way
To walk a path that brings me joy from how I live each day.
Yet nothing seems to work for me no matter how I try,
My heart is close to breaking as I hear my anguished sigh.
I need to know what drives me, what I really seek,
I'm tired now of walking through a life that seems so bleak.
I long to fill my emptiness, I long to feel fulfilled,
I long to find a peace filled life, so my fearful heart is stilled.
I long to find the answers to help my searching soul,
And quench this awful hunger through a higher, nobler goal.

Helen Gumienny Glowacki

Chapter One

THE NEIGHBORS

M ary awoke in the middle of the night, her head wet with sweat and her heart pounding with fear. It was the same nightmare she always had. She was, once again, a young girl walking to school. It was raining and she was wearing a rain parka over her head and shoulders, and clunky rubber galoshes over her shoes. She'd always loved walking in the rain, so that part of her dream hadn't been what had brought the fear and turned her dream into a nightmare.

In her dream, after walking a short distance Mary approached a large puddle and stepped up onto the curb to avoid the deeper water that could splash onto the calves of her legs. She wanted to prevent water from running down her legs into her socks and cause them to stay uncomfortably wet for most of the day.

As she balanced herself along the curb, carrying books in both arms under her rain parka, she suddenly slipped and knew she would end up walking through the puddle after all. The moment she felt her foot slip time stood still. The dream was always the same, always in slow motion from that point on, something she was watching happen.

The fear began as Mary looked down into the puddle and in the water saw the reflection of the trees that lined the street and the lampposts that lit the way at night. The sky was also reflected and from upside down the sky seemed to go on forever, be never ending, become a frightening abyss into which one could fall and from which one might never return.

Then came the realization that as her feet reached the puddle, there was no street under the water to stop her descent. Her body turned and she plummeted head first toward the endless abyss of reflected sky. It was the sensation of continuous falling, as if from a great height, at high speed that filled her with fear. It was the sense that she had no control over the fall or the acceleration, or of where her fall would bring her, and the sense that she was being hurled toward something sinister. It was this sense of evil and lack of control that turned her dream into a nightmare and brought the terrible fear and pounding heart that woke Mary.

Fully awake now, Mary looked at the clock and decided it was time for her to get up and make a pot of coffee. Kevin was beginning to stir and she knew that he too would soon be up and would look forward to their Saturday ritual of sharing their coffee time. Mary wouldn't tell Kevin about her dream because he would worry. It didn't come every night, only maybe every few weeks, and Mary had learned to live with it.

This morning Mary and Kevin would watch from their kitchen window to see if the young couple they had seen entering the house across the street every evening last week, would come again today. They wondered if the young couple would be moving into the house themselves or if they were investors, or perhaps people hired to work on the house for someone else. They both hoped the young couple might be their new neighbors.

Every Saturday, Mary and Kevin would start the day by making a regular pot of coffee but make their coffee time festive and reminiscent of their college weekends at the local coffeehouse, by adding a teaspoon of ground cinnamon, a square of rich dark chocolate, and two packets of stevia to each cup. These extras transported them back to Beeny Ben's Coffee House where they first realized they were in love.

There they had switched from another sugar substitute to stevia when they'd read that stevia was the healthiest calorie-free sugar substitute and the most natural. Mary added soy creamer to her coffee, but Kevin liked his coffee without cream. "More macho," he'd laugh, and flex his muscles. "Yeah, but what about the cinnamon and chocolate, huh, maybe not so macho?" Mary would retort. This morning, remembering, she hugged her "macho" man after placing his cup on the surface of the round table in the bay window of their kitchen where they would sit together and talk.

They were curious about the two cars that had appeared every weeknight except Wednesday at the house across the street. Both cars arrived around 6:30 p.m. and left about 10:00 p.m. This morning, however, only one of the cars appeared and Kevin and Mary wondered about the people who were coming so regularly. Were they investors, were they planning to move in, would they be looking for new friends, did they possibly share a similar philosophy about life? they wondered.

When the For Sale sign had gone up across the street, Mary and Kevin began hoping they would have neighbors who would become good friends. They didn't know the other neighbors very well except to wave hello and goodbye. The neighbors were always busy working or traveling and, being somewhat older than Kevin and Mary, seemed to have no interest in a closer relationship. Kevin and Mary wished for some good friends close by with whom they could share impromptu conversation and fellowship.

They lived on a pretty street in an established neighborhood with beautiful large older homes, some updated and elegant, others in need of updating with yards overgrown. They themselves had done a lot of work to whip their new home into shape. They had started by cutting back some of the huge shrubs, replacing others, edging the lawn, and creating some curving flowerbeds. Their efforts had made the house look more inviting and certainly more cared for right away. Inside the house they had added central air-conditioning, replaced the kitchen cabinets, counters, and appliances, and gutted the master bathroom. They loved what they had created and especially enjoyed the new kitchen with its hardwood floors, gleaming cabinets, and large bay window where they placed the kitchen table and chairs.

From their vantage point at the kitchen table they could look down the street from the three sides of the bay window and see the huge oak trees and lush plantings of their own property and also admire the old-world architecture of the houses across the street. The house they watched today needed lots of work, but its lines were magnificent and shouted its potential through its architectural detail, its setting among the huge old trees, and its placement at the top of the rise of the property.

As they spoke about the young couple they had seen entering and leaving the house all week, Mary said she thought the couple might be close in age to them, maybe a little younger, but close enough. She wondered aloud why all last week, the young woman, so very pretty and energetic, came in the one car and the tall wiry young man with sand-colored hair came in another car. Kevin thought that perhaps they drove to work in separate cars and came here directly from their workplace. This would explain the two cars. Today, however, they'd come together in one car.

As they talked and savored their coffee, they glanced out the window from time to time. Soon they saw both the young woman and tall young man come out of the house, walk back to the car to get what seemed to be a heavy cooler, and together carry it into the house. The couple then returned to the car for what looked like buckets of cleaning supplies and a third time for cans of paint. Finally on their fourth trip they carried a folding bridge table and two chairs into the house.

Mary and Kevin were excited by the prospect of new neighbors, especially a young couple that might be close in age to them. They laughed when they saw the table and chairs, remarking delightedly that it looked like the couple planned to stay. They themselves had moved into their house only a year before and were just completing their own renovations and redecorating. They had moved to this house because of Kevin's job transfer, coming from a rural area of Kentucky where they had grown up. They had dated since Mary was fifteen years old and Kevin was sixteen, then gone off to the same college.

Mary was very petite with hair as dark, shiny, and sleek as a newly chipped piece of blue-black coal. Her eyes were an exceptionally pale blue with a ring of black around the perimeter of the iris and a black center in the middle, giving her face an ethereal look. She had dimples too, not the round kind, but the kind that slanted about an inch along the sides of her cheeks. She wore very red lipstick, which contrasted brightly against her flawless and very pale and perfect ivory skin. She favored wearing deep red or yellow blouses over a long black skirt or black slacks and often wore a huge poncho over both. She disliked stockings and chose to wear socks, which were hidden inside boots, choosing ankle-height boots to wear with slacks and knee-high boots with her skirts. She always looked wonderful with her bright cheerful colors and unique style. She appeared quite fashionable even though she kept the same style over many years. The colors and clothing and bright red lipstick that she chose seemed to fit her perfectly.

Mary had a great personality too; she was smart and sassy and kind all at once, had a quick smile, and would reach out to touch an arm or shoulder to make contact and, in essence, to let the other person know she cared. It was a nice trait and made people warm to her. There was also something reticent about Mary, as if she could be two different personalities, one fun and outgoing, the other timid and withdrawn. There was an aura of uneasiness within her that you could somehow sense, yet never quite explain, that made one want to comfort her and at the same time be wary of approaching her when she was projecting this persona.

Kevin was muscular and stocky, with dark blond hair and light brown eyes. He was 5'10" to Mary's 5'0" but looked shorter because of his breadth. His hair was thinning, and he joked that it wasn't his hair he was losing, but his forehead that was growing. His happy face, instant grin, and bubbly personality made him handsome. He had a sort of jubilance about him that made people feel that everything was just right. He didn't realize it, but he literally beamed when he looked at Mary or spoke of her.

Kevin preferred wearing faded fitted jeans and pastel-colored plaid or striped shirts except when going to work. These casual clothes seemed to fit his personality and looked good on his strong, fit body. He wore a suit and tie to work, but while appearing more formal, his happy face, instant smile, and warm personality brought to mind his casual and fun side again.

Kevin found good in everything and everyone, so people naturally liked him because he made them feel instantly accepted. He had a great laugh and eyes that lit up his face when he smiled. He was kind and compassionate and liked to be with other people. Kevin adored Mary, and it showed, and after knowing them for a while people often turned to look at his face when Mary walked into the room. And they envied Mary for this.

They had been married for eight years, marrying while in their junior year of college and living in a tiny studio apartment, both working part time to make ends meet until they graduated three years later. When they left school they worked for two years in their college town before deciding to change jobs and buy their first house back in Florena, Kentucky, close to where their family lived. Last year, they moved from Kentucky to this house because Kevin had been given an excellent promotion at work that required their relocation. Kevin thought it would be a good experience for them and secretly hoped that Mary, in this new environment and beautiful old home, would find the happiness that was eluding her, perhaps by leaving the place where Mary had suffered so much would help her. And maybe here, Kevin hoped, they would finally be ready to start a family. Kevin wanted children. He was thirty years old now, established in a good career, and had a large home that could easily accommodate children and visiting family. He was ready.

Kevin had been working as a system analyst and in his new job would head up the department that would monitor the security of his company's computer systems. He loved his job and the challenges he faced and conquered each day. He had handpicked his team, trained them in his own efficient way of working, and was pleased by how well they all got along. He was especially pleased that his boss seemed to like his ideas and the progress he'd made.

Mary was an artist and worked at a studio where she did mostly graphic design. She enjoyed everyone at work and liked listening to the other employees as they talked at lunch, but she never really felt a part of the group, any group. She always felt . . . different somehow, as if she just didn't belong. She couldn't seem to chatter as everyone else did and couldn't seem to muster the same degree of interest in some of the things the others enjoyed talking about. She loved the fact that on occasion she could work from home and not have to go into the office.

But, sometimes Mary felt terribly alone, not lonely exactly, as much as alone and separate while listening to everyone's tales of life and experiences. She felt as if she was perched near the others yet could not be seen nor be a part of them. She didn't know why she felt this way. She thought that perhaps she was what people termed "a loner" and would never have that special girl-talk relationship that other women seemed to have. She'd wished for this for most of her life, but it had never come. She knew she was lonely, too, but she didn't understand why it seemed such an internal and personal experience that couldn't really be explained or fixed. She'd ask herself why someone could feel lonely in a room full of people, even attentive accepting people.

Mary secretly longed for the day when she would leave her job, stay at home, and paint. She hoped that when they had a child and she no longer worked, she would turn the second floor of their carriage house into a studio with skylights and there she would find refuge. In her child she would find someone she would always be able to trust and who would always be her friend. She knew that this wasn't right, that a mother shouldn't pressure her child to be her friend, but somehow it was just something she thought she needed and wanted.

Kevin worried about Mary. He knew that no matter how hard she tried, she never seemed to find what he described as "simple joy" in each day, nor in the people that entered that day. He knew she had experienced an inordinate amount of emotional pain in her early life and wished he could make those experiences disappear. He often found himself wishing that he would see Mary truly happy. But when he would ask her about her feelings, when he tried to talk with her, she said she was happy and would tell him that it was just that she was not able to express herself as openly as he did. This was frustrating to him, but he knew from past experience that if he kept going with this line of talk, she would get upset and feel even more insecure.

He knew she loved him, and he adored her. He knew they both loved their new home and had great expectations for their future, yet he still worried about Mary, still wondered if she meant what she said. He did not believe she had truly laid aside the old fears and felt strongly that someday, if not dealt with, these fears would come back to harm her, and maybe him. She still carried her trauma. She thought she hid it from him, but she didn't. He knew it was still there and worried that it would always be there.

Kevin was delighted to think that a young couple might be moving into the house across the street. Mary needed a friend. And so, with Mary's observation about the couple arriving again at the house, he suggested they pack a scrumptious little picnic lunch and go over to visit the young couple and welcome them to the neighborhood. Initially, Mary seemed delighted with the idea. But then Mary said that she thought they should wait until the following Saturday to plan the picnic lunch so they could have time to prepare and to bring a little housewarming gift with them . . . perhaps an indoor potted plant in a pretty bowl. Kevin knew that Mary's fear had surfaced again but accepted the week's delay because Mary had committed to a date and she always kept her commitments to him.

On Thursday evening, they took time to make their plans for what they would buy and what time they would walk across the street with their surprise. They planned that Mary would shop for what she needed on Friday and they would be ready to meet their new neighbors on Saturday. Kevin was pleased that Mary finally seemed enthusiastic about meeting the new couple.

On Friday after work, Mary drove to a popular market near their home to shop. The market boasted many outside tables around the exterior perimeter of its ancient dark red brick walls that were filled with everything from wallets and jewelry to freshly picked corn and homemade jars of jam. The block-square market, surrounded by sidewalks and huge oak trees towering over the building and across the narrow street, beckoned the buyer inside where there were little wooden dividers surrounding stalls and refrigerated cases filled with a huge variety of fresh produce, cooked foods, fresh meats and fish, and wondrous desserts. The atmosphere was charged with the exquisite smells of homemade breads and pizza and cooked sausage. There were also stalls with wall racks and tables filled with handmade clothing, craft items, magnificent cut flowers, elaborate hand-fashioned bric-a-brac, or potted plants. It was a fun place to shop.

Mary purchased a big tub of homemade potato salad, the kind where you could see the red skins of the potatoes, the small chunks of diced onions, and the thick creamy coating through the container. She also bought a huge loaf of braided French bread, crispy on the outside and soft on the inside, and asked how to preserve its perfect freshness until tomorrow. Then she purchased some wonderful deli meats, choosing turkey and roast beef, and some cheese, finally settling on thinly sliced muenster and a triangular-cut piece of brie in case she decided to leave some snacks with her new neighbors too. She bought fresh tomatoes so large that one slice would fill a sandwich-sized piece of bread. She also bought dill pickles, potato chips, crackers for the brie, and two bottles of exotic fruit-flavored white Zinfandel wine. After carrying her precious cargo to the car and with her head still spinning with plans for the lunch she would bring across the street the next morning, she returned to the market to purchase the potted plant that she thought would make a nice gift for the new couple.

Mary was amazed at how happy she suddenly felt. She realized that she hadn't felt this way in a very long time. She wondered why this nice feeling had come upon her so unexpectedly and wondered if it was just a feeling of hope. Perhaps it was the hope that she would find someone she could relate to, someone who wanted to be her friend as much as she wanted to be her friend, someone she could eventually trust with her fears and her feelings, maybe even someone who could teach her what was wrong in her life. Mary hated feeling so needy, but she knew the truth: she longed for a friend, just the right friend. She longed to be free of her fear and be as "normal" as she thought everyone else was.

Often Mary would try to analyze why she felt so different than everyone else and why she was always reticent around others. She asked herself if it was because she was afraid to trust anyone after what happened to her so many years before or if she was really afraid that they would judge her harshly if they knew the truth. She wanted to change, wanted this sadness to go away, and longed for a real true, loyal friend. But then she thought maybe it wasn't a good thing to want something so much. Maybe it wasn't right to want only that perfect friend who would understand her and fill her expectations. Life was, after all, filled with so much pain and so much disappointment, and to want something badly only set you up for disappointment. Intellectually, Mary understood that no one was perfect and her longing for that perfect friend was unrealistic. She had her faults and would want a friend to accept them, so why couldn't she overlook some of the things she saw in others? She hated the fact that she always seemed to have such crazy thoughts and a constant worry about everything she did and wondered if everyone's thoughts ran rampant like this. She felt that psychologically she was a mess!

Maybe it was better to keep apart, stay alone, and just have Kevin and, someday in the future, her own children with whom to build a relationship. Suddenly a pang of fear hit her heart as she wondered how she could ever tell her children about her past. They might hate her. But she drove that thought away knowing it could destroy her and went back to the safety of denial that kept her going. She knew that her denial was her safety net and knew she was good at it. She had to be to survive!

As Mary drove home, she successfully purged the negative thoughts from her mind and decided that she would just see how it went with the new neighbors and not have any false hopes. She had always been able to sense immediately what seemed right for her and what did not. She wished she was more of a risk taker, but she had learned to rely on her gut instinct and knew that she would probably not take any risks if it didn't "feel" right. So, with this settled in her mind, and everything tucked again in the proper corner of her mind, she busied herself with her tasks and thought no more of it except for the parting thought that she was exactly like the character Scarlett O'Hara in the movie *Gone with the Wind.* Scarlett had said, "I'll think about that tomorrow," when confronted with a problem she couldn't solve.

Finally, Saturday morning came. Mary and Kevin watched eagerly out of their kitchen windows sipping their cup of special Saturday morning coffee, enjoying the aroma of cinnamon, the true kind, called *Cinnamomen verum* and grown only in Ceylon, which was supposed to control blood sugar and possibly ward off diabetes, and the flavor of chocolate purported to keep the happy hormones going in the brain. Soon they saw the car pull up across the street and saw the young couple emerge from the car and begin to carry lots of boxes into the house.

Sipping his coffee, Kevin could see Mary's sudden indecision. When she saw the couple arrive, Kevin sensed her desire to cancel their lunch plans and just stay at home, safe. Kevin quickly jumped to his feet, ran to Mary, pulled her up from her chair, and whirled her around the room commenting on how proud he was of her and how much he loved her and how much he was looking forward to meeting the new neighbors. He saw Mary's resolve not to disappoint him battle to the forefront. He breathed a silent sigh of relief. She smiled, kissed him, and sat down again to finish her coffee, this time planning their excursion to the neighbor's house, locking her fear away once again.

Mary and Kevin had previously decided that at 11:00 a.m. they would prepare the picnic lunch and at 11:30 they would walk across the street to meet their new neighbors. They thought that by going over before noon, they would intercept the neighbors from going out to buy lunch or begin eating something they had on hand.

Kevin was excited. He hoped they would make two new friends and hoped that Mary would open up when she found someone whose company she could enjoy. But he could see that as they prepared the lunch, Mary was nervous. He knew she was struggling with her feelings, struggling with wanting to find a good friend and the risks this might entail. He knew she was thinking that it was so much safer just to stay home and alone. Kevin understood more about Mary than Mary realized. And he often felt at a loss because she would not talk about her fears and would not seek counseling about it. But in the end, Kevin's enthusiasm about today's lunch encompassed Mary, and she forced herself to think of all the positives that could come from meeting their new neighbors. Finally, the hour came, and the time was right. With a nice picnic lunch and the lovely plant to present, they walked across the street with smiles lighting their faces. Kevin's smile was as always natural and open while Mary's smile was slightly forced and fearful, yet with an unbidden hope beginning to blossom in her heart.

Kevin bounded eagerly up the front steps and pressed the doorbell. Mary followed a little hesitantly. Minutes passed. They waited on the front steps, knowing someone was inside but not responding, suddenly concerned about whether they would be welcomed or not. When they realized that perhaps the bell didn't work, they knocked to no avail since the old carved oak door was too thick for sound to penetrate, and their knuckles quickly became tender. Finally, Kevin climbed through some pachysandra and shrubbery to the front window and knocked on the glass. He cupped his hands along the sides of his eyes and peered through the dirty panes as best he could. He could see the young man respond to his knock on the window, call to the woman, and begin walking to the front door. Kevin quickly made his way back to the porch to join Mary. When the door opened, Kevin was immediately impressed with the young man. As the door opened and the young man saw them, he smiled the kind of smile that made his eyes light up, extended his hand to Kevin, and said, "Hi, I'm Matt, welcome, come on in." He called to the young woman, who was suddenly on his heels in the doorway, "Honey, we have company." She wedged herself into the doorway next to him and extended her hand to Mary saying, "I'm Sarah, hi!"

They liked each other right away. Mary and Kevin felt welcome, and Matt and Sarah were delighted to learn that they had such caring neighbors. Matt and Sarah raved about the potted plant Mary handed to Sarah as she entered the house. Sarah said it was the first thing to enter the house that made it look like a home instead of a workshop. Then Sarah made them all laugh as she ran to different areas of the room with the plant in her hands, asking them whether the plant would look best with the paint cans, or the ladders, or perhaps among the bristly paintbrushes, and even placed it delicately in the midst of the cleaning paraphernalia. Sarah finally decided to place the plant on the corner of the window seat where it would get the light it needed and make the bridge table and chairs more festive to look at. Sarah's delight in the gift was evident and genuine, and that pleased Mary.

Mary liked how silly Sarah had been about the placement of the plant and felt that she was natural, open, not afraid to be herself, and not worried about what Kevin or Mary might think, and Mary envied her ease and liked Sarah for it. Sarah made her feel comfortable.

As Kevin explained that the basket they brought contained lunch for all four of them if they would be permitted to stay and eat with them, Matt laughed aloud saying, "Wow, what a great excuse to take a break from all this work. We'd love it if you would stay, and we thank you for doing such a nice thing." Mary, too, seemed to respond to their open and genuine enthusiasm and finally began to relax under the warmth of their welcome.

Matt pulled their two folding chairs and single folding table closer to the window seat so they could all sit around the table. For a moment, Sarah wondered if asking Matt to bless the food would be awkward, but then Matt jumped in, saying, "Wait, let's make this meal together and our newfound friendship even better by asking God for His blessing and thanking Him for what He has given us." Sarah felt so proud of him, proud that he hadn't hesitated as she had. Matt bowed his head and folded his hands, and the other three followed his lead, and Matt prayed.

Mary was surprised by the content of the prayer. She didn't know anyone who prayed as if they were speaking to a friend. *Most people,* she thought, *were hypocrites who prayed when there was a major catastrophe or emergency and not regularly or so easily.* She admired Matt for it but still didn't understand it. She also thought that it was courageous of him since he didn't know Kevin and Mary or how they would react. Matt didn't seem to care actually, as if it was just something he would do regardless of how Kevin and Mary felt. This also impressed Mary.

Mary's thoughts shifted as they began to attack the delicious lunch and toasted joy in their new homes and in new friendships. As they all settled down to eat, Matt began to explain about their wedding plans and that they planned to marry in six months and hoped to get the house done before the wedding. Matt and Sarah asked Kevin and Mary about their wedding, and they all were off again into an animated discussion about the myriad of chores connected to a wedding, laughing and concluding that it was all worth the effort in the end.

All four were amazed by how easily they talked together and how much instant rapport they felt with one another. They would start on a subject, and the conversation would just fly with ease, and each of them would have something to contribute as the others listened raptly. After the first hour together, they realized that their cheeks actually hurt from so much smiling and using their smile muscles more than they had for a long while, and they all agreed and laughed some more. It was a great few hours. And as they finished lunch, wishing their time together hadn't come to an end so soon, they planned another lunch together on the following Saturday, this time with Matt and Sarah providing the food.

Trying to leave was difficult because as they walked to the door, another lively discussion would pop up and they would stand in place for another fifteen minutes then try again to move toward the door. And when finally they parted and each couple found themselves alone again, they each remarked about how wonderful their first meeting went and how much they looked forward to a friendship between all four of them.

Chapter Two

THE PROMISE

Kevin and Mary had had a fight two days after they met Matt and Sarah for the first time. For those two days, they had both been talking excitedly about their new friends and about how much they were looking forward to seeing them again on Saturday. But now this fight had occurred, on the one night they always spent together on a kind of "date." It was the same fight they'd had many times. This time it started because Kevin's sister had sent them a beautiful gift that had really pulled on Kevin's heartstrings because of its personal touch. The gift was a beautiful storage trunk that Kevin's sister had painstakingly restored. She had painted it in the colors she knew Kevin and Mary had chosen for their new home and attached new hardware that she had personally chosen and installed to match their style of decorating.

Mary did not want to keep the trunk in the house. She said that the trunk had eight sharp corners, four across the top and four on the bottom, and the rules of Feng Shui decorating that said sharp corners on anything inside the house sent poison arrows at the inhabitants of that house, causing them bad luck. Kevin felt this was ridiculous and said that his sister's kindness should override any silly superstition.

But Mary was determined to ward off bad luck in any manner that she could. She was adamant. Kevin realized that what had happened to her in the past made her need to take drastic and sometimes ridiculous steps to prevent problems in the future, and usually Kevin could go along with Mary's crazy schemes, but this made him angry. This was a beautiful trunk that his sister had restored for them out of love! He would not give in this time.

Mary wouldn't back down either. She was afraid, afraid of the bad luck that the trunk might bring into her life. Deep in her heart Mary knew that Kevin wanted her to confront her past experiences, meet the fear head on, and somehow move past what had happened, but Mary was afraid of counseling, afraid of the rejection she felt sure would follow if she told anyone of her experiences. Why couldn't Kevin understand that she'd never get over what happened, and she needed to be sure that bad things didn't happen again, and this was why she needed to obtain the good luck? She was angry with Kevin for not recognizing how important this was to her. She was angry that he didn't take her fears as seriously as she felt he should.

Mary knew she'd hurt Kevin by rejecting the trunk his sister had painted, knew that his sister had put a lot of thought, love and effort into it, and had painted it to please them, but she also knew that she was afraid of the sharp corners, afraid of the poison darts and bad luck she had been told the sharp corners would bring. Every time she looked at the trunk, she could almost feel the poison darts pierce her layer of protection and mess with her psyche. Didn't Kevin understand that she could not give in, even if she wanted to? If he *really* loved her, he'd understand!

As the fight continued, and neither one would give in, Mary finally offered to phone her Feng Shui advisor to ask his advice about the trunk, hoping that maybe, with certain other precautions, he would find a way to let them keep it. Mary thought that perhaps there was a preventive measure that could be found to counteract the poison darts.

Kevin hated that she had to "get permission" for him to keep his sister's trunk, but rather than fight, he agreed to a postponement of the issue until Mary spoke with this guy who Kevin had disliked as soon as he heard that he demanded his clients call him "master." That had really irked him! But Mary said that this was how it was done when someone had the experience that this Feng Shui expert had. She pointed out that they had relied on this man for the decorating projects in their house for the past year, and most of his suggestions had worked out well. Kevin agreed that he liked the way the house looked, uncluttered, clean lines, colorful, practical. But this was pretty far-fetched. No trunk for fear of poison arrows? Ridiculous!

Finally, they agreed that Mary would phone the Feng Shui master the next morning, and in the meanwhile Kevin placed the beautiful trunk in the garage atop his workbench and placed a blanket over it to protect it. He was still fuming but hoped this would blow over once Mary obtained "permission" to put the trunk in the house. In fact, Kevin pointed out a perfect little area for it in the living room where it would really look nice and blend in well with everything else in that room. But Mary had simply and noncommittally said, "We'll see what the master says." Kevin muttered to himself that this Feng Shui guy had better say okay, had better find a way for them to keep the trunk, or there would be trouble.

That night, still irritated by the thought that Mary seemed to fall prey to the advice of someone Kevin thought somewhat off the wall, Kevin thought back to the first night that Mary had been introduced to Feng Shui. Shortly after they moved into this house, Mary had attended an art exhibit at the local library and, as she was leaving, noticed that there was a lecture in one of the library rooms about how to attract good things into one's life. Curious, she peeked into the room and saw some empty seats, and when the lecturer beckoned to her and motioned for her to come in, she took an empty seat and listened to the remainder of the lecture. Mary had been fascinated by the master's explanation that bad things in one's life were a part of the Karma that people are born with but that special precautions could be taken to ward off bad Karma and other causes of bad luck. And thus began Mary's foray into the world of Feng Shui.

Mary was fascinated by the promises of Feng Shui. She longed to be free of fear and wanted to believe she could control her life and prevent any further pain and suffering. She felt that she and Kevin planned to buy furniture for the new house and do some decorating anyway, so what harm could there be in utilizing this method of interior design? She also liked the minimalist look and lack of clutter that Feng Shui encouraged and thought that this alone should recommend its use to Kevin.

Before she left the library that evening, Mary had arranged for the Feng Shui master to come to their home the following Monday and evaluate what might be wrong with the house and learn what they needed to do to make everything safe. It would be costly, but she felt it would bring so much benefit to their lives that it would be well worth the expense. Mary realized she would have to figure a way to obtain Kevin's approval for the consultation fee. She probably shouldn't have committed to it until she spoke with Kevin but had gotten so excited by its promise of safety and good luck that she wanted to do it right away.

Kevin wasn't a happy camper. He had been surprised by Mary's dissertation about luck and Karma and, after listening carefully, still had no trust at all in this master's claims. But by the end of the evening, he had given in to Mary hoping that once she heard all the mumbo jumbo she'd see the truth and may even be more open to them talking to a qualified counselor about her fear, and what now seemed like an obsessive need for protection.

Kevin wasn't particularly religious, but he did believe that at all times God was in control of everything and that "luck" wasn't in God's vocabulary, so he felt that luck shouldn't be in his own vocabulary either. Suddenly Kevin realized that he didn't really know what religious beliefs Mary held, and this surprised him. He thought he knew her so well, and he was surprised that they'd never had that conversation in all the years they'd been together. Kevin wondered if perhaps they needed to find a church they could attend from which to adopt a philosophy and life direction that they could both embrace. Maybe this would help Mary, Kevin thought, help her deal with her fear and realize that God could protect her and that she wasn't the only person in the world that this had happened to. Kevin resolved to bring this subject up one day soon with Mary.

But Kevin eventually accepted Mary's desire to consult with the Feng Shui expert, and little by little their home changed to one with less clutter and with furniture relocated and certain colors assigned to certain rooms based on the function of the room. Kevin didn't really mind, though he never understood what Mary tried to explain about why a certain item, placement, or color would bring them good luck. It seemed harmless though, and Mary seemed happier and the house looked quite nice. That was all he needed, although every once in a while Kevin would wonder if he were too complacent about some of the things Mary seemed to need to quench her fears. This crazy Feng Shui stuff caused him to worry, and he would once again think they should find a church or a minister that would lead them to a philosophy that would bring God into their lives.

But now, with the trunk his sister had so painstakingly created for them at stake, Kevin pondered the fight and decided that tonight wasn't the time to bring it up again but determined to return to this tomorrow night after Mary spoke with this Feng Shui guy. Kevin liked to pick his fights, make them count for something, and refused to fight over something he deemed inconsequential because he liked peace and was a pacifist at heart. While this was an important issue, he decided to let it ride for now. After that he'd decide what action he'd take. But he was not going to let this go. It was too important to him. He wanted his sister's trunk in the house.

All day at work, even knowing that he should be concentrating on what he needed to do in his job, his mind kept wandering, kept going to Mary and her fears and how her fears affected their life together. He loved her with every ounce of his being, knowing her heart to be sweet and gentle and her fears well grounded. But he also knew that the past was keeping Mary from her fullest potential and thus it was keeping him from having a happy wife. He wanted this. Badly. He also sensed that seeking resolution now was very important to him and could even be crucial for Mary.

As the workday drew to an end, he realized that because Mary hadn't called him, it would probably follow that the Feng Shui master's news wouldn't be news that he was going to like.

Spontaneously, Kevin decided to search the Internet for some quick information about Feng Shui. Maybe he could find an alternate argument. At first glance, everything he viewed seemed based on what he already knew: that Feng Shui was a simple, flowing, uncluttered method of interior decorating. This is what Kevin originally believed and was content with. But opening another site, Kevin, for the first time, learned about the use of astrology, numerology, the magnetic pull of the earth, the exactly balanced components of the five elements, the opposing qualities of Yin and Yang, and thus the need for the never-ending, ongoing advice from a "master" to obtain the protection Feng Shui offered.

Kevin wasn't comfortable with the complexity of some of these ideas but couldn't spend any more time reading about it since he was at work. He quickly printed the material he'd just found, signed off the Internet, and refocused on work, thinking that at some other time, after learning how Mary responded to this Feng Shui master, he'd investigate further. The thought also came to his mind that his parents once told him that he, as the husband, was responsible for the spiritual well-being of his family, and that meant Mary. He hadn't really done this.

Soon after Kevin left for work that morning, Mary went to the library to search for information about Feng Shui. She found five books and brought them home with her hoping to skim them as quickly as she could to gain some insight both before she called the Feng Shui master and before Kevin came home from work. She needed to win this argument. She needed the protection Feng Shui promised.

Three of the books were mostly pictures of rooms that were beautifully yet minimally decorated, and Mary enjoyed these and learned some of the basic tenets about eliminating clutter and about the psychological benefits of not arranging seating that placed your back to an open doorway. She was comforted to feel once again that Feng Shui made sense, that it was actually based in common sense. Feeling better, she finally telephoned the Feng Shui expert to ask about the trunk Kevin's sister had sent them.

The Feng Shui master told Mary she had to keep the trunk out of her home or she would suffer the consequences of poison arrows. He'd said that the poison arrows would cause a sort of imbalanced flow in the body that would bring her bad luck in the form of difficult circumstances or bad health. Mary knew that Kevin would not believe this. It was even hard for her to believe. In fact, she felt that this would upset Kevin and push him past his usual acceptance of her desires. She decided not to call him at work but to try to read some of the other books in the hope of having a more logical explanation for not to keeping the trunk in the house.

The fourth book Mary examined spoke about a nine-section square called a Ba Qua with its star-shaped overlay, which was used to determine the placement of furniture. Mary had known that specific placement of the furniture was said to affect a specific area of one's life such as health, marriage, children, finances, etc. However, this book was more detailed and described things Mary hadn't known. Did the Feng Shui master have to make these charts for her house before telling her what to buy and how to arrange the furniture in her home? Is this why it was so costly? It did sound very complex and scientific.

Mary read on, learning that it was necessary to understand the specific ways to combine the elements of water, wood, earth, metal, and fire in each room so that a special balance of nature would be created within the home. She also read that there were three cycles of life each containing five steps that determined the timing of what happens in life. It seemed terribly complicated but at the same time seemed to work with nature and seemed to make sense.

Mary laid the fourth book aside for the moment and took up the fifth book. As she read she knew she could never show this one to Kevin. Mary considered Kevin somewhat religious, someone who believed in the help of angels and in the evil and power of Satan, and someone who revered and honored the sacraments and the attached blessing from God. He was usually easygoing, but when they married he'd been adamant about a church wedding and adamant about their commitment to what the sacrament of marriage meant. That had been the one time he'd really opened up about his religious beliefs. But while he seemed strong in his beliefs then, he didn't seem to care now. She liked it better the other way because she felt he would provide a stronger direction for their lives the other way.

The fifth book was thick with many pages filled with fine print and very few drawings, none that pertained to interior design. In essence, this book said that the practice of Feng Shui embraced the enlisting of spirits to help you and described the characteristics of these spirits who preferred to be called "helpers." The author said that helpers were not angels, are invisible, and must be given a free hand to direct one's life. It also stated that to benefit from the helpers, one must not think of himself as a sinner or as born with original sin as these thoughts result in poison arrows that will poison the nature of that person and prevent the helpers from helping. Mary did not know much about the Bible, but she did know that this was diametrically opposed to what the Bible taught. Kevin wouldn't like this. Mary felt a sudden fear.

Reading further, though not fully understanding, Mary read about another book, which was called the I Ching, that contained a series of hexagrams that were purported to help people avoid bad luck through its ability to provide predictions. She also read of the use of yarrow sticks and coins to toss. The way these fell indicated which hexagram to read, which in turn explained what one needed to do or beware of in the future. Fear clutched at her heart as Mary read that Feng Shui must be practiced precisely in order to obtain the benefits it promises and that if Feng Shui countermeasures are improperly used, anger from guardian deities will fall upon the user. Did this mean that if she did not do everything the Feng Shui master told her to do, bad luck would claim her? Her heart was beating so fast now from her fear that she could hardly breathe.

She skimmed the rest of the book voraciously and read about the animal calendar, astrology, numerology, and chants and how these are also used with Feng Shui when it is properly practiced. Mary was suddenly terrified and knew deep in her heart that Kevin would never allow her to continue with Feng Shui if he knew these things. She tried to rationalize that Feng Shui was an ancient and well-proven method, used by millions of people, and that she'd never read anything negative about it before.

Mary continued reading and learned about the huge corporate world employing Feng Shui experts for the design of their buildings and the placement of furniture and fountains, statues and walkways to attract wealth and happy, productive employees. She read names like Citibank, Bank of America, the Bank of Canada, Trump Tower, MGM Grand Hotel, the White Sox Stadium, the Budweiser Brewery, I. M. Pei's Bank of China, and the Forbidden City and thought, *So many successful business people couldn't be wrong, could they?* These corporations were rich. Their luck seemed to work for them, so why should she be afraid? What harm could there be in trying Feng Shui for a while to see if it worked?

Mary was exhausted. She put the books aside and went upstairs to lie down for a little while to quell her fears. She didn't like to hide anything from Kevin. Maybe this sudden, crazy fear about Feng Shui was silly. After all, she thought, so much of what she heard in the lecture at the library spoke about common sense and the avoidance of clutter and how this benefited one's life. How could common sense be wrong? If she didn't get too involved until she tested the waters of Feng Shui, wouldn't this be okay for her? Many people in many countries practiced Feng Shui, so it had to be okay. Mary's mind fell into denial again, and she pushed her concerns aside.

In the end, Mary decided not to tell Kevin any of the negatives she'd read about, only the positives. Maybe he would allow her the freedom to try it out for a little while longer. Mary made Kevin's favorite dinner, changed her clothes, put on her makeup, and planned to convince him to help her for just a little while to see if the Feng Shui really worked. She'd beg him if she had to.

Mary had a sudden inspiration and quickly phoned the Feng Shui master again. She told him that she wanted to convince Kevin that Feng Shui really worked and wondered if the master could promise some small change that Kevin would be able to recognize as coming from Feng Shui. The Feng Shui master asked Mary a string of questions about Kevin's health and business. He finally told Mary to place Kevin's desk in the home office at a 45-degree angle to the wall to allow for his desk chair to back up to the wall and thus face the door to the room. He also told her to put a box filled with coins somewhere near or in the northwest corner of the room and to put a cover over the computer at night.

With dinner cooking, Mary struggled to move the desk before Kevin arrived home. The office looked beautiful when she finished with it, and she was anxious to show Kevin, but only after he'd had dinner.

When Kevin came home from work that evening, they had a wonderful meal together, both holding back the dreaded subject of the trunk until after they had eaten. Then Mary told Kevin that she had a surprise for him and took him by the hand to his office. He was pleased by how nice the office looked, very pleasing to the eye, and he said that he really liked that he could see the door while he was at the desk. Mary asked him if he was willing to take a chance on something for just two weeks if it would be something that would make him happy, and he said that he would. Mary told him that according to the Feng Shui master, Kevin would receive an award or some sort of recognition or bonus at work within the next two weeks because of the placement of the furniture and a few accessories. Kevin silently thought it all hogwash, but because of the joy and hope he saw in Mary's eyes, he didn't say what he really thought and agreed to wait and see what happened in two weeks.

Kevin was sure that this promise of a promotion would show Mary that Feng Shui didn't work the way she thought it would. "All right," he said, "but we need to face the issue of the trunk, and you need to promise me that it will come into the house in two weeks if there is no special promotion or recognition during that time." Mary gladly agreed to these terms, relieved not to have to face the question of the trunk now. Kevin felt better too and believed that in the long run, Mary would finally see the truth. He could wait two more weeks.

A few days later, their fight behind them, Mary and Kevin readied themselves for lunch with the new neighbors across the street. This time, Matt and Sarah were to plan the luncheon and supply the food. Kevin was excited about seeing their new friends and thought that he and Mary could surprise Matt and Sarah by arriving in work clothes and offering to help for a couple of hours after lunch. Kevin, excited as a little child going to a birthday party, had made signs for his and Mary's shirts that said, "CHEAP LABOR, WILLING HANDS," and planned to let Matt and Sarah see these pinned to their shirts by pointing to them when they opened the door. Kevin had such fun getting ready that Mary caught his mood and overcame her social anxiety for the moment. When they were ready, they walked hand in hand across the street looking forward to a wonderful afternoon of fellowship.

Kevin tried the doorbell and found it had been fixed. When the door opened, Kevin used outlandish and exaggerated gestures to point out the signs on his and Mary's shirts. Seeing the signs, Matt and Sarah burst out laughing and laughed so hard that Kevin and Mary wondered why. When Matt and Sarah recovered from their laughing, they brought Kevin and Mary into the house and showed them the sign they had placed on the card table in front of the window where they would eat.

Braced up against a platter of rolled roast beef, lettuce, and sliced tomato was a cardboard sign that read, "NO WORK FOR THREE HOURS, SPENDING QUALITY TIME WITH FRIENDS." All four of them laughed together and were secretly pleased to think how nice it was that each couple thought to please the other. When they finished laughing and commenting on their signs, Kevin said, "Let's compromise: two hours for a great lunch and wonderful conversation and two hours of slave labor as dictated by Matt and Sarah!" They all laughed again. Kevin beamed at Mary, so happy to see her at ease and so thankful for these new friends with which they seemed to have so much in common. The four of them shared the next four hours eating and working, talking and laughing. During this time, Mary did not experience even a hint of fear or panic.

Chapter Three

THE DANGER

Sarah was lying in bed, wishing she could fall back to sleep for a few hours before Matt was scheduled to pick her up for another Saturday's work on the new house. Sarah's brothers and Matt's uncle were coming to the house to help install crown molding in the living and dining rooms and hopefully the study and porch. They'd planned for a pizza delivery for lunch. Kevin and Mary would not be coming over because they were attending a function at Kevin's boss's house. Mary had been excited when she shared the news that they would attend a party to celebrate a promotion for Kevin, which he had not expected. It wasn't another raise in pay, but meant a more important title and a company car. Sarah and Matt were happy for them.

Sarah didn't know why she was awake; the clock said it was only 5:00 a.m., and she didn't have to get up until 8:00 a.m. As she lay unable to sleep, yet trying at least to rest, her mind was filled with thoughts about the renovation of their new home. She remembered that her grandmother once told her the story of how she had been awakened at two or three in the morning by the sound of tapping. *Tap, tap . . . tap, tap, tap . . . tap.* When her grandmother recognized the sounds that had awakened her, she was comforted and turned over to sleep once again. The tapping was the sound of a hammer driving nails into the wall. It was done gently, as quietly as possible. It was her mother rearranging the pictures on the living-room walls.

Now, years later, Sarah was following in the footsteps of both her grandmother and great grandmother by renovating a house in the style they had both loved. Sarah remembered that her grandmother's earliest memories were those relating to interior design and how shopping as a little child with her mother inevitably led to a wonderful new find for their home. Grandma said that in just a short time, even though still a child, she had learned to notice statues, pictures, glassware, throw pillows, clocks, and furniture and identify which styles would work best with one another. Grandma loved to tramp through the various stores with her mother and look at all the lovely room settings and looked forward to having lunch in the department store. Sometimes her aunt would join them and make her feel very grown-up by asking her what she liked best out of all the things they had looked at that morning.

Sarah reminisced that both Grandma's parents enjoyed their home and gladly labored to make it a Bethany for their family. Even as a child, Grandma said she had known that the word *Bethany* meant a happy place. Later, she learned that it also meant a place of refuge; a place where one can gain renewed strength to again face a harried and difficult world. Grandma had taught Sarah that the meaning of the word *Bethany* evolved from the times described in the Bible where Jesus went to Bethany, a town where His friends Lazarus, Mary, and Martha lived. Jesus loved to spend time in Bethany where He could rest and regain His strength in fellowship with those He loved and trusted and those who loved and trusted Him. Sarah wanted their new home to be a Bethany for her and Matt, and knew that Matt felt the same way.

Grandma's mother, Sarah's great-grandmother, had not been a trained designer, but had a gift for color and proper proportion that enabled her to create a beautiful home. This trait seemed to have been passed on to Grandma and then to Sarah. Grandma often recalled how her Dad joked about being sure to turn on the lights before entering a room since he never knew where the furniture might be placed that day. But the truth is, he loved his wife's desire to make the home as comforting and beautiful as their budget allowed.

Sarah also recalled Grandma telling her that her great-grandmother had chosen traditional furnishings in an elegant but eclectic blend, which allowed for many different configurations. Grandma said that though there were lots of accessories in her mother's home, it was the sense of balance through placement, color, and style that gave these numbers legitimacy rather than a feeling of clutter. Grandma said that this balance produced a feeling of harmony and a sense of well-being and that as she watched her mother move furniture and accessories until the room seemed "just right," she learned about balance and the influences of different cultures on the various furniture designs. Pagoda-style lampshades, silks, and lacquer finishes from China; graceful curved legs and rich wood grains influenced by French and English design; and wood carvings reminiscent of the old European churches, especially of the Byzantine period, were some examples of the various styles. Sarah thought, *This sense of balance and peace and beauty is what I want in our home.*

Sarah realized that these thoughts were sparked by her concern for Mary. Mary had confided how important it was to her to be able to convince Kevin of the benefits of following Feng Shui rules for decorating because it was imperative that she take steps to ward off bad luck. Sarah didn't know much about Feng Shui but worried about Mary's seeming obsession with luck. Something didn't seem right to Sarah, and she thought that perhaps she should learn about Feng Shui so she could respond to Mary properly. Sarah recalled Grandma saying that through trade and travel, fabrics such as silk and fine linens, fabric dyes, marvelous architectural influences, and a variety of furniture styles made their way from one culture to another as did herbs and medicines, spices and foods. She'd said that even the pasta thought of as Italy's claim to fame actually originated in China and indicated that our world becomes smaller from the ease of travel and trade, even more so now with all the information available through the Internet. This results in fewer and fewer distinctions so the styles and artifacts, discoveries and mores of many cultures easily converge.

As Sarah lay daydreaming, she thought that time itself was different than it was just a few generations ago. Without a myriad of television shows, computer games, long hours at the office, or driving children to lessons or sporting events, there used to be plenty of time to devote to the betterment of a home and family life. *I think we all feel somewhat desperate because we can't seem to do all we feel necessary, and what we can do we do hurriedly on the run,* she thought.

There is a tremendous difference in the amount of spare time between the generations of grandparents and children, Sarah thought. *In today's world, we can barely keep afloat just to provide the necessary things in life, let alone the things that truly bring us relaxation and joy.* She remembered a scripture that seemed to predict what was happening in the world now.

The time of the end: many shall run to and fro,
and knowledge shall be increased.

—Daniel 12:4

From the Internet to television, from shopping centers to the local grocery store, we are bombarded with offers of the miraculous quick fix that will change lives. And sadly, Sarah thought, *we never seem to lose faith in the marketing promises of these quick fixes. We know better than to think there are quick and easy solutions to all our problems, but our busy lives cry out for that one miracle that will bring us the help we want and bring it right now.*

Sarah wondered what made a person buy into one type of quick fix and not into another. *Do people really think there is a quick and easy way to guarantee financial success, good relationships, happy family life, and continued good health? Is there really a quick fix for obtaining these things?* she wondered.

When Mary told her that she needed, really needed, to ward off bad luck, Sarah sensed not only an urgency in Mary's voice but also a pained look on Kevin's face. It seemed to Sarah that Kevin felt something akin to fear but felt it for Mary. *What happened?* Sarah wondered, *Why did Kevin react so strongly, yet differently, to Mary's words about bad luck?*

As Sarah stretched before rising from her bed, she realized that there must be something that Mary was afraid of. She wished that she could help or at least direct them to the Bible where she and Matt seemed to find their answers. *Why do so few of us reach for the Bible and search scripture to find comfort in our concerns? Perhaps,* she thought, *because in scripture the verses applicable to our worries are not always easy to find, especially when we are driven frantic by our time constraints and when we don't know where in the Bible to search for what we need.*

The truth is, Sarah thought, *few know what the Bible says. We are a generation of people, creating a new generation of people, who have not learned what the Bible says. We have no time to learn these things or to teach our children about them.* Comparing her parent's life to her life, Sarah could see the difference in the amount of "running to and fro." She found herself so busy that she never had the time anymore just to relax. *Because of our hectic life,* she thought, *sometimes Matt and I find ourselves ill equipped to cope, not knowing where to turn except to the false promises of the quick fix. Our hopes and our energies can easily go into these quick fixes. Where would we be if it weren't for Grandma's legacy?*

Then Sarah remembered Matt talking about the pitfalls of trying to serve two masters and how they had made a commitment to adopt a special verse as their guide in life.

> *As for me and my house, we will serve the Lord.*
> —Joshua 24:15

How blessed she was with Matt, she thought. *We've just bought our first house, will be married in six months, we have the next five months to renovate the house, and have met two neighbors we really like.*

Brushing her teeth, now hurrying to be ready in time, she couldn't help but worry about Mary and Kevin because they seemed so adamant about decorating a home according to the tenets of Feng Shui, believing this would guarantee them peace, protection, and harmony. Mary believed that Feng Shui promised, through its art of placing furniture and accessories in a manner that is in harmony with nature, that their lives would become better and they would be protected from harm. *Was that serving two masters?* Sarah wondered. *Did this way of life negate God as the source of hope?* Sarah knew that if so, this was a one-way trip to disaster.

After Sarah finished dressing, she went to her computer and looked on the Internet to see what she could learn quickly about Feng Shui and thought that perhaps she could print some information to share with Matt while they worked on the house today. The first site she opened explained that Feng Shui originated in China, was called the art of placement, and promised a beneficial change in one's fortune when the home or office environment was outfitted by following their tenets. As she skimmed some of the sites she found, she could see that Feng Shui imparted some excellent and practical advice for bringing the home environment into harmony with nature, but then as she jumped from site to site, she began to suspect that despite Feng Shui's many benefits, it seemed to have a dangerous side too. She was suddenly worried about this for the sake of Kevin and Mary. Quickly she printed some material to bring to the house so she could show Matt. Then she made her bed and packed a little bag of snacks before Matt arrived to pick her up.

As Sarah waited for Matt, she remembered the old trunk she had taken from Grandma's house. After Grandma died, they'd found a little manuscript inside the trunk about Feng Shui, astrology and Vastu, which Grandma had handwritten. Grandma said that she'd done a study on Feng Shui because she had purchased some large oriental vases to make into lamps and had chosen the beautiful pagoda style shades for them. She'd also purchased some small chests painted in the black and gold chinoiserie style as accent pieces and a large secretary-style drop-leaf desk in the red-and-gold chinoiserie style. She wanted to learn about the origin of this style and had accidentally learned of the existence of Feng Shui.

Matt and Sarah had never read the little manuscript because they'd placed Grandma's trunk directly into storage thinking they'd read everything once they were settled in their own home.

When Grandma died, Sarah struggled not only with grief from her loss but also with a previously unrecognized anger that surfaced only after Grandma died. Because these struggles took a long while to reconcile, it had been difficult to move Grandma's possessions from Grandma's home to Sarah's apartment or the storage unit. She had not been ready to go through Grandma's possessions thoroughly, but she now remembered seeing the yellowed manuscripts among some letters from Grandma's friends.

Sarah also remembered the journal she had helped Grandma write just before she died. In this journal, Grandma related a story about a friend suffering through a bad marriage who turned to astrology as a way to find solutions to her situation. Grandma supported her friend's ideas for a while, but as she saw destructive patterns emerge in her friend's life, Grandma began to search the Bible to find whether or not this path was the right one to take. Grandma compiled a great deal of information about astrology and tarot because she had been so worried about her friend. *Maybe*, thought Sarah, *this information will also help Kevin and Mary.*

Even though Sarah hadn't read the Feng Shui manuscript in Grandma's old trunk, she knew she'd be fascinated by it and hoped, because it surely would have come from scripture, it might contain information she could use to evaluate Feng Shui. While Sarah hadn't known anyone who decorated their homes according to the rules of Feng Shui, she felt uncomfortable with some of the things Mary said and certainly by some of what she'd just read on the Internet.

Sarah didn't fully understand what Feng Shui really was and thought that maybe she should read Grandma's manuscript as soon as she could, or at least look into the concordance for more guidance. Sarah decided to ask Matt if it would be okay to get the trunk from the storage unit and bring it to the new house so they could read whatever Grandma had gathered about Feng Shui.

But first, Sarah thought, *I ought to read a few books about Feng Shui. Like Grandma, I should gather the facts, then compare these facts to what the Bible might say about it. Yes,* she thought, *I'd better get my facts straight before I jump to conclusions. This way, when Matt and I speak with our new friends, we'll be informed enough to draw some conclusions about Feng Shui.*

Sarah didn't want to ruin this new friendship by assuming Mary and Kevin were doing something wrong without having the proper information. After all, maybe Feng Shui was harmless, maybe even beneficial. Sarah would talk with Matt about this, and together they could investigate, gather facts, and discuss them while they were working on the house.

When Matt arrived and Sarah had settled into the car, she asked Matt if they could swing by the library on their way to the house. She told him that she wanted to run in and just randomly grab three or four books on Feng Shui without taking time to look at them in the library. She said that she didn't think it would hold them up for any longer than fifteen minutes. They were a little early, so Matt agreed and drove to the library. He double-parked the car, leaving the motor running while Sarah ran inside. After Sarah returned to the car, she asked Matt if it would be okay to run to the storage unit when they took their lunch break so they could get the trunk that held Grandma's old manuscripts. Matt agreed, but suggested Sarah keep the trunk carefully covered at the new house because of all the dust they were still creating from the renovation.

A few days earlier, Matt and Sarah had made plans to meet Sarah's two brothers and Matt's brother-in-law at the house today so they could help Matt install the crown molding in the living and dining rooms, the study, and the porch. The crown molding and corner blocks had been delivered during the week and Matt had precut triangular blocks to use as a backing to better support the moldings. Both Matt's brother-in-law and Sarah's older brother brought their nail guns and compressors to make the work go quickly. The four men planned to split into two teams of two. With the use of corner blocks, there were few cuts and no angles to worry about so the work would be much easier.

As the five of them worked, they chatted about the house, commenting that the house seemed to fit Matt and Sarah so well and that it would have made Grandma proud. To tease Sarah, the men began to tell Sarah where she should place her furniture in the new house. They knew Sarah had taken Grandma's furniture and exactly what those pieces of furniture were. With each outlandish description of where everything should go, Sarah laughed, saying, "You guys have it all wrong." After they finished, Sarah began to tell them where those pieces of furniture should really be placed, teasing them back. Sarah jokingly described how she wanted to place the big canopied bed in the center of the dining room and the living room couch in the kitchen. They beat her at her game, however, by appearing to accept and ponder her own outlandish placement of the furniture. Finally, she told them that she felt the dining-room hutch should be placed in front of the bay windows of the turret in the study and when they still didn't respond negatively she knew they were teasing her again. They told her that she might have thought she'd tricked them, but they knew all along what she was doing.

"Fat chance," Sarah said. "We all know which gender is better at decorating." They calmly took a vote, and all four men decided that men were definitely the superior decorators. Matt reminded Sarah that God, "presumably a man" he added, designed many a structure requesting such things as wood carved with the figures of pomegranates and curtains of blue linen! "And don't forget," he said, "King David, King Solomon, and Noah!" Almost in unison, the men said, "Yeah, Sarah, top that one!" And Sarah conceded, being outnumbered and outmaneuvered.

> *Moreover thou shalt make the tabernacle*
> *with ten curtains of fine twined linen,*
> *and blue, and purple, and scarlet.*
>
> —Exodus 26:1

Sarah spent the morning bantering with the men, handing them the molding and the blocks as they needed them, kept their compressor hoses from getting tangled, and moved ladders for them to step across from one to the other so they didn't have to climb up and down as they moved around the room nailing the molding in place. She also gave them bottles of cold water when they were thirsty and extra packets of nails for the nail gun as they ran out. Soon it was time to break for lunch.

The men decided that they would rather have subs than pizza, so Matt suggested that he and his uncle run to the deli for the sandwiches while Sarah and her brothers go to the storage unit to get Grandma's trunk. They made plans to meet back at the house in forty-five minutes and have lunch together. Matt reminded Sarah to bring another two folding chairs from the storage unit as well. The men laughed, asking Matt if this was because he expected them to help him again another day! Matt, of course, said, "Yes, I'd planned for you to come every weekend for the next six months." The guys replied, "Only if you catch us first." Sarah interjected, "But that's what a family is for." They were all laughing as they left the house to run their errands.

Over lunch they talked and talked, easily and comfortably, as the wonderful, close family they had already become. They reminisced about Grandma's clocks and commented how great they'd sound in this house. They discussed the wedding and the excitement that the women felt about all the plans and preparations.

Sarah's older brother asked Matt if he had cold feet yet. Matt said that he was thinking of backing out but was afraid that Sarah might seek him out one cold dark night for revenge. Sarah reminded him that she was the best thing that ever happened to him. Matt said sheepishly, "Yeah, you're right, you are," and leaned over and kissed Sarah on the cheek. The men guffawed and teased Matt for being a sissy, loving every minute of it, even though each of them knew they felt the same way.

After they ate, they worked a few more hours and finished with just a few nails to spare. They walked from room to room admiring their handiwork, commenting about how talented they were, how great a job they did, giving Sarah specific instructions for spackling the nail holes and joints between block and crown. She teased them back, letting them know she was a pro at minor stuff like that. It was the supervising work she'd had to do all day that made the job tough! The men grumbled that one could never win with a woman so they might as well give in right away. They hugged Sarah and slapped Matt on the back the way men do and left, promising to return for the really macho work again whenever Matt needed them. Their parting words to Matt were "Remember, Matt, when you get married, you have to practice the four 'gives' of marriage: Give, Forgive, Give in, and . . . Give up!" Sarah ran after them to give each of them a gentle, but meaningful, punch in the arm.

Matt and Sarah decided to take a short break to have some cookies and chocolate milk and to sit a while together. They were pleased with the elegant look the crown molding gave to the rooms and felt that the house was beginning to look like a home. Sarah grabbed the manuscript she'd gotten from Grandma's trunk and began leafing through it, quoting different passages as they ate their cookies and drank their milk.

Sarah read that Feng Shui is at once practical, ancient, and interesting, and must be practiced precisely in order to obtain the benefits it promises. As Sarah continued to read, they learned that if Feng Shui countermeasures are improperly used, anger from guardian deities will fall upon the user. Matt and Sarah didn't like that part at all.

If their friends were lulled by promises, perhaps led to the apple of the Garden of Eden, believing what should not be believed and practicing what should not be practiced, should she and Matt try to warn them? Should they risk the friendship this way? Grandma had shown them that the Bible clearly said no one can serve two masters and that our trust in good times and in bad should be placed only in God. Matt and Sarah believed that the only real quick fix for their lives is God. They had learned that God is so very gentle and loving that He never closes one door without opening another and to a far better place to be and never allows us to carry a burden greater than our strength permits.

> *No one can serve two masters; for either he will hate the one,*
> *and love the other; or else he will hold to the one, and*
> *despise the other. You cannot serve God and mammon.*
> —Matthew 6:24

Sarah read that *harmony* was a word often used in conjunction with Feng Shui and recognized that this is what drew so many to the practice of Feng Shui, yet she and Matt also knew that without the protection God offers, without living with Him at your side, there could be no harmony, no peace, and no rest here and certainly none after we die. They would have to learn more and figure out how they could approach Kevin and Mary about their concerns.

Time for their break had run out. Now it was time to get back to work. They put the manuscript aside and decided to stop for Chinese takeout on the way home, bringing the manuscript and library books home with them so they could read more once they were back at Sarah's apartment. With these plans in mind, they swept up the sawdust and folded the ladders and the extra chairs and carried them to the garage. Then they positioned the folding table back into the window seat niche with the remaining two chairs at the table, ready for their next meal. They decided that over lunch again next week with their new friends, they would discuss Feng Shui and learn a little bit about Kevin and Mary's knowledge of it and perhaps even a little about their spiritual life. By that time, Matt and Sarah would know more about Feng Shui and could perhaps discuss it intelligently with their friends.

They wanted to take things slowly. Matt warned Sarah to try to curb her natural desire to "get things done" because they could easily harm their new friendship by pushing their own opinions too quickly. "It's better," Matt said, "to let people draw their own conclusions." Sarah said that body language gave great hints for these types of conversations and that she would watch and she would be careful.

They worked another two hours, then left and stopped at the China Dynasty to purchase two meals, asking for the take-out containers. They walked around the buffet tables and filled their containers with their favorite items and brought everything home to Sarah's apartment. When they had finished eating and cleaned off the table, they brought the library books, Grandma's manuscript, and their tired bodies to the couch and stretched out with their legs on top of the cocktail table to learn more about Feng Shui.

They found that Feng Shui, pronounced "Fung Schway," is the art of placement, a method of interior design used in China for over three thousand years. In the Chinese language, Feng Shui means literally "wind, water," and its basic goal is to bring the home into harmony with nature, advocating that the achievement of perfect selection and placement, encourages positive forces and inhibits negative forces that abide in a home. To fully employ Feng Shui and gain the promises of happiness, success, health, and harmony, one must use Chinese astrology, symbols, and magical numbers for luck and good fortune. With that last sentence, Matt and Sarah were convinced that this could be something that God would not approve of and felt a terrible letdown as they thought of the danger to their friends.

Sarah read that in the Chinese culture and philosophy, Feng Shui is considered to be to the home or business what the physician is to the human body, and that studies of nature and its cycles, of animals and their strengths and weaknesses, and even the magnetic fields of the earth are included in the Chinese quest for harmony with nature. Further, the elements found in nature provided the early proponents of Feng Shui the tools with which to discover the natural order of things in the universe. These tools require the application of one's date and time of birth (astrology), one's lucky numbers, element, and animal, and the use of a divination tool, the I Ching (Book of Changes) and its coins or yarrow sticks. Here Feng Shui prescribes following a specific course of action meant to change significant events in one's life.

Matt and Sarah were afraid for their new friends. Mary had called her Feng Shui advisor a master and said he acted in the various capacities of designer, astrologer, geomancer, and diviner. They looked at each other, reading one another's thoughts. *What is the power behind this? Is it the master, the procedure recommended, luck, coincidence, or some unseen being?* Scripture told them that Satan wields a great deal of power on earth and can indeed better one's fortune.

"Do you think Mary and Kevin use the components of Feng Shui we've just read about?" Sarah asked. Matt replied, "Well, even if they don't, remember that God warns of His anger toward those who are "lukewarm" and cannot or do not draw the line between what is pleasing to Him and what is not, so even doing 'a little Feng Shui' may be displeasing to God."

> *I know thy works, that thou art neither cold nor hot.*
> *I would thou wert cold or hot. So then*
> *because thou art lukewarm, and neither cold nor hot,*
> *I will spue thee out of my mouth.*
> —Revelation 3:15, 16

Matt said, "Consider this hypothetical situation showing how one may become a strong advocate of Feng Shui: Miss X was having extensive medical problems. One day a friend told her that according to Feng Shui principles, she could be cured if she moved her bed to the left far corner of the room. Miss X went home and moved the bed. Within a week she began to feel better, her symptoms went away, and she was thrilled to have tapped into a method that worked for her." Then Matt asked, "Would you follow the same advice and move your bed?"

Sarah answered by saying, "If my problems were long-term and I wasn't a stickler about the décor of the room, I might very well try it if I had no knowledge that it might displease God. If I began to feel better and if some of my symptoms went away, I would, of course, be very happy. I could see how one might attribute the change in health to moving the bed, especially if it were explained in terms of the earth's magnetic influences, something I know nothing about. Also, having heard about copper bracelets for arthritis and magnets in knee braces, I might conclude that this bed moving, this theory, works."

"Another one," Matt said. "John was suffering from anxiety. The duties of his job were massive, and he had deadlines to meet. He was feeling exhausted, overwhelmed, and constantly battled anxiety. Susie stopped by his office and, knowing he was losing his ability to cope, mentioned that she received relief from her problems through Feng Shui. John ran to the bookstore, bought a Feng Shui book, and read through it quickly. He learned within an hour that he should move his desk so the chair behind the desk faced the door rather than having its back to the door. John noticed a reduction in his anxiety level that same day. If this remedy worked for you, you could easily be enchanted with the simplicity of Feng Shui fixes. Wouldn't you?"

Then Matt read that if one placed a box of coins in the northwest corner of your home or work office, one could increase their potential for financial success. Matt reminded Sarah that Mary and Kevin hadn't come to the house today because Kevin received an unexpected promotion and was attending a luncheon at his boss's house. Had Kevin placed a box of coins on his desk? Had Kevin been hooked into believing that this could have brought him this unexpected promotion?

Now they felt an urgency to learn what Feng Shui is, from where it came, what it requires, what it promises, and does it work. They also wanted to know if it offends God and causes us spiritual harm. They thought they'd make a list of what they wanted to know about Feng Shui and from what they'd already read, they listed Qi, Yin and Yang, the five elements, the Lo Pan, and the cycles of life. They also wanted to know more about how astrology, magic numbers, yarrow sticks, animals, and chants fit into Feng Shui and more about the I Ching, the helpers, and the Ba Qua. They needed to learn what the Bible might say about these things.

In the meanwhile, they could pray for wisdom and pray for their friends and ask God to help them all recognize His will in this matter.

Many of them also which used curious arts brought their
books together, and burned them before all men: and they
counted the price of them, and found it
fifty thousand pieces of silver.

—Acts 19:19

I will cut off witchcrafts out of thine hand; and thou shalt have
no more soothsayers: Thy graven images also will
I cut off, and thy standing images out of the midst of thee;
and thou shalt no more worship the work of thine hands.

—Micah 5:12, 13

For the heart of this people is waxed gross,
and their ears are dull of hearing,
and their eyes have they closed.

—Acts 28:27

There is none that understandeth,
there is none that seeketh after God . . .
There is no fear of God
before their eyes.

—Romans 3:11, 18

Chapter Four

THE HOUSE

It was almost Spring and we were still working on the house. There were pieces of wood lath, chunks of plaster mixed with the horsehair they used so many years ago, and plaster dust all over the kitchen and in two of the three bathrooms. Cans of varnish, brushes, cleanup rags, and window scrapers were scattered throughout the house. Eight-foot-by-four-foot pieces of Sheetrock leaned against the kitchen walls ready for installation and were also in the bedrooms where new closets had been framed and awaited the wallboard. We were pleased with our progress. The house was beginning to feel like home to us, and we were excited to think of the day when it would be finished. Sometime in the coming year we would be married and finally living here!

We had both accumulated extra days at work that we needed to take or lose and decided to take them together so we could put in another full day's work on the house. When we broke for lunch, we sat together on the window seat and ate huge Dagwood sandwiches and began to think about the way the house would look when it was decorated for Christmas. It would be beautiful! We wished we could have decorated this past Christmas, but our renovation was just too messy; not enough was completed to even think about it.

Whenever we thought about Christmas, we thought of Grandma and all the things she did for Christmas. She made such exquisite displays they took your breath away. Each display highlighted a different aspect of Christmas and each one was unique. She loved to assemble the decorations, placing pinecones and Christmas flowers and greens throughout the displays. She had an incredible talent, and everyone wanted to visit her home at Christmas to see what she had created. I thought about how much the children I hoped to have someday would have loved seeing them, loved to experience the fairyland she created.

We'd been telling Kevin and Mary that Grandma always held an open house for church friends and neighbors when she completed her decorations. Her friends looked forward to being with her and enjoying her famous "glogg" and Christmas cookies. Grandma's aunt had given her the recipe for glogg and told her it had been handed down for generations from her uncle's family in Norway.

Glogg was a hot drink, made from port wine and whiskey and heated in a big pot with a mesh bag placed into the pot that had been filled with orange peel, raisins, almonds, ginger, cloves, cinnamon, and cardamom seeds. Grandma would add a thin fresh curl of orange peel, a few raisins and some almond slivers to each cup and pour her mixture over these as she served it. This would look, smell and taste so festive.

It was potent, but she would add half orange juice to the cup of those who preferred it a little less potent. Heated slowly on the stove, the warm glogg filled the house with the smell of Christmas as the clove and cinnamon aroma swirled over the stove, were caught by the air ducts and circulated from room to room. It made everything feel so "Christmassy." The minute anyone entered the house from outside, they noticed the wonderful aroma and were immediately put in the Christmas spirit, breathing deeply to draw in the savory smells associated with this beautiful and precious holy day.

I'd copied Grandma's recipe into my computer using a fancy script and printed it onto a special paper with scrolls of flowers and ivy intertwined and circling its perimeter, and yesterday I'd given Kevin and Mary a copy of it. I had framed my copy using an oval matt in the same burgundy color that was in Grandma's rugs and placed the matt and recipe into a thick, somewhat ornate cherry-stained frame. It looked like an heirloom. I loved it!

The recipe read:

For one quart of Glogg:
Pour one pint of port wine into a pot,
add ½ cup raisins, ½ cup skinless almonds slivers, 4 cloves,
½ cup sugar, 3 figs cut into pieces, 2 four-inch-long cinnamon sticks,
6 cardamon seeds, 1 small piece of ginger about the size of a nickel,
and the peeled skin from one orange (wash first). Soak for fifteen minutes.
Slowly heat until hot. Do not boil. Add one pint of your favorite whiskey.
Heat until hot, still not letting the mixture boil. Let cool.
Store in a tightly sealed wide mouthed container until ready to serve.
Pour through a strainer, reheat, not allowing the mixture to boil,
and serve in a clear glass cup preferably with a handle
and add a few fresh raisins, an almond,
and a small piece of fresh orange peel.

Grandma's tree was filled with tinsel, lights, and garlands so thick you could hardly see the tree. These were interspersed with her collection of vintage-looking Santa faces and miniature teddy bears, and large hand-painted ornaments in between. Grandma created a sea of poinsettias under the tree to hide the tree stand, and electric trains ran through the little village nestled in snow that graced the perimeter of the tree. The leaves of the poinsettias looked like a primordial forest behind the uphill slope of the tiny village.

Two forty-eight-inch shelves in Grandma's bookcases were used to create a village of taller ceramic houses and shops. There were sidewalks made of miniature bricks that were filled with people and gates and fences that surrounded a miniature park with a skating pond and skaters. Pine trees loomed lush above snow-covered streets that held tiny old-fashioned automobiles and a horse and carriage. Chestnut vendors and fresh-flower vendors further enticed villagers carrying precious gifts home to their families. Puppies sat at the feet of old men on benches under ornate lanterns. Creating this lovely village, Grandma seemed like a little girl again, her eyes alight with the innocence of a fairy tale come true. Watching her with her village always reminded me of how she must have played with the little paper dolls she cherished as a child and which I wrote about in her journal *When God Broke Grandma's Heart.*

I'd told Mary that when Grandma was a young bride preparing for her first Christmas in her own home, she created a sled and four reindeer out of wood she cut to shape with a saber saw. Years later, she refinished the sled by placing thin sheets of gold leaf over a burgundy base color then staining the gold leaf and varnishing the entire surface. She hand-painted old-world curlicues along the edges of the sled. It was elegant. She painted the reindeer white and rolled them in silver and white sequins and added colored sequins for eyes and nostrils. She'd purchased a uniquely dressed Santa, outfitted in bow tie and shirtsleeves, lush burgundy velvet pants, and black leather boots, seated on a bench playing a fiddle. He was in perfect proportion to the sled and reindeer. She found little Christmas elves that were also perfectly proportioned and placed them on ladders and pathways or atop the sled where they appeared to be loading amazing little gifts onto the sled for Santa's long trip.

Tiny packages, teddy bears, sleds, and rocking horses lay on the snow awaiting careful placement by the elves onto the waiting sled, and a snowman sang his Christmas song in the background when the key in his back was wound. A row of little green Christmas trees formed a backdrop for the sled and reindeer. Little children visiting Grandma's house during the Christmas holiday couldn't help reaching for the tiny rocking horses and sleds on which the elves were working.

Grandma hung gold angels with billowing sleeves and flowing hair from the edges of the mirror over her couch, and they were reflected in the mirror, their lights and their ribbons doubling. Grandma said the angels were watching over her house and her guests, making sure everyone was safe and happy. Their skirts, long and full, were elegant. The ribbons they held in their hands complemented the color scheme of Grandma's room and flowed gracefully, being held in place by the wire along their edges. The angels were perfectly placed to balance the Christmas tree on the opposite side of the room.

Her largest display, the most important in her eyes, was her nativity scene. The papier-mâché figures were two feet tall and wore exquisite robes in the jewel-tone colors of green and burgundy and gold and blue. They, like the angels, had deep sleeves and full skirts. The three wise men wore shapely crown hats with gold trim and carried shining gifts, one a chest filled with precious pearls and gold chains, which spilled out over its edges and cascaded to the feet of the Christ child.

A manger held the Christ child as he lay in a bed of greens ringed with pinecones that were intertwined with delicate gold ribbons and tiny silk rosebuds. His arms were lifted toward His mother, His beautiful crocheted wide-sleeved gown slipping down one of His outstretched arms. Grandpa placed a spotlight on the ceiling above the nativity scene and directed it at the child and His mother. The light showcased the beauty and importance of the nativity scene, which became the focal point of all the rooms. Next year, we would hang that light in our home when we placed all Grandma's lovely things in their own special niche next Christmas! How special that would be for us! We were so blessed to have found this house. It would be a showcase for Grandma's things.

Mary asked us how we had found this house, and Matt told them both the whole story of what a mess we had made with our lives when we first bought this house. We'd looked for months to find just the right house, and in doing so we had learned a strong and important lesson in humility.

Just before we began to search for a house, we had completed an extensive study of the Bible. We wanted to start our life out right and wanted to obtain God's blessing on all that we did. We'd both been upset after Grandma died, and then Matt's brother had died soon thereafter; and we needed to find a way to understand God's will. We did as Grandma had taught us and turned to the Bible for our answers and from this had written our own journal, which we called "When God Took Grandma Home."

We had been fascinated by what we found in the Bible and learned things we never knew before and were amazed. That experience strengthened our faith, and we truly believed we would not ever have to face a faith challenge again! We were sure that we had everything down pat and would be able to stay pretty much on the straight and narrow. To our surprise, as soon as we ran into our first problem, our first disappointment, we'd messed up, big-time. We were embarrassed to admit, especially now in front of Kevin and Mary, that we even became angry with God for a short time.

When we purchased our home and then lost it, when we hadn't gotten our way, we'd grumbled and grumbled and grumbled! We knew better than to behave that way but nevertheless still acted badly! We were blessed to have recognized what we were doing before it was too late.

We recalled how ecstatic we were when we'd finally found this house! We had dedicated all our spare time over a period of three months to look for a house and had considered over one hundred houses, none that we really fell in love with. We'd gotten tired and discouraged but kept on looking. Finally, we found it, the home of our dreams, and we were ecstatic! It looked like a Tudor-style home, but had a granite turret located to the right of the entrance door and a gabled gray slate roof that was a slightly darker shade than the turret. The house was filled with beautiful chestnut woodwork, which had never been painted. The one-inch-thick baseboards were over ten inches high. We'd always loved the warmth of natural wood moldings, so finding the wood unpainted was a real plus to us.

We planned to scrub all the woodwork clean and prepare them for a new coat of varnish to give them a face-lift. We considered this an easy chore compared to stripping layers of paint from them. Matt gloated about how little work he would have whenever he wanted to repaint a room and didn't need to paint the trim! He had winked at me and gave me a thumbs-up when we walked into the house for the first time and saw the unpainted trim.

The floors were a mess, but they were solid oak, and we knew we could have them sanded, stained, and revarnished to bring them back to life. This would be especially easy to do while the house was empty. We planned that I would stay in my apartment and Matt would give up his studio apartment and move into the house as soon as it was livable. This way he could continue to work on the house whenever he had time, and I'd come over whenever I could to help him. We smiled at the thought of stocking a cooler with the ingredients for huge sandwiches, juice, and bottled water, and having impromptu picnics while we worked on the house.

When we first took Kevin and Mary on a tour of the house, we pointed out the perfect little entry foyer that would accommodate a mirror and a bench or console table on its only solid wall. There was a tall slender window on the opposite wall, and the outside entry door was located on the wall between these two. An inner archway with intricate wood fretwork filled the fourth wall and led from the entry hall to the parlor. An antique light fixture hung from the eleven-foot-high ceiling.

The first room to the right around and behind the entry was the turret, so it was round in shape and had lots of windows and lots of light. We thought we'd make this room a study and build low bookcases along the bottoms of the windows, creating a series of curved window seats. We planned to furnish this room with a huge desk and desk chair and a pair of comfortable wing chairs, with a table and lamp between the two chairs, with the window seats providing whatever extra seating might be needed.

Straight ahead and on the left was the living room, which had two tall narrow windows on the wall opposite the entrance to the room and three windows in the bay on the left wall in the front of the house. This double-arched entrance into the living room was also framed in a beautiful wood fretwork with little spindles and balls and curved pieces of wood stained to match the other woodwork in the house.

There was a central parlor with a stairway on the right side with a huge carved post marking the first of three steps that led to the landing, which peeked into the turret room. The steps turned to the left as they ascended from the landing and climbed toward the upper hallway. The steps were of natural oak to match the floors, and each had a slight depression in the center indicating years of use. Matt joked that we would have to climb the steps with our feet placed widely apart so we could wear down the outer area of the steps to match the inner area and said that when we were old we could tell our children we had worn the steps even!

On the left side of the parlor was a corner fireplace with an oak façade about eight feet tall that contained two columns, a lovely curved mantle with an oval mirror above, and a curved shelf above the mirror. Through the parlor was a huge dining room with a window seat under a pair of corner windows on the left. On the wall opposite the entrance into this room was a built-in cabinet for storing dishes that was flush with the wall and had its top shelves open for display and the bottom enclosed by doors. Unfortunately, this cabinet had been painted with multiple coats of oil paint and might be difficult to strip. On the right wall of the dining room were French doors leading to a screened porch with a floor of thick gray slates and three skylights across the ceiling. Some of the slates were reddish in color and some slightly gold and were interspersed in no particular design between the gray slates. We felt that the floor would probably be incredibly beautiful once it was cleaned and sealed. The porch was my favorite room in the house!

Walking through the right side of the dining room toward the opposite wall brought us to a narrow hall which led to the kitchen. Off this hall on the left were two doors, one to a bathroom, and the other to a laundry room. Traveling further, we entered the kitchen and were surprised by how bright it was. To the far left was an eating area that reminded us of an old-fashioned solarium because of its high mullioned windows along three walls, perhaps ten or twelve feet given to each wall of windows. It was a picturesque area, and though the windows were in a state of disrepair that would either be a huge expense to replace, or a lot of work to repair, we felt it would be worth it to keep its original splendor. To the right of the kitchen was a tiny family room with a fireplace. Straight through the kitchen was a door to the garage, which we thought had once been a covered portico for a horse and carriage to pass through.

Upstairs were two bathrooms and four bedrooms. There were no closets. Not one closet in the entire house! The original occupants of the house must have used armoires and cupboards to store clothing. We thought we would build a wall of closets in each of the bedrooms because the rooms seemed large enough to accommodate them.

The master bedroom was in the front of the house. Off to one side there were three large curved windows which were in the bay created by the upper part of the turret. This formed a sort of niche that would make a perfect little sitting area. A very small master bathroom had no windows and no room for expansion and was the main drawback of the house. However, there was an area where we could build a master bedroom walk-in closet by taking some space from the bedroom adjacent to the master bedroom.

The large attic had wood floors which would be perfect for storing all of Grandma's exquisite Christmas decorations and other items needing storage. The attic entrance was located in the hallway with access through a hatch in the ceiling and would require a ladder to reach. We thought we could add a set of pull-down steps to create an easier method of access.

The house was over a hundred years old and needed its three bathrooms, kitchen, and laundry room completely gutted. We'd also need to update the old, nonconforming electrical system and install a new heating system and an air-conditioning system. The windows in the eating area of the kitchen and the skylights on the porch would need a lot of work and possibly even need to be replaced. The basement, with an entrance to the backyard, was dark, and dirty and one of the beams holding up the first floor was sagging from termite damage and would need to be replaced. We thought that someday we could add a bathroom and create additional rooms, maybe even a separate apartment in the basement.

The house would take a lot of money and a lot of work to bring it back to what it once was. However, the asking price was low, and we felt we would enjoy the work and be able to put our personal stamp on the house by renovating and restoring the grand old place ourselves. We would have over eight months to make the house ready for us to live in.

We were delighted with the house. We loved the neighborhood, the huge old oak trees reaching across the street, the curving sidewalks, the overall look of the house, the size of the lot, and the floor plan. We talked for hours about our ideas for the renovation, and when we did, we would laugh as we made the sound *ka-ching, ka-ching* of a cash register every time we came up with another project/idea for the house.

We were so excited and couldn't wait for the purchase to be finalized. We'd given the realtor our signed contract and a big down payment to show we were serious. We had stipulated no contingencies except the inspection, which had just been completed, and the contingency was therefore waived. We asked for an inspection because we wanted to know what else we might have to do on the house before we moved in, not because we would not buy it.

We explained to Kevin and Mary that the house had been one of ten properties owned by an investor who had gone bankrupt. He desperately needed to sell something quickly or go into foreclosure on all ten properties, one of which he wanted to keep. He was very pleased with our offer and had signed the papers. When our realtor telephoned with the news that he accepted our offer, we celebrated. Our very first house! We thought about Grandma's lovely things and how elegant they would look in the house. We knew Grandma would be proud of us!

The inspector had come to look at the house and told us the house was relatively sound, just needing what we'd planned to do anyway; the electrical, air, and heating systems, the basement beam, and the windows in the kitchen nook and skylights on the porch. Luckily the slate roof seemed in good shape, needing only minor repair and gutters. The inspector told us that the windows in the kitchen and porch could be saved but would need a lot of work. If we were willing to put in the work, we could save a great deal of money. He suggested that in five or ten years, we consider having new windows and skylights installed so we'd save on heat and air-conditioning bills. But he warned us that this would cost quite a lot of money to do.

We talked it over and decided to do as much of the work as we could do ourselves and were willing to make another investment for new windows in the future because we loved the house and thought a second investment and the long-term savings on heat and electric well worth it. So we celebrated and thanked God for bringing us to just the right house and giving us such a wonderful blessing. We told each other that God had blessed us because we had made the decision to follow Him and had studied His word and committed our lives to our faith. We were very proud of ourselves! Now of course, looking back, we remembered the old adage that "pride goeth before a fall."

A few days after we purchased the house, our realtor called to tell us there was a problem. According to the realtor, the owner's bank claimed that the ten properties couldn't be separated. Evidently they had been placed as a group of properties into foreclosure the same day we made the purchase. Therefore all ten properties would have to be sold together or foreclosed together, and the deal with us had to be cancelled.

We were devastated. We'd looked for so long for a house. We'd been getting discouraged and tired and impatient. We wanted to have everything perfect for the day we were married. We wanted to move into a house that would already be set up with all the things we cherished. This had been the first house we looked at that we both felt fit us perfectly. We were heartbroken to lose it. Then devastated, then angry. Then, sadly, we felt resentful.

We easily let our human nature get in our way and were not happy campers. Instead of trusting God, we surprised ourselves by feeling angry. We even dared to comment that we felt as if a carrot had been dangled before us and whisked away. For a few days we complained to one another, to the realtor, to every relative and friend, to every co-worker, and even complained when we prayed. Matt told Kevin and Mary that they were lucky not to have known us yet.

We had growled, grumped, and grumbled. We questioned, queried, and quarreled. We let everyone know we were heartily disappointed to lose the house and couldn't understand why this had to happen to us. Our bad attitude was reflected in everything we said and did. Our loss took over our lives, and our bad attitudes affected everyone, and even our prayer life. We felt anger, and even resentment at times, and knew this was wrong. We felt out of control and couldn't seem to prevent our feelings yet were secretly ashamed of our reaction, and this contributed even further to our anger.

But within a day or two, a little sense returned. We began to realize that we should not have behaved the way we did and saw that we'd been the worst possible example of a child of God. We hadn't given God the benefit of the doubt at all. *After all*, we reasoned, *perhaps there is something wrong with the house and God is protecting us. Perhaps there is something much better, safer, more important for us if we would trust and wait.* And we wondered, *Ahh, patience, where are you?* We recalled that the trust we believed we had, had flown out the window as soon as we didn't get our way, as soon as we met up with disappointment. We felt guilty but were also still heartily disappointed.

As we talked about what we should do, we changed direction with our thoughts, shooing the bad guys from our heads and trying to say "thank you" to God for what had happened, even though to us it still felt like bad news. It wasn't easy for us because we wanted *that* house. Finally we did what we felt was right (gritting our teeth at first), and eventually we felt better for it. We used Grandma's old trick of yelling "No!" whenever we'd start complaining about losing the house, so we could rid our mind of the bad thoughts. We tried to focus on what would come into our future another day. When I would start grumbling, Matt would yell to me "NO!" and I'd laugh with the realization that I was grumbling again even though I hadn't realized what I was doing just a minute ago. I'd do the same to him when he started grumbling and complaining.

We began our search for a house again and tired ourselves by putting more of our free time into the new search. Within a few weeks we found another house, a little smaller than the first, not as pretty, and not in such a lovely setting. When the inspection was completed, we learned of a few unexpected and serious problems. The house needed a new roof and would need the pointing replaced between the bricks on the entire outside of the house. There was also evidence of water leakage into the basement. We asked our realtor to give us a few days to think this over before we made our final decision. We weren't perfectly happy with the new house, but we were tired and impatient, and it was, after all, the second best house we'd seen out of over one hundred we'd looked at.

A few days later, our realtor telephoned, and we thought she called to ask for our decision about the purchase of the second house. But instead, she sounded excited and rushed, talking a mile a minute. She asked if Matt and I could both get on the phone at the same time, so Matt went into the bedroom and picked up the second phone.

Our realtor told us that one of the officers of the bank holding the mortgages on the first property we purchased had just telephoned her. He told her the bank would be willing to split up the ten properties if the buyers met four criteria. The first was to make an immediate offer, the second was to pay cash for the house, the third to purchase the house "as is," meaning no inspection and no contingencies, and fourth to go to settlement in no more than four weeks. Our realtor explained that she could easily cancel the contract we signed for the second house because it had been contingent on a satisfactory inspection and the inspection had uncovered many unexpected and serious problems.

We jumped for joy. Our house was available again! We quickly decided that we could meet the four requirements the bank requested by borrowing from our families and repaying them when we took the bank loan that would include the money we needed for the renovation. We did have a couple of resources from which to get the quick interim money. We had been prequalified for a loan, so we knew that obtaining the loan after settling on the "as is" sale should be no problem other than the added expense of two settlements. Thank goodness! So we said, "YES!" And the realtor came right over with the papers, and we signed.

When we read the papers the realtor brought, to our absolute amazement, the price she listed on the contract for the house, as is, no contingencies, quick settlement, was twenty thousand dollars *less* than what we offered the first time! The realtor told us the bank had suggested the price. She added that the bank reasoned that they needed the money immediately to get the other properties unencumbered and, unaware that we had already had an inspection and concerned that an inspection on such an old and unoccupied house would uncover a lot of problems, wanted to ensure by the low price that we buy the house. They wanted a quick and a sure settlement and had simply offered the house to us at a price that they were comfortable with and which they felt would make us agree to the purchase under their terms.

We were thrilled, and it was absolutely a jumping-up-and-down kind of thrilled. This savings would pay for some of our renovations! When the realtor left, we grabbed one another and danced around the room. We used words like "ecstatic" and "miracle" and "incredible" and "I can't believe it"! Then "wow," "golly," "unbelievable," and finally, "What a blessing!" "Golly gee whillickers," I yelled liked Grandma always did when she was excited.

When we calmed down we suddenly felt ashamed that we had initially complained so much. We were mortified to realize that we had been angry with God because we thought we'd lost the house. We felt embarrassed by our actions, chastised, and repentant. We felt that we'd gone through a test and had failed miserably. We also realized we had been arrogant. We thought we deserved the house and had somehow earned the right to have it. I was frightened and told Matt that for the first time in my life I really understood what the word *humiliated* meant. I was truly humbled by what had occurred, by my reaction.

But while Matt agreed with me and felt that we had behaved badly, he also looked at the situation a little differently, always with the glass half full. Matt explained that he felt we would always be sinners and God knew that we had to learn this so we'd be more careful in the future, not so sure of ourselves, and certainly not feel entitled. He said that if we learned with each mistake we made, we'd eventually get to the point of growth and development that would bring joy to God's heart. He reminded me that with God's grace we had come to our senses in two days, and in our hearts we did finally accept gratefully whatever it would be that God deemed right for us. Matt felt that God rewarded us for our final attitude, for our struggle toward that attitude and, despite our disappointment, for finally doing what was right in God's eyes. And I began to cry, happy for forgiveness, sad that I knew I'd disappointed Him, hopeful that I would do better in the future. Perhaps they were tears of humility.

"So," we told Kevin and Mary, "we prayed. And prayed, and prayed. And we were sorry, really sorry, that we hadn't measured up to the kind of person we wanted to be, or immediately felt what we wished we could always feel or think in our relationship with God. It was a humbling experience, one that we really learned from. We hoped we'd do better the next time we were faced with the choice to complain or to accept what God allowed into our lives. And we were thankful, so thankful for a new beginning and for the gift that Christ gave us so we could be forgiven."

As we discussed what we experienced, we also touched on the fact that we'd also learned the value of Holy Communion. Without this, we would have had to carry the burden of our mistakes forever. Thankfully, we could be forgiven because of the sacrifice Christ made for us. Matt remembered that there were six things we needed to remind ourselves so we could be sure we were taking Holy Communion worthily. They were to:

- Acknowledge our sin and our sinful nature
- Sincerely repent and gauge our sincerity by the remorse we feel
- Earnestly resolve to do our best not to repeat that sin
- Have a longing in our heart to be right with God
- Recognize the sacrifice Christ made for us for the forgiveness of our sins
- Forgive those who have sinned against us

We appreciated that we could have this gift because of the sacrifice that Christ made, by His perfect life, His suffering for us, and His ascension. We also had to be able to forgive others as we were being forgiven.

And forgive us our debts, as we forgive our debtors.
—Matthew 6:12

He that humbleth himself shall be exalted.
—Luke 18:14

Now I rejoice . . . that ye sorrowed to repentance . . .
For godly sorrow worketh repentance to salvation.
—2 Corinthians 7:9, 10

Wherefore whosoever shall eat this bread,
and drink this cup of the Lord, unworthily, shall be guilty . . .
But let a man examine himself.
—1 Corinthians 11:27, 28

Because God was so good to us, we had a new beginning, were now in our new home, bank loans were finally in place for the renovation, the beam had been replaced in the basement, the radiators were steaming beautifully with a new burner in the basement, and we had bright new copper water pipes, and . . . we had made two new friends!

We were so happy and wanted to live our life in a way that pleased God and yet were humbled enough to now recognize that this may be an ongoing battle for us for the rest of our lives. We also recognized that the evil one, Satan, would still be coming at us, sometimes subtly and sometimes with an out-and-out easily recognizable onslaught. We knew that we needed to recognize these times and resolve to keep watch on ourselves and keep our prayer life strong.

Meanwhile, our new air-conditioning system would soon be installed and I was proud of myself for coming up with a great idea for the new system. When I arrived at the house one evening during the week to help Matt with the woodwork, he was talking with the man who would be installing the air-conditioning system. They were discussing where the ducts would be placed throughout the parlor, entry, and dining rooms. As I listened, I was worried because what they were suggesting would take away from the beautiful architectural lines of these rooms by introducing clumsy boxes running across the ceilings. These were deemed necessary for housing the ducts that would carry the cooled air from the air handler.

Understanding the principal that hot air rises and cold air falls, I suggested that the air-conditioning unit be placed in the attic. "If a duct was placed over the top of the stairwell," I said, "since cold air falls, it will naturally travel down the stairs into the parlor. This room is our main esthetic problem in terms of adding ducts. The air will be coming down the stairs and will circulate to the entry and dining rooms, especially if the ducts through the bedroom closets to the living room, study, and kitchen provide cool air that will also be circulating through these rooms toward a return duct." I wasn't concerned about the kitchen, study, or living or family room because there were places for the ducts to travel from upstairs that would be relatively hidden, mostly through the new bedroom closets we were installing. But the parlor, entry, and dining rooms were causing an aesthetic problem if we had to build those ugly boxes across the ceilings.

Matt and the air-conditioning consultant looked at me, surprised, and for a moment were silent, pondering what I'd said. But then, they smiled, and I knew they liked the idea. I could see the wheels turning in their heads, and when they walked around the rooms one more time, they had worked it out. They came back to stand next to me, looked at me, shook their heads, and jokingly said, "Don't tell anyone that we didn't come up with this idea!" I was as proud as a peacock, and the pretty architectural details I loved so much were saved from the ugly intrusion of boxy ducts! I smiled at Matt and said, "I won't tell toooo many people, my dearest-darling-sweetheart-love." And Matt grinned.

When Kevin and Mary arrived for lunch the following Saturday, we told them our neat idea for eliminating some of the air-conditioning ducts, and they wished they had thought of the idea because they never liked all the ductwork that broke up the ceilings in their own house. Mary said she was concerned because their ductwork presented the sharp angles and corners that Feng Shui told them would send poison arrows at them and bring them bad luck.

Mary and Kevin stayed to help us after lunch, and we discussed their concern about "bad luck." We told them we searched the Bible to help us with any given problem because we had learned that God's protection was more powerful than any other. Matt challenged Kevin to see if the Bible gave any clues about the practice of Feng Shui explaining that we'd often been surprised by what amazing information the Bible provided when we looked for specifics. Kevin grinned and quickly agreed. We liked this couple so much and wanted the best for them.

Chapter Five

THE SUBTLE HOOK

We were relieved that Kevin and Mary had not gotten angry with us when we asked if they would study the Bible with us to look for God's word about Feng Shui. In fact, Kevin seemed excited about the prospect, even somehow relieved. They had come for lunch and stayed the rest of the day. We all worked in the same room and talked and talked. Matt and I had armed ourselves with information about Feng Shui and were determined, through an open discussion, to try to shake their faith in Feng Shui as a major luck giver.

We talked about the many people who thought that ancient wisdom, by virtue of having survived for so many years, was valued and protected. We spoke about the awe that can exist about the mystical knowledge held by ancient civilizations. We admitted that we felt it prudent to keep an open mind toward much of the ancient wisdom and that the original form of many ancient practices were based on studies of nature and mathematics.

But we did tell Kevin and Mary we learned that the Bible tells us to be cautious of some ancient practices despite the fact that they seem benign and promise us solutions to pressing problems. Matt explained that the Bible never refutes the claims these practices make, only warns us who can manipulate situations to appear to control its power, and how that can seriously harm us. He explained that the Bible reiterates many times over that God asks that our loyalty and trust be placed in Him and not in anything else. Matt used the three wise men as an example of an ancient practice providing a benefit. The Bible tells us that the wise men forecast the birth of Christ by the stars and followed a star to locate the Christ child. However, emphatically and in many areas of the Bible, we are told that because of the danger to us, we are not to place our trust in the practice or predictions of astrology or the apparent signs of astronomy.

We told Kevin and Mary that we realized Feng Shui is an ancient practice that makes many promises that cover important areas of our lives, but we worried about remedies that seemed in some cases to be so complex and in others too easy. I told Mary that I made a list of the problems that Feng Shui indicated its practice could solve and how. I tacked my list to the wall where we were washing down the woodwork and suggested we read them and discuss them while we worked.

The first item I'd copied from one of the library books stated that for better health, one should move their bed to the corner of the room that is across and diagonal to the bedroom's entry door. As we discussed this, we agreed that this may reduce stress by allowing the occupant of the bed to easily identify who came into the room and could possibly protect them from a draft, so it may indeed have a practical application. We also agreed that a bed usually looked best on the far end of the room as well. We also agreed that this action certainly could not alone cure a serious illness. We addressed the power of suggestion and the power of the mind but agreed that nevertheless there was no basis for making the claim of a cure.

Mary read the second item which said that to obtain lifelong friendships, one was to place a painting of mountains filled with pine trees in the entry hall or the living room. We could not think of a practical reason why this would work. Kevin observed that mountains were immovable and that pinecones lasted a long time, so perhaps it was simply that connection, a sort of symbolism.

Kevin read the next one, which said that to increase wealth, one should place coins in a metal box on a cabinet behind the desk or atop the desk. Kevin and Mary mentioned that when Mary did this a few weeks ago, Kevin had received a promotion. None of us could think of a practical reason why this would have worked, so Matt suggested that we keep this one in mind and return to it later because he was concerned about what power may have made the coins appear to work for them. Matt told Kevin that he wanted to show him what the Bible said about the power of Satan.

I went on to read that for a happy marriage, one was instructed to hang a red-and-gold double happiness sign written in Chinese calligraphy in the southwest corner of the bedroom. We didn't see any practical consideration in these suggestions and had to agree that it seemed more superstition than anything else.

The list continued, promising that to obtain greater endurance, use chrysanthemums, bamboo, or pine trees in the home's décor; to enhance a career, place a clear quartz crystal paperweight on the desk and keep wastebasket bins out of sight; and for a long life, incorporate tortoise-shell patterns into the décor. Once again we could find no practical application or reason why these things should work as promised, except again as symbolism and very possibly a means through which Satan could work.

Surprisingly, Mary commented that all these suggestions did seem too easy somehow. She said she'd never heard the promises grouped together before and sounded worried that the solutions seemed so simple. I went on reading, and we learned that to increase wisdom, use elephants in the décor and paintings containing clouds on the wall; and to obtain specific strengths, incorporate into the décor those animals which represent the strength you seek. To gain peace, use vases as ornaments in various rooms or as the subject of paintings on the wall, and to have fidelity from others, place a statue or picture of a crane in the home. For protection from harmful people, place an eight hollow-rod wind chime in the northwest compass direction of your room; and to live an upright life, use the lotus flower in your décor.

As they listened to me rattle off the rest of the list, Kevin and Mary agreed that life couldn't possibly be arranged that easily, and we all asked, "Aren't these promises too good to be true?" and we all answered with an unequivocal, "Yes." *Nevertheless,* I said, *these are claims and promises given by Feng Shui, and most Feng Shui followers believe them.* Mary noted that when they didn't work, the Feng Shui master would find other solutions by using charts and other materials to guide him. Again Matt asked, "What if when they do work, a dangerous power may have made them work?" For the moment we were all quiet, wondering at the importance of his statement.

Matt went to get our Bible. He had marked a few passages he wanted Kevin and Mary to hear. The first one he read was written by the apostle Peter and said:

But there were false prophets also among the people,
even as there shall be false teachers among you, who privily
shall be in damnable heresies, even denying the Lord
that brought them, and bring upon themselves swift destruction.

—2 Peter 2:1

And the second Bible verse that Matt read, which was from Jeremiah in the Old Testament said,

They prophesy unto you a false vision
and divination, and a thing of nought, and the
deceit of their heart.

—Jeremiah 14:14

Matt said, "Here God clearly warns us to watch carefully for those who teach false doctrines. When we believe and follow these false doctrines, we can lose our soul's salvation." Mary and Kevin were quiet for a moment, but then asked if we agreed that Feng Shui seemed based on the requirement that we seek and find the way to live in harmony with nature and that when we are in harmony with nature, we'd be happy. Matt suggested that to adjust all the things Feng Shui mentioned seemed daunting and impossible to fulfill and asked, "Who is to say we are living in harmony with nature? Who and how can one make that determination? If something goes wrong in our life, it is not only an easy scapegoat to say it is because we moved out of harmony with nature, but also a great moneymaker for the one who supposedly helps us get back into harmony."

Mary explained that she had just read that Qi, Yin and Yang, the five elements, the proper symbols, one's personal "magic" number, their animal, astrological chart, and personal chant must all be in place to create perfect harmony, especially when a changing circumstance would require an adjustment of these items frequently. Matt commented that this is why he would become leery about Feng Shui and would think of it as a moneymaker for the advisor.

He added that if the practice of Feng Shui were something God did not want us to do, we would be serving the spirits of the world that God warns against. If we practiced Feng Shui only for the so-called practical parts, we'd still be taking the chance that even more spirits would enter our lives further separating us from God. Matt found the verse in Matthew that had always fascinated him and also indicated that the people of our time would also have this occur to them and read,

> *Then goeth he, and taketh with himself seven other spirits more wicked*
> *than himself, and they enter in and dwell there,*
> *and the last state of that man is worse*
> *than the first. Even so shall it be also unto this wicked generation.*
> —Matthew 12:45

Mary felt that Feng Shui encompassed an incredible view of how the various parts of nature worked together and didn't believe it was all that bad. She said that for instance, Qi is expressed by a written two-part Chinese symbol that represents steam or clouds rising above a grain of rice, and the cloud denotes the nourishment (water) provided to the field that grows the rice that sustains life. The water falls as rain to feed the rice then, as the field dries, evaporates to feed the cloud. The water, which is vital to both the cloud and the rice, is symbolic of the Qi, which flows everywhere.

She explained that Qi is believed to be both a spiritual and physical form of universal energy, which cannot be seen or measured. According to Chinese philosophy, the energy of the earth, which is sometimes called the cosmic breath or more commonly Qi, and the earth's elements must be funneled, grouped correctly, and balanced in order to promote health and wellness.

Mary explained that Feng Shui is, in essence, the study and perfection of how to encourage Qi to enter and flow through our environment, moving in the proper quantity, with the proper propulsion. Her master told her that the proper placement of decorating elements causes natural energy (Qi) to pass through our environment properly, bringing improved health, wealth, and happiness.

We could see that Mary had learned a great deal about Feng Shui by how her arguments appeared well developed. But Kevin was uneasy, not realizing that Mary knew so much detail about Feng Shui, yet he wanted to understand it himself so he would know what to do. Kevin wanted what was best for them both and felt they should continue these discussions until they could make the right decision. He didn't want anything in their lives that would harm them.

Mary explained that *Feng* meant wind or air and represents our breathing process: inhaling fresh air and exhaling stagnant air. Without this process (the taking in of air), we would die in minutes. *Shui*, meaning water, represents the fluids within the body. Water makes up 60 percent of the human body, and without water we would die within days.

She told us that the Feng Shui master can recognize those areas where the flow or movement has stagnated, is in excess, or is deficient. In essence, the master "diagnoses" what needs to be corrected and "prescribes" the remedy to eliminate or at least lessen the problem encountered. Matt and I looked at one another and instantly understood that this could be likened to the work of the sorcerer and astrologer we are warned about throughout scripture.

> *And it shall be unto them as a false*
> *divination in their sight.*
> —Ezekiel 21:23

"We need to know what God says on these subjects," Matt said, "see if there are guidelines and if there are warnings. We need to find how God wants us to live and be an example of godliness to those who are entrusted to our care and ask if Feng Shui could be a way of keeping us from calling on the Holy Spirit, separating us from God, or making us depend on another source of help."

Matt conjectured that it was possible that in ancient China, when the principles of Feng Shui were first developing, the proper flow of Qi, or air, was imperative to the health and well-being of the people. They were without the benefits of antibiotics and modern-day medicines or the benefits of the four or five-person household of present times. Then it was commonplace for ten or fifteen person households to be crowded into small quarters. Because the general population did not understand science, they believed largely in luck, magic, and the mystical. They did heed mystical advice or one purported to bring good luck. Therefore an astute medicine man, clan leader, chieftain, or religious leader seeking to help his people might have couched the practical in terms of the mystical to ensure the people's acceptance.

Perhaps in this light, we could better accept the mystical essence of how Qi came to be regarded as a flow of air and health. "But," Matt said, "could something good become an avenue of use to Satan, and could the divination parts of Feng Shui possibly have evolved this way?"

Some trust in chariots, and some in horses;
but we will remember
the name of the LORD our God.

—Psalm 20:7

But let all those that put their trust in thee rejoice: let them
ever shout for joy, because thou defendest them:
let them also that love thy name be joyful in thee.

—Psalm 5:11

Matt tried to explain that those whose faith revolves around scripture believe that the Bible not only records the historical words and deeds of God but also gives helpful advice, direction, and warnings needed for our lives. "God means the Bible to be the help manual we rely on when we have important decisions to make or problems to solve that are affecting our lives. It also teaches us that good spirits [the Holy Spirit and angels] and bad spirits [Satan and his helpers] have a tremendous impact on our world and our lives as they battle for our souls. Therefore we need to discern carefully what is good for us and what is harmful."

Mary asked Matt about the force of opposites, such as good and evil, God and Satan, and told us that patterns of opposites, studied in great detail by the Chinese, are symbolized as Yin and Yang, which literally means shade and light. In Feng Shui, the Yin and Yang of a home must be brought into harmony, so Qi can flow smoothly throughout the home in the quantities required by the particular occupants of the home. The flow of Qi is encouraged by the friction or action between Yin and Yang. Matt thought that an analogy to the action between Yin and Yang would be the action of a fan pulling or pushing air through a room.

Mary went on to explain that a room that does not have the harmony (balance) required to encourage the movement of Qi, due to the improper combining of Yin and Yang, is said to be Sha Qi, which means imbalanced. Anything less than the optimum distribution of Yin and Yang objects (opposites) will inhibit the Qi from flowing properly. While they are opposites of each other, they work in synergy when correctly balanced. If that balance is disturbed, trouble arises in one's life, and the Feng Shui master must be called in to correct the balance of Yin and Yang.

Matt said the same is true with God, that when we are out of balance or out of step with what He teaches, trouble arises in our lives. While God hears our prayers and sees our troubles, He is bound by certain rules due to His righteousness. This is why we can know with certainty that if we strive to follow Him, we can always obtain His help and the forgiveness of sin. However, the impact of sin on our lives can hold us back from proper communication with God and thus from obtaining God's help. God's protection against the evil (negative forces) of Satan through the use of the good (positive forces) of the Holy Spirit of God brings us into a properly balanced life. He reiterated that Satan takes things similar to what God says and turns it into something that eventually causes confusion, doubt, or apathy.

As the hours slipped away and our discussion came to an end, Kevin told Sarah and Matt that he was so grateful for their open mind and willingness to try to understand Mary's interest in Feng Shui. He also thanked Matt for wanting to share his faith with them. He told Matt that he wanted to do what was right but needed to know what that was. Kevin and Mary both hugged us as they left for the day and made plans for us to see each other again the following Saturday.

Chapter Six

IT'S COMMON SENSE

When Mary and Kevin arrived home after spending the afternoon with Matt and Sarah, Kevin said that as he listened to Matt and Sarah, he began to remember some of the Bible studies he'd attended as a young boy. He felt that he wanted to move back to these beliefs and that for him to do so he needed Mary to put aside the Feng Shui mumbo jumbo she was hooked on.

Mary was suddenly afraid. She was torn, not knowing what to believe anymore. She trusted Feng Shui despite the doubts that Matt and Sarah placed in her mind. *What if Matt and Sarah were wrong? What if bad luck came back and engulfed her once again and something terrible happened if she stopped using Feng Shui? Where was she supposed to turn, what was she supposed to do about her fear, where would she get the help she so desperately needed? How could she manage this without Feng Shui?*

"Common sense! Doesn't it make sense to believe in common sense?" Mary asked Kevin. "So far, that's the only so-called hook of Feng Shui we've experienced, and it's all so, well, natural," she said. "And no sharp edges? Well of course that's practical if it prevents someone from hitting their shin or their head on a sharp edge! Hearing the sound of water or watching tropical fish move through a fish tank *is* relaxing! I can understand that too. And what Feng Shui says about fire, air, water, earth and metal, well, they are a natural part of the earth, aren't they? Compasses always point north, doesn't that have something to do with the magnetic pull of the earth? And the cycles of life really opened my eyes to nature, Kevin. That makes sense too! Feng Shui really seems to know what it's all about, so it can't be all that bad! Why does it upset you?" Mary asked. Kevin could see her fear and how upset it made her.

Softly, Kevin responded by telling Mary, "It's true that there is an appearance of 'naturalness' in Feng Shui, and some things do not seem to conflict with the Bible, at least not yet," he said. "As Matt and Sarah explained the Bible to us, even you had to see a warning in God's words. What if it is wrong in God's eyes?"

Badly frightened about the prospect of being forced to give up Feng Shui, Mary accused Kevin of relishing and encouraging the discussions of the Bible. She had listened carefully to what Matt and Sarah said and was angry now because she felt threatened. If Kevin made her stop using Feng Shui right now, she had nothing to take its place, nothing that could help her, nothing that could make her feel safe. The old familiar panic began to rise in her throat, making her sick with fear.

Kevin saw her reaction, recognized her fear. To placate her, he suggested that perhaps they could study both Feng Shui and the Bible for the next few weeks while continuing to seek the counsel of Matt and Sarah. He told Mary that he felt Matt and Sarah seemed to understand a great deal about Feng Shui and they ought to listen to all that Matt and Sarah believed about these subjects. "But then," he said, "we will have to choose for ourselves." He told Mary that he felt strongly that Feng Shui and the Bible were not compatible with each other and that, while he understood that Mary felt pushed into a corner and resentful of Matt and Sarah, at the same time she had to see that it was a conversation that was long overdue between them. He also told her that it was important for them to be doing what was right even if that choice would be difficult for Mary.

As they prepared for bed, Mary felt that her only recourse was to learn as much as she could about Feng Shui so she could persuade everyone that it was okay to use. She asked Kevin if he would agree that he and Matt and Sarah would listen to her side of the story too, and then they could all decide what was right or wrong together. Kevin agreed to this and, for the moment, Mary felt her panic begin to subside. Maybe it would all work out.

She began her serious research at the library and on the Internet the next morning and learned that the Feng Shui master would incorporate the five natural elements into the interior design of the home through the symbols of those elements. These would act as an agent for change when a problem needed to be corrected. The five elements were wood, fire, earth, metal, and water.

> *For he maketh small the drops of water:*
> *they pour down rain according to the vapour thereof:*
> *which the clouds do drop and distil upon man abundantly.*
> —Job 36:27, 28

According to Chinese studies, there were set relationships between the five elements. Through the careful study of nature and its cycles, the Chinese recognized how the elements worked together and how the cycles seemed to be repeated, with each cycle ending and beginning anew. These studies were one of the many tools employed by Feng Shui masters to determine the proper remedies for each negative influence they found in a home. They believed these negative influences are what caused illness and misfortune to the occupants. They believed that the proper use of symbols countered the negative influences and brought specific benefits into the home.

Feng Shui taught that using wood increases benevolence, loyalty, and forgiveness; using earth increases honesty and faith; using a metal element increases righteousness and meticulousness; using a water element provides insight and motivation and increases social contacts; and using a fire element increases wisdom, reason, and etiquette. These studies also determined that there were set relationships between the elements and that each element could have a strengthening or weakening effect upon one another.

Mary's library books described how wood is assisted by water, hurt by metal, weakened by fire; yet wood causes weakness to earth. Similarly, fire is assisted by wood, hurt by water, weakened by earth, yet will cause weakness to metal. Earth is assisted by fire, hurt by wood, weakened by metal, but causes weakness to water. Metal is assisted by earth, hurt by fire, weakened by water, but can cause weakness to wood. Water is assisted by metal, hurt by earth, weakened by wood, but causes weakness to fire.

This began to boggle Mary's mind, and she couldn't help but think back on how everything seemed so easy before. *God wouldn't have planned the elements of nature to confuse mankind and make him crazy with worry,* she thought. Doubts about Feng Shui began to frighten her, for if she lost faith in this, where was she to go, what would she do? She struggled to read more, wanting to believe, wanting to find more that she could defend. Then she could continue in her belief that Feng Shui could really protect her and that God wouldn't object to it.

Mary knew that the principles stating the interaction between the elements raised fascinating and thought-provoking questions, and she asked herself if she could believe that the strengthening or the weakening influences of one element upon another could have an impact on her life. *Can an element really affect me in any way?* she wondered.

She knew that metal exposed to moisture would rust; this information can affect building methods. Water running with force or rising from the rain can have a detrimental effect on the soil or the planted field, causing us to build a dike or a dam or to build our homes higher than the flooding level of a river. She knew that many people felt that wearing a copper bracelet brings them relief from arthritis.

Suddenly Mary felt too tired to study anymore, yet she needed to get these questions answered. If she didn't, it was going to destroy her relationship with Kevin. Kevin was her best friend and the only one she could talk to about the past. He'd never judged her; he accepted her and loved her and had always been willing to listen and to comfort her and assure her when everything overwhelmed her. She was lucky to have him and worried that she wasn't being fair to him.

Kevin wanted children. She did too. But she was still afraid that so much would eventually have to be said about the past once other people entered the picture. She knew it was time for change, knew that Kevin deserved more. While she wanted to make changes, was she ready? Could she do it now? If Feng Shui were to leave her life, maybe she would plunge into the terrible abyss she feared. Should she trust what Kevin said, that she would be surprised at how everything would be okay?

Mary decided that she had to try to trust Kevin and also to trust Matt and Sarah because Kevin trusted them. Perhaps she should encourage their discussions to continue and accept wherever they led. Perhaps she should talk to Sarah. Maybe this would help her stop this horrible fear of rejection and more hurt and pain. Little by little, Mary convinced herself that she would go along with their discussions about Feng Shui with an open mind and be willing to give it up if she had to. She would also begin to feel Sarah out to see if she could trust her with why she was so afraid.

Kevin and Mary walked across the street on Monday night to surprise Matt and Sarah who were thrilled to see them and didn't mind at all continuing their discussion. They began by jumping on the question of whether or not there could be a detrimental effect on those who live atop a gold mine or any other mineral deposit, thereby being surrounded by metal. Or on those who live on a tiny island surrounded by water. Or on those who lived in the dense woods in a log cabin and were surrounded by wood. Would this cause an imbalance in their lives? Had the scientific community reported any benefit or detriment to anyone living near the north or south poles? Have there been any scientific findings regarding the electromagnetic forces of the earth or its elements and their effect on us?

Mary asked Matt if he believed an imbalance could be corrected by Qi simply picking up energy from an element that had been placed in the room to offset elements already built into the room. Matt said that Eastern cultures seemed to believe that life is based on the timely birth, life, death, and rejuvenation of the elements that make up our physical world. They believe that understanding the cycles of life would help one discover how to influence the effects of that cycle on an individual and that there are three cycles of life, described by the Chinese as the Production Cycle, the Destruction Cycle, and the Reduction Cycle. They are expressed in terms of the five elements of wood, fire, earth, metal, and water. Each cycle moves through its five steps and then repeats the cycle again.

The Production Cycle includes wood that burns to produce fire, which then produces ash or earth, which then compresses to produce metal and which then produces water, which then nourishes the vegetation which grows into more wood. The Destruction Cycle shows that water destroys fire, which melts metal, which destroys the tree whose wood puts roots down to feed on earth, which absorbs water. The Reduction Cycle demonstrates that earth controls fire, which controls wood, which controls water, which controls metal, which controls earth.

Kevin noted that by using this information about the cycles, it would appear that an office with a wood desk and metal file cabinets would not be in harmony. According to the Destruction Cycle, the metal would injure the wood. Yet according to the Reduction Cycle, it appears that to add a water element would offset any negative effect by diminishing the strength of the metal. Thus, according to Feng Shui, because this is how nature works, this is how we should view our environment and adjust it accordingly. "But," said Kevin, using the Destruction Cycle as an example, "the premise is that in the home, metal file cabinets will destroy a wood desk." "However," Matt countered, "in the home environment these elements are no longer in the compressing or cutting or expanding stages of their development in nature. Their 'life,' and thus their ability to function in these roles, has ended, or at least been suspended until they are thrown into a dump to recycle." They had to conclude that these are questions that Feng Shui does not seem to address, except that all things have a primordial energy with predictable patterns.

Beware lest any man spoil you through philosophy
and vain deceit, after the tradition of men, after the rudiments
of the world, and not after Christ.

—Colossians 2:8

Mary found what she thought was a great debate for them. It was about the use of Feng Shui in the corporate world. She explained that there is a special draw in Feng Shui for the corporate world. According to Feng Shui, the proper placement of entry doors, windows, and even the desks in office buildings entice wealth to these businesses. Therefore, Feng Shui masters are in demand throughout the Asian world and command high fees, often into the millions of dollars.

Even the somewhat dated library books listed a number of examples. Bank buildings belonging to Citibank, Bank of America, and the Bank of Canada, and Trump Tower in New York City, MGM Grand Hotel in Las Vegas, the White Sox Stadium in Chicago, and the Budweiser Brewery in Budvar, Czech Republic, use Feng Shui. Interestingly, in Hong Kong, there are buildings that are considered to need Feng Shui to "offset" the bad luck that another building produces, such as I. M. Pei's Bank of China building with its "bad luck" triangular shaped construction. So ominous is the luck emanating from this building that the building opposite installed cranes to reflect the bad luck back to I. M. Pei's Bank of China. There is also a hotel designed by a Feng Shui master with a hole in its top as an entrance for a dragon to bring good luck. The Forbidden City in China, built by the Ming Emperor and rebuilt by the Qing ruler, was based on Feng Shui's geomantic principles, as are many of today's businesses and offices in China and Japan.

The corporate world uses Feng Shui not only to attract money (high profits) into their buildings and success into their endeavors but also to promote good will and good health within their employees. *Why would the corporate world put so much faith in Feng Shui?* they wondered.

Sarah felt that the hope of financial gain is one of the appeals. A corporation will hire an interior designer, paid for by corporate funds, so why not choose one who makes promises to draw wealth to the company as opposed to someone who simply decorates? That's practical and makes sense as long as the decorating gets done in the same pleasing and efficient manner and, possibly, costs no more. Cynically, Kevin said, "Yeah, if finances go well, great! Suppose they go well for a while and then diminish. If the Feng Shui master comes back, introduces a 'water element' such as a fountain, and business picks up again, who gets the credit? Feng Shui? Certainly not the sales force unless it were said that they excelled because of Feng Shui." Kevin observed that because of these "successes," trust in Feng Shui grows and the Feng Shui consultant is paid again. If business slumps the following year, the Feng Shui master is called in once more. When changes are made, the master gets paid again. Perhaps business picks up and it's a vicious cycle with the consumer paying for all these consultations.

Matt asked, "But how does this work? I think that the most serious question remains to be answered. Is it possible that the power we spoke of earlier, Satan, could cause a positive reaction to the suggested mumbo jumbo? Or should we attribute the success or failure of a business simply to the fact that it did or did not use Feng Shui principles? Is it because the building faces a certain direction or because the doors to the office are positioned a certain way? Is it because desks and chairs are facing a particular direction or because a wind chime hangs in a certain corner? Or could these successes be due to good business sense or even coincidence because we have done our homework when making major decisions? Have we chosen to build a business in the heart of a growing business district or built a home taking into consideration the way the winds come off the mountain and how the roads leading to the house are laid out? Have we planned a garden based on the amount of sunlight it will receive? All of these will naturally play a large part in the success of the endeavor."

Sarah felt that most of these choices were either common sense or utilized knowledge available about a particular area, neighborhood, or situation and thought that most of the Feng Shui master's advice came from using that information or possibly from psychological studies that have been proven to benefit us by reducing stress.

Hast thou given the horse strength?
hast thou clothed his neck with thunder?

—Job 39:19

"Okay," said Kevin, "let's regroup. So far, we understand that through the art of Feng Shui, one can direct the movement of Qi and enhance that Qi by balancing Yin and Yang through the proper distribution of the five elements. Feng Shui claims to have identified ways to help rather than hinder us as we travel through life. Feng Shui seeks the way man can be harmonious with the natural laws of the universe, and this supposedly contributes to his health and wellness."

Kevin asked how this compared to biblical teachings. Matt told him that according to scripture, God provided the Earth and all in it for man. He gave us a certain amount of power over the earth. He showed us the secrets of fire, how water can control a fire, and how water will nourish the earth for the harvests, to name a few. Since the beginning of time, man has desired to enjoy the fruits of his labor by exacting control over his environment. In essence, this is a self-preserving mechanism.

While we hunger for diversity and change in our lives in terms of the clothes we wear, the foods we eat, how we seek to express our creativity (for instance in how our homes are decorated), we also thirst for predictable elements in areas of human interaction, safety of home and hearth, and a certain sense of stability in our lives and our future. Psychologically we need this structure and hunger for it. Scripture tells us that this can be achieved only through the proper relationship between God and man, which keeps evil at bay and allows us to recognize when evil comes.

Matt explained that we believe that God maintains complete control over all the earth and its elements and thus has the power to control the forces of wind and water, fire and earth. Whether these elements manifest themselves as a hurricane, volcano, earthquake, or a gentle summer breeze, it is God who controls these forces.

Both the Old Testament and the New Testament tell us who controls the elements. For example, in the Old Testament, in the book of Job we can read many verses that ask who gives power to the various elements. Here are a few of these passages:

By the breath of God frost is given:
and the breadth of the waters is straitened.

—Job 37:10

Knowest thou the ordinances of heaven?
canst thou set the dominion thereof in the earth?

—Job 38:33

Doth the eagle mount up at thy command,
and make her nest on high?

—Job 39:27

In the New Testament book of Revelation, we find God commanded the angels to hold back any harm that these elements can bring upon earth:

And after these things I saw four angels standing
on the four corners of the earth, holding the four winds
of the earth, that the wind should not blow on
the earth, nor on the sea, nor on any tree.

—Revelation 7:1

Kevin asked, "Does the Bible speak of anyone other than God and His angels who might exercise power? And Matt answered, saying, "As we mentioned earlier, throughout the Bible we are told about Satan and the power he wields on earth for a limited time. One of the most shocking examples of this power is in the promises Satan makes to Jesus if Jesus would but kneel to him. Satan comments on his power, saying, "That is delivered unto me."

Jesus . . . was led by the Spirit into the wilderness, Being forty days
tempted of the devil. And in those days he did eat nothing . . .
he afterward hungered . . .
And the devil, taking him up into a high mountain,
shewed unto him all the kingdoms of the world in a moment of time.

And the devil said unto him, All this power I will give thee,
and the glory of them: for that is delivered unto me; and to whomsoever I will give it.
If thou therefore wilt worship me, all shall be thine.
—Luke 4:1-2, 5-7

Satan does have a lot of power. For an example from the Old Testament, the story of Job tells how Satan had the power to take away all Job had.

But put forth thine hand now, and touch all that he hath,
and he will curse thee to thy face. And the LORD said unto Satan,
Behold, all that he hath is in thy power;
only upon himself put not forth thine hand.
—Job 1:11, 12

In other areas of scripture we see how evil prospers here on this earth. As a result of Satan's power, we can all fall prey to his wiles. Satan can also give rewards to those who follow him, and this is why those who follow Satan often prosper.

Matt explained to Kevin, "We are tempted every day as well. Also, the devil is extremely subtle. He was direct with Christ because Christ knew him and knew God's truth. With us, Satan is as sly, subtle, and enticing as he was with Eve in the Garden of Eden. As a result, we are not always aware of how one simple decision or one simple act can lead to another that leads to another, each moving us progressively and unknowingly further away from the word of God.

Feng Shui claims that to offset an imbalance, one must follow certain strict protocols to offset the problems this promotes. God is surely stronger than that in our lives. And what of the person who knows nothing of this philosophy, such as the man living in the forest in a wood shack? Is he doomed to live a life filled with problems?"

They feared the LORD, and served their own
gods, after the manner of the nations
whom they carried away from thence.
—2 Kings 17:33

Mary asked, "Would God help me if I asked?" Sarah and Matt answered simultaneously with a "Yes, of course He will!" Mary said she wanted what Matt and Sarah had, an unshakable faith in God that He was understanding, kind, and just and that He protected those He called His own. She was tired of trying to figure out the mumbo jumbo and running to the Feng Shui master with every concern, she was tired of hiding things from Kevin, and she wanted more than anything to do what was right. She even realized that she wanted God to love her, and she didn't think He would if she wouldn't be willing to do things His way. She was almost there, almost ready and willing to make that leap into the unknown.

But privately, Mary realized that she had entered the most important battle of her life, and she'd need to master her fear to continue on the path she had now chosen.

Chapter Seven

BENIGN AND BENEFICIAL

Have ye suffered so many things in vain? If it be yet in vain.
He therefore that ministereth to you in the Spirit,
and worketh miracles among you,
doeth he it by the works of the law,
or by the hearing of faith?

—Galatians 3:4, 5

I wondered if Mary felt that the three of us, arguing against her trust in Feng Shui, had ganged up on her and were urging her to give up its practice. I didn't want her to feel that we had taken something from her. I wanted her to form her own conclusions from our discussions, and this might take time. God didn't want us to be forced to love Him and follow His ways, and this is the reason he gave us our free will. We needed to give Mary her free will in this decision. She seemed so willing to try.

I wanted to be alone with Mary. I wanted her to realize that I would not ask questions or talk against Feng Shui until she was ready. I wanted her to trust me. I wanted her to believe that I just wanted to be her friend, comfort her, and not pressure her in any way. I wasn't sure how I could accomplish this because I knew there was something she feared. I didn't know what she was afraid of, and naturally I wished I could get her to open up and tell me, but I also didn't want her to have regrets later. If I pushed too hard, she could begin to resent me; and if she felt she had said more than she was comfortable telling me, this could drive her away from our friendship. If she gave up Feng Shui because we had pressured her, she could end up resenting us for it.

I was glad when Mary asked if I wanted to look at the color of her kitchen walls, which she thought was the exact color I might want for my living room. It would mean some time with her alone. So we decided to take a break, leave the men working, and walk across to her house with the paint swatches Matt picked up at the hardware store and which I thought close to the right color.

I'd already let Matt know that I wanted to talk with Mary and that he should leave us alone for as long as it took. He'd understood and was willing to keep Kevin in conversation but had warned me to let Mary talk and not ask any questions. As we left, I sensed somehow that Kevin understood my motives and approved, even hoped, Mary would open up.

As we were leaving, we heard the men expounding on the differences between soccer European style and football American style and bobbing their heads as if passing a ball back and forth between them. Sometimes they'd run a few steps back as if trying to catch a ball somewhat off course. Mary and I left laughing at their antics and commenting that they better not break any windows tossing that ball around so recklessly!

Once in Mary's kitchen, I looked at the wall color, which was indeed similar to what I wanted in our living and dining rooms. Then I placed the paint swatches against the wall and chose the one that best matched. Mary asked if I would mind taking a short break from the renovation work and sit for a moment to have a cup of tea with her. I was delighted. As she made the tea, I told her how difficult it had been for me when my mother died. I was only eighteen years old at the time and moved through the days denying the pain and trying to make my grandmother into my mother. I told her of the agony of that experience and how anger toward the people who had so hurt my mom and grandma had festered in me.

Mary said she would never have guessed that I had been through so much because I seemed so happy. She expressed compassion for the loss of my mother and admitted to being terribly angry with her own mother for many years, explaining that her mother had responded to a situation in Mary's life in a manner that hurt her so badly she never recovered from it. She said her mother had forced her into a decision when she was only fourteen years old that had ruined her life. I could see that suddenly Mary felt she had said too much and started to close down.

I didn't want her to feel uncomfortable, so I steered our conversation to the mistakes we all seem to make, parents especially, and joked about parents needing a school to teach them how hard it is to raise a teenager and help solve the problems a teenager sometimes encounters. My line of work taught me that most parents do make many serious mistakes with their kids because they don't always know what is right or wrong and don't know how to find answers to their problems.

Mary asked me if I knew how we are supposed to know right from wrong all the time, and I told her that Matt and I struggled with these same questions, especially when Matt's brother died, and his death, even the struggles he had had in life, had seemed so unfair. I described how we decided to search the Bible for our answers as my grandmother had taught us to do and how amazed we were to find the answer to every question we asked. Mary scoffed, saying that she didn't think anyone could find their answers in the Bible, a book written so many years ago, and today's problems so much different, so much harder than in the days when the Bible was written. I told her that we did find our answers there.

I told Mary that God never said life would not be unfair or filled with troubles, but He did promise us a way out, gave us answers about how we could protect ourselves from our real enemy, and taught us about that enemy. I told her that the experiences Matt and I lived through taught us that God could turn every tragedy wrought by Satan into a personal triumph. This surprised Mary, and she asked how it was possible to turn a real tragedy into a triumph.

I told Mary about Grandma's life and how much she had suffered. I told her about the journal we wrote together which we called "When God Broke Grandma's Heart." I told her how God turned Grandma's tragedy into an incredible triumph by creating a beautiful heart in Grandma that God would cherish forever and how He restored to her what she had lost and longed for. I told Mary she was welcome to read Grandma's journal. It explained who our enemy is, what he wants, and how he goes about harming us. "But more importantly", I said, "the journal also explains God's plan for us, what we should strive to do in life, and the wonderful peace and joy and future that God wants to give us." Mary wanted to read the journal right away, and I promised to bring it to her tomorrow.

Hesitatingly, Mary began to tell me that she suffered from panic attacks and bouts of incredible fear and sometimes had to use all her strength just to keep the fears at bay. "Sometimes," she said, "I am completely exhausted from the effort. I don't understand why you believe and trust God so much, why you feel He will take care of every person and every circumstance."

I remembered a verse I love and told it to Mary to comfort her and show her that God promises His help.

For he hath said,
I will never leave thee nor forsake thee.

—Hebrews 13:5

And another where God says,

When thou passest through the waters, I will be with thee;
and through the rivers, they shall not overflow thee:
when thou walkest through the fire, thou shalt not be burned;
neither shall the flame kindle upon thee.

—Isaiah 43:2

I remembered that Matt and I carried a little calendar where we listed all the things we needed to do each day and in the back of the calendar had stapled a list of Bible verses for us to refer to on those days we felt discouraged or tired or wanted to encourage someone else who felt that way. I asked Mary to wait a moment while I ran to the car to get the calendar. Mary said she was surprised to think I would ever need to refer to any list because she thought of me as so strong and never afraid of anything. I told her that looks are deceiving and most people were fearful from time to time.

When I returned with the calendar and had turned to the back page, I handed it to Mary and asked her to read it out loud. Mary began by saying,

I will put thee in a clift of the rock,
and will cover thee with my hand.

—Exodus 33:22

These things I have spoken unto you,
that in me ye might have peace.
In the world ye shall have tribulation:
but be of good cheer; I have overcome the world.

—John 16:33

And a man shall be as an hiding place from the wind,
and a covert from the tempest; as rivers of water in a dry place,
as the shadow of a great rock in a weary land.

—Isaiah 32:2

I explained that these verses demonstrated the protection that God offers us, but for God to help us, we must first call on Him in humbleness acknowledging that we cannot fix our problems ourselves, and believing that He can and will help. I explained that scripture tells us how to come to God, what to expect from Him, and also what He expects from us. For example, God says,

Call unto me, and I will answer thee,
and show thee great and mighty things, which thou knowest not.

—Jeremiah 33:3

I explained that when you hunger for righteousness and see only unrighteousness around you, you know that Satan is near and desirous of breaking you. God knows this; He sees your hunger for what is good and right, and is glad for it, and promises that if you hold on, trust Him, He will make it right.

Blessed are they which do hunger and thirst after righteousness:
for they shall be filled.

—Matthew 5:6

God also knows that you are afraid and He understands what you have been through. He also has compassion for our inability to trust Him when we are new to our faith and tells us,

Prove me now herewith, saith the LORD of hosts,
if I will not open the windows of heaven,
and pour you out a blessing,
that there shall not be room enough to receive it.

—Malachi 3:10

I explained that when Matt and I read this verse for the first time, we felt that we could see into the heart of God and the wondrous love and forgiveness He has for us. Through scripture we finally came to understand that He longs to help us.

We must go through tribulation here on earth, for it makes us pure. It teaches us compassion and why we should forgive others. These things make us strive to be a worthy bride for the Lord Jesus. God tells us that from our trials and tribulations, He makes pure gold of us.

Scripture tells us that God directs all forces and creates or allows all experiences for the good of those who love Him. Therefore, for our benefit, there may be difficult experiences that are necessary to our spiritual development and that give us the opportunity to become more pleasing in God's eyes. Difficult circumstances can be a catalyst for creating a noble and loving heart. Scripture often describes these challenges as similar to the process of ore refined by fire to become gold. Three verses from scripture that describe this process are

But he knoweth the way that I take;
when he hath tried me,
I shall come forth as gold.

—Job 23:10

And I will bring forth the third part through the fire,
and will refine them as silver is refined,
and will try them as gold is tried:
they shall call on my name, and I will hear them:
I will say, It is my people: and they shall say, The Lord is my God.

—Zechariah 13:9

I counsel thee to buy of me gold tried in the fire,
that thou mayest be rich; and white raiment, that thou mayest be clothed,
and that the shame of thy nakedness do not appear;
and anoint thine eyes with eyesalve, that thou mayest see.
As many as I love, I rebuke and chasten:
Be zealous therefore, and repent.

—Revelation 3:18, 19

And those tribulations will pass, for God tells us:

Thy sun shall no more go down;
neither shall thy moon withdraw itself:
for the Lord shall be thine everlasting light,
and the days of thy mourning shall be ended.

—Isaiah 60:20

We also have the angel protection. God gives us his faithful angels who look after us and keep Satan from harming us. I also explained that in some cases when scripture speaks about giving assistance to those who fear God, this might not refer to fear as a sense of jeopardy. Rather, it is similar to the anguish we feel when we disappoint someone we love. It is like loving someone so much that we fear to hurt them in any way. A scripture that came to mind was

The angel of the LORD encampeth
Round about them that fear him,
and delivereth them.

—Psalm 34:7

Here God tells us that He sent His angel to surround, protect, and deliver those who love Him so much they never want to disappoint Him. They "fear" the sadness they will experience if they disappoint Him, so they strive to be pleasing in His sight, but not because they are afraid of Him. Of course, there are some who *should* fear God because the judgment that will come upon them for their continued ungodly behavior and lack of remorse.

For thou hast been a . . . strength to the needy in his distress,
a refuge from the storm, a shadow from the heat.

—Isaiah 25:4

When we think we have an impossible situation to contend with, when we see no way out, God promises that it is through this circumstance that He will show us His power and care for us. Jeremiah knew this and said to God,

Thou hast made the heaven and the earth
By thy great power and stretched out arm,
And there is nothing too hard for thee.

—Jeremiah 32:17

Therefore, we can trust God and heed His words:

And we know that all things
work together for good to them that love God,
to them who are the called according to his purpose.

—Romans 8:28

I told Mary that Grandma always had to pray for peace because her heart was so troubled. She reminded God of Jesus' promise that she could retain her own peace within her and He would give her His peace as well. He says,

Peace I leave with you, my peace I give unto you . . .
Let not your heart be troubled, neither let it be afraid.

—John 14:27

To reap all these blessings, we must do our part. We must seek God and desire to learn of Him and follow His direction.

Come, and let us go up to the mountains of the LORD . . .
he will teach us of his ways,
and we will walk in his paths.

—Micah 4:2

I told Mary that my favorite song in church is based on the verse:

> *The LORD is my light and my salvation;*
> *whom shall I fear?*
> *the LORD is the strength of my life;*
> *of whom shall I be afraid?*
>
> —Psalm 27:1

Mary was amazed and said that she thought she knew what religion was all about. Although she hadn't gone to church, she believed in her own way, but she had never before heard these verses that I provided her. She wanted to read them again and asked if she could make a copy of the list she'd just read. Since Mary had a copy machine, it was easy to accomplish. Matt and I had made this list when we ourselves were struggling to believe and trust God, trying to understand why Matt's brother died.

But Mary also said that while the things I'd just told her sounded wonderful, to her they were still intangible. The wind chime in her hallway brought her comfort because she could see it and hear it and know it was there as a form of protection. The chime wasn't something intangible; it was real and "spoke" to her by its very presence. "God," she said, "seems intangible." I told Mary that as she learned of God, He would give her what we called experiences of faith that would make their relationship tangible to her, but this would take some understanding and faith on her part.

I knew that Mary would need to investigate on her own and come to her own conclusions, but I was happy that we had made this breakthrough. She had confided in me, and we'd had this discussion about the promises God gives. It was truly a wonderful start. God was already working in her life.

When we rejoined the men, they were deep into a discussion about Feng Shui, so Mary and I jumped right in. Mary said, "I'd like to continue our discussions about Feng Shui because I am now very curious about all these parts that I hadn't previously understood, but I also want you to know that I am willing to listen, debate, and learn about the Bible too."

Matt and I were ecstatic, and we could see that Kevin was amazed, but rather than make a big deal of it, we thought it best to keep the conversation going so that Kevin did not ask questions or ask what had happened. As we continued talking, Mary again provided information about Feng Shui explaining that in one of the Feng Shui lectures she attended she'd heard that if you think you may have a calling to become a Feng Shui expert and want to know whether or not you have the necessary sixth sense to "feel" Qi, there was an exercise to try. She told us to rub our palms together for fifteen seconds. After fifteen seconds, with palms facing each other, she asked us to spread our hands apart by about eight inches and lower our hands to our navel, keeping them about eight inches from our body. Slowly we were to move our palms closer together until a magnetic pull of one palm was felt. Then slowly move our palms closer to each other and then apart from one another, but by no more than eight inches, and assess the resulting magnetic pull. The magnetic pull sensation is purported to be the Qi, and this exercise is supposed to demonstrate one's ability to feel the Qi.

We felt more at ease about Feng Shui now because the focus of our discussion had changed and it was more of a discovery than a challenge between us. When Mary finished her explanation of the experiment, we noted that we all could feel something in our hands but thought this to be a physiological response of the body to the static electricity generated between the hands. Matt explained that we often experience similar reactions when we brush our hair in a cold dry climate or when we move across a rug with socks on and touch a lamp and see sparks between our hand and the lamp. This is static electricity generated naturally by the friction, the air, and our bodies.

Mary told us that her Feng Shui master used a compass called a Lo Pan to locate underground water and mineral deposits. Geomancy was the art of finding and providing an optimal situation in which to live in harmony with the natural setting and energy of the earth. Mary explained that the Lo Pan, also spelled Luo Pan, is a bowl-shaped geometric compass with thirty-six concentric rings and twenty-four points and was developed in the eighth century. According to Chinese philosophy, just as animals and plants have a specific environment where they thrive rather than struggle, so too should mankind. Thus, the Lo Pan is used to locate the specific area where a given individual will thrive.

Many assert that the use of a compass and the measuring, recording, and matching of outcomes in Feng Shui make this art a scientific method, meaning it is repeatable and seen through the senses. Matt advocated that while the compass, in terms of pointing north and assisting in navigation, does indeed afford that science, the recommendations and outcomes of Feng Shui do not fit the criteria for scientific method.

Mary pointed out that the Lo Pan helps define the negative or positive influences on the occupants of the home. The Lo Pan is used to locate the five elements of metal, wood, water, fire, and earth in any given area where they cannot be seen by the naked eye. The diagnoses and cures of Feng Shui rely on assessing the strengths and balance (Yin versus Yang) of wood, fire, earth, metal, and water in the home by use of the Lo Pan.

In conjunction with the Lo Pan, a chart called the Ba Qua was developed as a tool for using the magnetic fields of the earth and incorporating the interaction of the five elements to locate rooms and place furniture. This chart uses a series of nine squares to represent the nine areas of life and the five elements. The nine squares are placed three abreast in three rows to form a larger square (the Ba Qua), and a star shape is overlaid on top of the nine squares. The Ba Qua is used to indicate the counterbalances or augmentations and placement needed that will correct, direct, or control the flow of Qi and avoid those things which disrupt harmony, thus bringing good luck, good health, and success.

There are eight areas of life, each represented by a square that surrounds the center square. These areas of life on the Ba Qua are wealth and resources, health and family, career and destiny, fame and status, children and projects, wisdom and skill, marriage and relationships, and finally travel and people.

The cycles of life that the Chinese discovered from the study of nature led them to believe that there might be cycles to the life of man that were also predictable and therefore possibly controllable. The result of such thought and purportedly the markings on the shell of a tortoise resulted in a mathematical approach to the way the world works, and thus the I Ching was born.

When a Feng Shui client is in need of specific help for a problem, the Feng Shui master and the client might sit together, establish an environment of calm, and concentrate on the single question that they have decided to bring to the oracles for resolution. Five coins of the same denomination (e.g., all nickels or all dimes) are placed in a bowl or cup or in your two hands. The coins are shaken gently but thoroughly. With eyes closed, the coins are shaken again and arranged one by one horizontally on a table in a straight line. Then, the eyes can be opened and the heads and tails pattern of the five coins can be noted left to right. The Feng Shui master then consults a chart to match the coin pattern to the simplified thirty-two-verse representation of the verses in the I Ching, a book of verses described in the next paragraph that is used for divination or direction, for the answer to your problem. Yarrow sticks can be used in the same manner instead of coins.

The I Ching (pronounced "yee jing") is also known as the "Book of Changes." Through the use of sixty-four hexagrams, the I Ching addresses all of the changes and stages of life and guides in avoiding or minimizing negative influences. The I Ching's verses are used to direct one's actions in times of trouble. Tossing a set of sticks or coins provides a series of numbers that indicate which verse in the I Ching to use when looking for guidance for any given circumstance. Many scholars consider the I Ching an incredible mathematical way to view the universe. It relates the natural cycles to quantifiable terms using a sequence of broken and solid lines. It is, in essence, a mathematical approach to the cycles of the earth and man's interaction with the earth and is believed to have merit by virtue of its mathematical basis.

Each of the sixty-four different hexagrams in the I Ching is made up of six lines, stacked in upper and lower sets of three. Each set of three lines is called a trigram. Each line can be either broken or solid. The broken lines represent Yin forces (negative, passive, and destructive), and the solid lines represent Yang forces (positive, strong, and constructive). The eight possible combinations of broken and solid lines in a set of three lines yields eight trigrams. These are the fundamental units of the I Ching, representing the primary forces in all life. Each of the sixty-four hexagrams is a result of the combination and interaction of two trigrams.

The hexagram in the I Ching appropriate to fit the circumstances of the one looking for the answer to a problem is located through the use of the coins or yarrow sticks. The way the sticks or coins fall when tossed reveals not only the hexagram but also the particular lines in the hexagram that will help the seeker learn what life will bring and how to avoid and minimize its difficulty.

However, it is thought that the I Ching, like Feng Shui, became distorted over the centuries. It was put together as a coherent text in the ninth century BC and sought to show a way (Dao) that man could avert wrong decisions, avoid failure, escape misfortune, or conversely make the right decisions and achieve success and good fortune. In essence it was used as a divination tool.

Matt and I told Mary and Kevin that we found a manuscript in Grandma's trunk that contained a little history about some of the men who discovered and augmented much of the ancient discoveries. Grandma had done some research on this subject many years ago to help a friend.

Shew me thy ways, O LORD; teach me your paths.
Lead me in thy truth, and teach me: for thou art the God
of my salvation; on thee do I wait all the day.

—Psalm 25:4, 5

Grandma's manuscript briefly and without much detail described the origins of the I Ching. Grandma wrote that Fu Xi of remote antiquity was purported to have invented the original eight trigrams, and King Wen of the Zhou, who reigned from 1171 to 1122 BC, developed the hexagrams out of those trigrams, with these becoming a coherent text in the ninth century. While Confucius contributed to the I Ching during the period from 551 to 479 BC, the work of Wang Bi from 226 to 249 BC is thought to have had the most impact on the translations and interpretations of the text. Many other commentaries, interpretations, and translations followed.

The "way," also called the Tao or Dao, is often associated with the directions found in the I Ching. Many believe that the I Ching and Buddhism are linked because of the use of the words "the way." This is not accurate. Buddha warned against divination. (The word "Budh" means "to wake up," and "Buddha" means "the Awakened One.") Buddha said many things that clearly indicated his opposition to divination.

Buddha was born in 563 BC in the region of Nepal and was named Siddhartha Gautama. His father was a king, and Siddhartha, handsome and intelligent, knew every luxury. His father summoned fortune-tellers to determine his son's future and tried to direct that future to "world conqueror" rather than "world redeemer" as prophesied by the soothsayer. Despite his father's efforts, Siddhartha eventually left the riches of his father's house to seek a higher realm of existence. In time, Siddhartha overcame the lusts and emotions of the flesh and through meditation, rigorous thought, and concentration, was able to conquer his body and his human nature. He was tempted by "the evil one" and resisted that temptation and was able to become "enlightened."

From this point on, he traveled for a half century preaching his sixfold doctrine: a religion devoid of authority, devoid of ritual, devoid of tradition, a religion that skirted speculation, a religion of intense self-effort, and interestingly, a religion devoid of the supernatural. Buddha condemned all forms of divination, soothsaying, and forecasting.

Thus, Buddhism in its pure form should not be linked to the I Ching. Buddha suggested that man could elevate and extricate himself from the emotions and desires that plague and divert one's life. By rising above these materialistic and physical needs and reactions, one reaches the highest pinnacle of spiritual development and can then implement the necessary ability to show love and compassion and cease any form of harm to all living things. Where and how people conduct themselves in these matters during their lifetime, or how effectively they strive to overcome these desires and emotions, results in a rebirth to a better or a worse state for the next life cycle.

In most cases, Karma, which will impact the status or level of one's reincarnation, is a part of the Buddhist's belief. Reincarnation into human or animal form is purported to enable the spirit of man to develop with each differing circumstance.

Grandma noted that just as the stars may indeed provide a message, the I Ching may also provide a message. God does not say anywhere in the Bible that these "discoveries" are not based in truth. What God does say, clearly and emphatically, is that through our use of divination, astrology, prognostication, soothsaying, witchcraft, idolatry, other gods, and other forms of knowing the future or trusting something other than God with that future, we place ourselves at great risk. Because the I Ching is used as a divination tool, God warns us through scripture not to use it to guide our lives. Again, scripture does not say divination or any of the other tenets used in Feng Shui are not valid. God never says they do not work, but clearly, adamantly, and repeatedly He warns against employing these methods in our lives. God also clearly warns that Satan can use these tools to destroy our spiritual lives and that God Himself is angered by our use of them.

Grandma's manuscript also mentioned the same book we'd found that said the I Ching spoke of its employment of "helpers" and its definition of who or what these helpers are. According to the book we'd found, *I Ching, The Oracle of the Cosmic Way*," by Carol K. Anthony and Hanna Moog (I Ching Books, Anthony Publishing Company, Stow, Massachusetts, 2002), helpers are aspects of the Cosmic Consciousness, invisible, proficient in varied areas, are not angels, must be given a free hand in how to help, and must be thanked afterward for their help. Additionally, in direct opposition to biblical teachings, it is stated that to benefit from the wisdom of the I

Ching and to draw the helpers into providing their assistance, man must not think of himself as a sinner or as born with original sin. "Mistaken" ideas and beliefs such as these will result in poison arrows that poison the true nature of that person. When man believes himself a sinner, neither the helpers nor the I Ching can be of any use.

These beliefs are diametrically opposed to scripture as God clearly tells us that we were born sinners and remain sinners. The sacrifice of the Lord Jesus allows us to partake of Holy Communion for the forgiveness of sin. In denying that we are sinners, we deny the great sacrifice of Christ; thus we deny Christ himself. Matt and I felt that denying that we are sinners was a very dangerous position to take spiritually, and we could see that Mary was visibly shaken by our explanation.

Mary quickly changed the subject to explain about the Chinese calendar based on a twelve-year cycle and representing a different animal for each of the twelve years with each animal depicting the various strengths and weaknesses of those born in that year. The twelve animals are the Rat, Ox, Tiger, Rabbit, Dragon, Snake, Horse, Goat, Monkey, Rooster, Dog, and Pig. After the Pig, the animals rotate again in the same order.

However, the twelve-year calendar is not accurate enough for astrological calculations. Instead, the calendar upon which Chinese astrology is based uses a sixty-year cycle obtained by pairing the "Ten Heavenly Stems" and the "Twelve Earthly Branches." The "Ten Heavenly Stems" are usually associated with the five elements, while the "Twelve Earthly Branches" are associated with the psychological aspects of man and are now represented by the twelve animals as discussed above. Because of the pairing of the stems and branches, the cycle is stretched to sixty years before the cycle starts repeating. The interaction between the stem and the branch makes the sixty-year cycle more complex but more accurate than the simpler animal-only cycle.

Using the astrological calendar and charts, the animal, element, number, compass direction, and Yin/Yang balance are determined for each individual. Used in conjunction with the magnetic compass, the Lo Pan and the Ba Qua, the astrological components become pivotal to directing the Feng Shui client toward a better life. Matt commented that once again, employing astrology, charts, and other tools for the purpose of divination are what scripture warns we carefully avoid, areas that the Bible teaches us is where Satan rules.

Feng Shui employs numerology as well. The Kua (or "magic") number is determined for each occupant of the household. This number identifies the best and worst directions for the Feng Shui client to sit or face in order to achieve maximum benefit. For example, if your Kua or magic number is 1, southeast is your best direction, west your worst.

Mary said that the Feng Shui master generally recommends that their clients compose a chant affirming what they want or need and place a handwritten copy on their nightstand. Every morning when arising and every evening when going to bed, this affirmation is to be chanted three times in succession. Performing this ritual will draw positive energy to you and cause your wants or needs to be fulfilled.

I felt that seeking a solution to problems through image placement or through the use of the verses in the I Ching could result in a dependency on these things, a sin in itself, yet lead us to a form of paganism and idolatry and the acceptance that one not view himself as a sinner.

The idea that man should not consider himself a sinner opposes both Jewish and Christian doctrine. If man does not consider himself a sinner, then both atonement and the forgiveness of sin is unnecessary. According to scripture, God requires man seek forgiveness for his sins in order for him to enter the kingdom of heaven.

> *For there is no man that sinneth not.*
> —1 Kings 8:46

> *For there is no man which sinneth not.*
> —2 Chronicles 6:36

> *If we say that we have no sin,*
> *we deceive ourselves, and the truth is not in us.*
> —1 John 1:8

> *But God commandeth his love toward us,*
> *in that, while we were yet sinners, Christ died for us*
> *. . . we shall be saved through him.*
> —Romans 5:8, 9

Kevin said that since Feng Shui employs the use of astrology, magical numbers, yarrow sticks (and divination), animals, and chants to achieve its end, it is important to examine what scripture says about these practices. It would also be helpful to know what various Bible scholars have to say about employing these practices.

Matt and I loved an old book of Grandma's titled *Many Infallible Proofs* by Dr. Henry M. Morris, and we told Kevin that in this book Dr. Morris says, "Astrology is unequivocally condemned in the Bible (see Deuteronomy 4:9; Isaiah 47:11-14; Kings 23:5; Acts 7:42, 43; etc.); therefore, we must by all means avoid any association with these particular teachings."

Matt also said, "In fact, Dr, Morris states that astrology is synonymous with ancient polytheistic paganism and akin to the worship of fallen angels or demons. He further considers many so-called ancient myths and religions to be a corruption of the original revelation, rather than the raw inventions of men." I told Kevin and Mary that Dr. Morris wrote that book in 1974, and Grandma had kept it all those years. His examination of scripture applied then and still stands today.

Matt explained that we are striving to live as God desires us to, striving to trust Him above all other things and to know His word through scripture. Once we know what scripture tells us in regard to the various practices in Feng Shui, we would clearly be warned against it and make the choice to stay away from it. Matt felt that Feng Shui can work against the relationship between God and man if we were to accept and live by the superstitions and divinations embodied in it.

> *For thou wilt light my candle:*
> *the LORD my God will enlighten my darkness.*
> —Psalm 18:28

> *Beware that thou forget not the LORD thy*
> *God, in not keeping his commandments, and*
> *his judgments, and his statutes . . .*
> —Deuteronomy 8:11

A certain man called Simon . . . used sorcery . . .
believed Philip preaching . . . and Simon himself believed . . .
Repent therefore of thy wickedness, and pray God . . .
The thought of thine heart may be forgiven thee.

—Acts 8:9, 13, 22

Abstain from pollutions of idols.

—Acts 15:20

As we finished our work for the day, we concluded that while trust in our Heavenly Father and not in superstition is primary in our lives, we do know that the forces of nature exist, that they are given and controlled by God, and that they sometimes act in ways that we do not fully understand. Sometimes however, God gives temporary and limited control of these elements over to the angels and to Satan.

There is a fine line in terms of where we can safely walk in seeking to interpret the meaning of these elements. We felt it is better to err on the side of caution and put our faith not in a chart or specific placement of furniture but in our Heavenly Father and the prayers and supplications we bring to Him to help us.

Chapter Eight

THE HEARTBREAK

Mary had finished reading Grandma's journal and was amazed by what Grandma had lived through and by how God helped her. She said that she wanted God to help her too but did not think she could develop the kind of trust this would require. Matt and Kevin had left the house to purchase the wood trim for the outside edges of the newly constructed bedroom closets. As soon as they left, Mary asked me to sit with her in the window seat so we could talk for a little while. She was breathless and nervous and began to speak as soon as I sat down next to her. She wanted to tell me her story before she lost the courage to do so. I sat quietly as she talked.

Mary began by explaining that she had been born in a small rural farming town that years later grew immensely because of plans to move the airport from the city to the suburbs about ten miles from them. Though financially Mary's little hometown was struggling, many held on, knowing that in a few years the airport would come and bring a boost to their economy. But when Mary was a teenager, the airport relocation was still a hope in everyone's heart but in actuality probably five to ten years in the future.

When Mary was growing up, the town consisted mostly of single farms where most of the people were struggling to eke out a living while at the mercy of the weather and the prices and quality of what they grew. When all went well, their crops would allow the farmers to make their way, but when drought or floods, wind, fires from lightning strikes, pestilence, or any of the myriad other problems that can befall a farm occurred, money was scarce.

Most children worked, either by helping their parents on the farm, by selling and delivering the products they grew, or by helping other farmers bring in their crops. Some had jobs with the local shops delivering merchandise, stocking shelves, feeding livestock, or cleaning out barn stalls. Age was no consideration, and even very young children worked wherever they could. The very lucky children found work with someone skilled in carpentry or machine repair and could learn a trade as well as earn a salary.

Mary was one of the lucky ones. She was only fourteen when she found a job that could also teach her a skill. She accepted an after-school job with the local dentist working from 3:00 p.m. until 6:00 p.m. three days a week and one day a week from 3:00 p.m. until 9:00 p.m. The dentist drove her home when they finished with the last patient to be sure she arrived home safely. She was happy with the prospect of earning some spending money and learning a skill. She'd been tired of babysitting for such little pay and had been looking for another way to earn money for a long time. She had been thinking about becoming a nurse someday and felt that becoming a dental assistant was a good start in the medical field.

In the first week, Mary learned how to greet patients, log them in to the appointment book, and, if new, have them fill out an address and medical history form. She learned how to seat the patient in the examining room, apply the patient's bib, adjust the chair and headrest, and explain how to use and refill the water cup and how to operate the water in the basin correctly. Within a few weeks she learned the name of each instrument, how to mix the various types of filling materials, and how to operate the sterilizing machine so she could have all the instruments ready for use again the next day. Mary learned that most payments for the dental services were in cash, but some were a promise to pay when the patient could. Other payments were made in the form of produce from the farm or meat the farmer had butchered. Entering these payments into the general ledger was at first a challenge to Mary.

Mary felt very grown-up to be doing such responsible work and to be learning so many different things that related to an office. She was also proud to wear the stark white, crisply ironed uniform that the dentist had provided so she would "look professional" while at work.

The dentist seemed to be a kind man, happy with Mary's work, and she saw how considerate he was when he would always remind Mary to call her parents if they were running late with a patient. He would drive her right to her door and wait until she entered the house before he drove off. He often spoke of his son who was away at dental school and lived for the day when his son would return from school to help with the practice, perhaps even take it over when the father retired.

Mary was pleased with the extra money she was earning. She was saving one-third, giving one-third to her parents to help with their bills, and using one-third for her own needs. She found that she could study or complete her homework whenever a patient didn't show up or when one patient finished before the next patient came in. If Mary hadn't finished her homework, she completed it at home after work, so her grades would remain good and she would be eligible to apply to a good college in a few years.

On Saturday evenings, Mary would bring the dentist's white jackets and her uniform home to wash and iron and bring them back with her on Monday so they would both have clean, crisp uniforms. She had purchased a pair of white shoes to match her uniform and left these at the office so she would not have to carry them back and forth to work. She wore socks with the shoes at first but then felt that white stockings would look more professional. She felt very grown-up and responsible with the stockings on. And for the next six months everything went well.

The dentist lived in an old two-story house on the outskirts of town and had converted the lower-level rooms into his office and the upper-level rooms into living quarters. He'd married late in life. His son had been born when he was forty-one years old and became the apple of his eye. His wife had died many years ago, and he had been devastated by the loss. A year after his wife's death, it was time for his son to go to college, and his loneliness became overwhelming once his son left. His joy in life had been his son, and he missed him terribly when he left for college. Yet he'd wanted the best school, the best dental program he could get for his son and for the future they would have together.

It had taken every penny he had to send his son to school, but he felt it a good investment in both their futures, especially since the town would grow quickly when the airport was moved from the city to the suburbs as it was projected to do.

Sometimes, if they had some time between patients, the dentist would tell Mary about his son, and his eyes would light up with pride. But over time, Mary noticed that the dentist would seem upset when she asked about his son, and finally one evening he told her that his son never called him or wrote to him, not even a birthday or Christmas card. But the dentist still phoned his son and let him know he loved him and was counting the days to his return.

A few months after Mary began working at the dental office, she came to work to find that the dentist had been crying. He told Mary that his son had met someone at school and was thinking of marrying and moving to her hometown and not coming back to his father's practice. The dentist said that he had given his son every penny he had and had heavily mortgaged his house to put him through school. He didn't know what he would do to get out of debt. That was the first time that Mary smelled alcohol on his breath, and she worried about him.

She worked hard to increase the dentist's income by trying to rebook all cancelled appointments and to be courteous to everyone so the patients would want to come back. She tidied up the waiting room after each patient and brought more up-to-date magazines from home to place in the waiting room. She was punctual and polite and always looked crisp and clean in her uniform. She stored her uniform, shoes, and stockings in a small closet in the hall next to the x-ray room where she changed from her school clothing to her uniform and, after work, from her uniform back to her school clothes.

One afternoon the dentist entered the x-ray room when Mary was putting on her shoes just before exiting the room with her school clothes to place them in the little closet. The dentist told her that the first patient had arrived and offered to put Mary's clothes away while she settled the patient in the examining room. Mary hurried so she would not keep the patient waiting, and his help to get her to the patients as quickly as possible became a routine for them.

As time passed, Mary saw a change in the dentist and learned that his son had graduated from college, had married, and set up a practice in another state with financial help from his new father-in-law. Mary recognized the high and low emotions that the dentist went through as he was torn between his happiness that his son was doing so well and was happily married and his distress that his son would not be coming home to be with him, and had, in fact, seemed to abandon him after all he had done for him. The dentist had not gone to his son's wedding, feigning a sudden bout with the flu. The reality was that he was hurt and angry and could not afford either the airline fee or the new suit he would need for such an occasion. What Mary did not know was that the dentist had slipped into a deep depression and had given up his desire to live.

As she watched him suffer, Mary took on more and more of the work, even began doing the cleanings and x-rays, having watched the dentist do these things so often. Nevertheless, she saw the dentist slip further into depression and withdrawal, but she didn't know how to help. She was only fourteen years old. One evening as Mary changed into her uniform, she heard what sounded like a broom fall to the floor. The sound seemed to emanate from the closet outside in the hall. She placed no significance to this, but as time went by she often heard the broom fall or begin to slide when she was changing. One evening Mary decided to move the broom so it would not fall again, and as she did she noticed a bottle of scotch on the floor behind the broom and a small hole in the wall between the closet and the x-ray room. She wondered if the dentist leaned on the broom when taking a drink and this caused the hole to develop in the wall. But in the end, she decided to put the broom back in its original position so the dentist would not know she found the bottle of liquor.

One night, Mary noticed that the dentist was exceptionally drunk. There had been torrential rains most of the day along with bouts of thunder and lightning, and this caused many patients to cancel their appointments. Mary thought it best to ask the dentist to drive her home early and tell him that he did not have to pay her for the day. She knew that money was tight for him. He agreed to take her home, and she went into the x-ray room to change from her uniform to her school clothes. As soon as she had taken her stockings off, the dentist burst into the room, pushed her to the floor, and raped her.

Later, still in a drunken stupor, he cried, babbling that he was sorry, that it would never happen again. His wife had died, his son had abandoned him, he was distraught, almost bankrupt, he would lose his license if she told anyone what he had done and would face destitution in his old age. He begged her not to say anything. Mary was in shock. She could not speak. She felt horror and shame because she didn't know what to do, what to say, how to react. She felt sorry for him. She wondered if she should try to get him help. She wasn't sure what this meant to her body. Her mind worked quickly to shield her from the trauma. Denial of its horror set in, and she began to wonder if it was her own fault. Like so many children do, she automatically blamed herself when others were at fault.

The dentist saw her hesitation and took advantage by trying to soothe her, telling her it would all be okay as long as she did not tell anyone what had happened. He would not let her go home until she gave her word not to say anything about what had happened. He would make it up to her, and no one needed to know. It would be better for her too if no one knew. Mary couldn't think for the moment and thought that perhaps his advice was best. Slowly, as if in a daze, she nodded her head in acquiescence. He told her to dress and said he would drive her home. Again she slowly nodded, unable to understand what it was that she should do about this situation. So she did what he told her to do.

Mary did try to tell. That night she attempted to open a conversation with her mother about what had happened. Mary's timid hints about what she wanted to say went unnoticed by her mother. In fact, her mother exuded such a strong distaste for the subject that Mary was afraid her mother would blame her for what happened. When she broached a similar subject to her dad the next day, he said something to the effect that the way most women dressed today, they invited men's attention and that most problems of this sort were the woman's fault.

Mary went to her room to think and wondered how this incident could have been her fault. Thinking about what her father said, she wondered if it was possible that the long loose jeans, long-sleeved shirt, and baggy sweatshirt could entice anyone. In fact, she didn't even have any so-called attributes to show off even if she wanted to. Maybe it was her fault on some level; maybe she did do something wrong. She also reasoned that the dentist had so many problems and so much sadness in his life that he allowed the drinking to cloud his judgment, so perhaps it was not really his fault either. Maybe it was not fair to hurt him any further by telling anyone what had happened. Maybe she should simply never go back there.

Mary stayed away from work for a week, telling her parents that the office was closed for vacation. Finally, after two weeks, the dentist called and asked her to come back. He said he could not run the practice without her and was desperate for her help. He promised her all would be different and that he would lose the practice if she didn't come back, for already patients were canceling far too often. He pleaded with her to help him. So, softhearted Mary went back. She kept quiet about what had happened, and the dentist was very kind to her, acted in a very professional manner, did not appear to drink anymore, and didn't say more about it. Mary now locked the door to the x-ray room when she changed her clothes, and after a few weeks she began to relax and believed that everything would be all right and it had just been a horrible mistake.

Three weeks later, Mary was changing back to her school clothes after getting the office ready to close for the night. She had just removed her white stockings when she heard a key in the door to the x-ray room. Before Mary had time to react, the dentist entered and raped her again, this time with more force because she fought back with every ounce of her strength.

When it was over, the dentist told Mary that since she hadn't told the first time, if she told now, everyone would believe that she was the one who wanted a relationship with him, and everyone would blame her, not him. He told her that everyone would think badly of her and her reputation would be ruined. Mary was frightened and sick with shame. She realized she had made a terrible mistake in judgment when she decided to come back to work. She grabbed everything that was hers, ran out of the office, and walked the five miles to her house in the dark of night. She was filled with shame and remorse. She was horrified to have made such a stupid mistake in going back to work for him. Guilt enveloped her and stole her self-confidence. It also stole her courage the minute she accepted the premise that there would be no justice for her. Without her courage and belief in a just system, she began to experience her first panic attack.

Mary never went back. She told her parents that the dentist had hired someone else because she had explained that her schoolwork had to come first so she could get the scholarship she wanted. Since her schoolwork was getting progressively more difficult, she'd had to make this choice. She reiterated how much she had her heart set on college and needed good grades for a college to accept her and even better grades to get a scholarship. She cheerfully rambled on about how important college was, and this made her parents accept her decision.

This became the point in Mary's life where she began perfecting the art of burying her experiences in her subconscious to avoid the pain. This was where Mary lost her faith in the goodness of life and in people. But the story didn't end here. There was more, much more, Mary said.

Our conversation ended when the men returned with their supplies. Mary said she would finish her story another day. I knew it was best not to push her and gave her a hug and told her I loved her. She smiled and hugged me back. I was so glad to have had this breakthrough with Mary, and I was determined to find a way to help her.

The men wanted to resume our Feng Shui discussion. Matt had copied a list of dos and don'ts from Grandma's manuscript and tacked it to the wall. Since I am a psychologist, I was interested to learn the psychological and practical ideas that Feng Shui offered and was fascinated that Grandma had done all this research. We started with the first item, which addressed the entry area of a house. According to Feng Shui, the driveway should not be used as the walkway to the house, and no walkway should be laid out in a straight line. Rather, the walkway should be a gracefully curving path from road to door to control the flow of Qi, primarily to cut down on negative Qi entering the house. My argument was that a curving walkway looks appealing and provides many little nooks for plants. Kevin noted that whether or not a walkway curved or ran straight from the driveway or road, it wouldn't reduce the strength of the wind toward the front door. No one could think of any other comments.

Then we addressed the front door. According to Feng Shui, bright colors attract Qi, so the front door must be painted a bright color, such as red, should open easily, but not be too large. This is because large doorways cause both loss of the positive Qi from the inside and allow too much negative Qi in from the outside. My response was that in good design, bright colors are cheerful, add a decorative touch, and highlight where the door is located. Extra large doors are costly in terms of loss of heat or air-conditioning. Easily opening doors demonstrate good carpentry and good quality and contribute to feelings of security. Matt observed that Qi must be like wind, but more self-motivated.

In the living room, Feng Shui admonishes that the floor not be sunken, that seating arrangements face the door, that furniture should have rounded edges, and that the fireplace must not be visible from the front door. The room should contain a healthy live plant or nine healthy live fish and a picture of a peony. Qi will "stagnate" in or "pass by" a sunken room and not move through properly. A fireplace visible from the front door allows Qi to rush directly up the chimney and be lost. A live floor plant or live fish represents life, and peonies represent peace and long life and activate romance. Matt said that good airflow will prevent the stagnation of the flow of heat or air-conditioning and that considerable heat can be lost up a fireplace flue when the front door is opened so it might be best for it not to be located near the door. We also agreed that plants or an aquarium are a pleasant and soothing addition. So far, no mumbo jumbo! But Matt warned that even if we didn't think of it as mumbo jumbo, it was the significance we were willing to attach to it, it was the promise of "luck" that made us fall into idolatry.

In the dining room, Feng Shui requires that family members sit with their backs to the wall, facing specific compass directions based on astrology charts. Round tables are best, as is a mirror on the north wall, and a painting of a bowl of fruit on another wall. A north-wall mirror ensures that one will never lack for food. A bowl or a painting of fresh fruit brings prosperity. Matt said that he thought seating should be optional, perhaps giving preference to the head of the household or elderly or honored guests as a gesture of respect. Table shape should be based on room proportion, but round tables are best for conversation, and the choice of pictures or wall hangings is personal and should simply be in keeping with the room's décor.

Mary admitted that she never viewed the restrictions and promises of Feng Shui in this light and hadn't realized there were so many. She admitted that the way Grandma presented them made them appear merely symbolic. Kevin felt there was definitely a sense of superstition in these admonitions.

Matt was sure that God did not put us on this earth to allow some to understand the tenets of Feng Shui and therefore have a good life and others never to know about Feng Shui and therefore have a bad life. It didn't make sense. I agreed with Matt that God would not create an earth that was so alien to man that he had to worry about all these special locations, furnishings, and seating arrangements. What about the days when people didn't use pictures and aquariums? While I could agree with some of the practical aspects, most suggestions seemed controlling and subjective and not something that would come from God.

Mary went on to read how accessories are specifically addressed in Feng Shui and read aloud that moderate use of mirrors is recommended, but no wall-to-wall mirrors and none hung opposite the front door because Qi bounces off mirrors and changes direction. Pairs of mirrors connote balance since happiness comes in twos. Feng Shui purports that the strengths of animals are imparted to those in the home if a picture or statue of these animals is used as decoration. Which animals and which strengths are determined by the needs of the individuals living in that home and this is gleaned from one's astrological chart. Matt said that God never tells us that there is power or strength in an inanimate object. It is simply an object for practical or adornment purposes only.

As we read, we learned that the choice of color in Feng Shui design is strictly dependent upon the direction of the walls and calls for the use of a magnetic compass to determine the direction of at least one outside wall of the house. That wall can point to or face one of the eight compass directions: north, northeast, northwest, south, southeast, southwest, east, or west. Once the location of one wall is determined, other walls in each room can be labeled, and the color of the room would be designation by that label.

But we all agreed that we wouldn't want to be told to paint a room a color we didn't like. We felt that good design allows one to choose colors they do like, colors that are in harmony with the fabrics and décor of the room and flow from room to room for continuity. The only consideration we felt important is that some colors relax and others stimulate. We felt that we should never assign any luck or beneficence to a color other than the generally held opinion that reds, oranges, and yellows are stimulating while blues, greens, and violets are restful.

> *Through wisdom is an house builded;*
> *and by understanding it is established.*
>
> —Proverbs 24:3

We went back to the subject of symbols. It was interesting to note what attributes Feng Shui assigned to the various symbols used to ward off problems. As an example, to gain longevity, incorporate tortoise-shell patterns into the home. To gain prosperity, use coins decoratively. To gain wisdom, use elephants and clouds within the home. To gain heavenly blessings, introduce a water fountain into your décor. To gain fidelity and honesty, use a crane in your decorating theme.

We strongly disagreed with the idea that objects could give power to someone and felt this may truly be a part of the idolatry that God warns against. We felt that objects, if they have no practical application, should be used decoratively only, if used at all. They should not be used for the purpose of fulfilling a desire or initiating some change. Believing that an inanimate object has the power to grant one's desires is dangerous. Using an inanimate object for this purpose is not only playing with idolatry but also opens a channel through which Satan can gain control of our lives . . . so subtly we often cannot recognize it.

> *Gird up thy loins now like a man; I will demand of thee,*
> *and declare thou unto me.*
> *Wilt thou also disannul my judgment?*
> *wilt thou condemn me, that thou mayest be righteous?*
>
> —Job 40:7, 8

We discussed how the diagnoses, cures, and chants of Feng Shui come directly from the Feng Shui master and is usually quite costly to the homeowner seeking this advice. The Feng Shui master is first hired then spends a great deal of time performing the tasks involved in determining Qi flow, Yin and Yang, the five elements, the cycles of life, symbols, astrology, lucky number, best direction, etc. After this information is gathered and processed, a "diagnosis" is made regarding negative influences and problems. Further investigation is often necessary to recommend a "cure." This may include changing or moving furniture, changing rooms, hanging wind chimes and crystals, remodeling, purchasing symbols, etc. The "cure" is said to take as little as three to seven days to produce a noticeable change in the life of the recipient and reach its fullest effect within six months. Once the cure is determined, the Feng Shui "master" will usually advise the client to perform a chant or mantra twice a day asking for whatever is needed. This is also called an "affirmation" ritual.

This is diametrically opposed to scripture. In good design, prayer and an understanding of God's word helps us make sensible and godly decisions. Prayer is an important part of one's religious life. Prayer can, in some ways, be compared to affirmations, chants, or mantras. God has promised to hear all prayers. Could it be that this gift to His children is manifested as a natural law that grants this benefit to the chants of Feng Shui followers? Or could it be that chants produced as a result of following tenets such as Feng Shui are answered by Satan and acted upon by the power he wields? Viewed in this light, we must ask to whom we would want to pray. If we thought a chant, mantra, or affirmation could be labeled a prayer, and that it may be answered by a power other than God, would we engage in this practice?

> *Then I beheld all the work of God,*
> *That a man cannot find out the work that is done under the sun:*
> *because though a man labor to seek it out, yet he shall not find it;*
> *yea further; though a wise man think to know it,*
> *yet shall he not be able to find it.*
> —Ecclesiastes 8:17

We asked ourselves if any of these practices really work. If so, we must also ask, is there a mystical power that can be induced, persuaded, or forced into helping us by implementing any of these practices? Certainly many of these practices can have natural consequences. Certainly it is well known that a beautiful and harmonious home or garden where we can escape the din and stress of daily life can bring us peace and contribute to better health and a longer life. While we can do the best we know how to enrich our lives, God does have the final say as to what each of us must go through in the course of our lives. Many of the hardships we endure build a stronger faith and a more noble heart. We want to exit these hardships a better, more loving, more understanding person.

We could also concede that good or bad "luck" can indeed come in cycles, that there are forces in nature we do not understand and certainly cannot control. But scripture commands that we place our trust only in God, that we accept His will for us. When we experience difficult times, we believe what we go through molds us into a more loving and compassionate person, and through these experiences we learn that we can, indeed, trust God.

If we seek a strong relationship with God, we ask Him for His help and guidance and to provide what is needed to make our soul a worthy soul, pleasing in His eyes. While education, health, good relationships, and a happy family life are good things to pursue, the most important is our relationship with God. First and foremost, we need to apply ourselves to a higher goal, to an intimate relationship with God wherein we constantly strive please Him. Using and believing in inanimate objects to bring us good luck and improve our lives will destroy this relationship and separate us from God.

Is there any alternative to Feng Shui? Is there a God-pleasing method that offers similar benefits for our lives? Is there a quick fix that will help our stressed time-restricted lives? Yes. Not only is there an alternative with benefits but also step-by-step instructions that can be easily implemented and a list of guarantees that come with this implementation. Our homes are guaranteed to become joyous, and our lives guaranteed to be protected. The guarantee is real and all-inclusive. Not only can we attain harmony but also serenity, focus, direction, expectation, and protection for our lives and our homes. This is the ultimate quick fix that pleases God.

Both the book of Job and many passages in Isaiah challenge man to examine who really controls the power of the universe and asks who we would follow by also asking who we think has the power to provide for us.

Wilt thou trust him, because his strength is great?
or wilt thou leave thy labor to him?
Wilt thou believe him, that he will bring home thy seed,
and gather it into thy barn?

—Job 39:11, 12

Who hath measured the waters
in the hollow of his hand . . . and weighed the hills in a balance?
—Isaiah 40:12

Beware lest thou forget the LORD . . .
Thou shalt fear the LORD thy God, and serve him . . .
Ye shall not go after other gods, of the people which are round about you.
—Deuteronomy 6:12-14

Trust in him at all times; ye people,
Pour out your heart before him:
God is a refuge for us.
—Psalm 62:8

Our only drawback is our own ego, our desire to do it our way, or in a way we believe science has negated scripture, but God bluntly tells us:

Ye stiffnecked . . . in heart and ears,
ye do always resist the Holy Ghost:
As your fathers did, so do ye.
—Acts 7:51

Chapter Nine

THE POWER

Or who shut up the sea with doors, when it brake forth,
and if it had issued out of the womb

—Job 38:8

In Grandma's manuscript we found reference to a book on the I Ching that spoke of "helpers" of man that are invisible, are not angels, require that man never think of himself as a sinner, require free rein to do their will to solve problems, and must be thanked for what they do. We wondered who these helpers are and what power enables them to perform. This same book spoke about God (in capital letters) saying that it is okay to speak of God as a loving energy, but that God must not be considered the supreme authority nor protector, nor able to give man the job of being overseer of the earth. Grandma's manuscript said that this book further stated that these concepts are mankind's arrogance in viewing itself, and that sin or guilt is only an invention of society designed to keep the individual under its control. I said that frankly this is frightening to me because it is entirely contrary to scripture and to the doctrines of many religions.

The I Ching is part of the Feng Shui tenets, so we had to ask ourselves, if one has to adopt Feng Shui, does one have to adopt the I Ching? Matt said that a good analogy for that question would be to consider the person who decides to go to Europe, makes reservations, purchases tickets, and brings to the airport a driver's license, birth certificate, and credit card complete with picture ID, but not a passport. That person is clearly identified but nevertheless cannot board the plane without the passport. The rules state that you must have a valid passport to travel; if you do not, you cannot travel. I reminded Matt that he had used that analogy when we were writing *When God Took Grandma Home,* and it had also fit the concept of what the requirements were for entering the kingdom of heaven.

Matt said that another analogy would be to consider the clean white garment that scripture says is worn when we enter heaven. Whether there is one spot or three hundred spots on the garment doesn't matter because if it isn't spot free, it isn't clean. Using these analogies, one would have to admit that if the tenets of the I Ching belong to Feng Shui, then those who embrace Feng Shui also embrace the I Ching and the "helpers." To say one embraces only a part (has one spot on the garment) does not negate its association with the other parts (has many spots on his garment).

> *Thou hast a few names even in Sardis which have not defiled*
> *their garments; and they shall walk with me in*
> *white, for they are worthy.*
> —Revelation 3:4

We explained to Kevin and Mary that scripture tells us a great deal about astrology, soothsaying, divining, symbols, and trust. Once we learn what God says, we can seek and obtain His full protection and not become endangered by the spirits that govern these practices. As we learn that astrology and divination are a form of idolatry that subtly claims God is not in control of all things, we can recognize how strongly mankind contrives to exercise his control.

"In the book of Job," Matt said, "scripture poses questions that show Job that he [and, by extension, all men] does not understand or control the universe around them. For example,

> *Canst thou send lightnings, that they may go,*
> *and say unto thee, Here we are?*
> —Job 38:35

Here God is asking if man himself is powerful enough to cause and command lightning and if not, who is.

Have the gates of death been opened unto thee?
or hast thou seen the doors of the shadow of death?

—Job 38:17

Here God asks what man has seen where the dead go or even the doors that encompass the dead.

Take ye therefore good heed unto yourselves;...
Lest ye corrupt yourselves . . .
And lest thou lift up thine eyes unto heaven, and when
thou seest the sun, and the moon, and the stars, even all the host of heaven,
shouldest be driven to worship them and serve them, which the LORD thy God
hath divided unto all nations under the whole heaven.

—Deuteronomy 4:15, 16, 19

In this verse God warns us to be careful that our admiration for the wonders about us does not drive us to worship (follow, trust) them. God reminds us that He is the one who made the heavens. Why would we worship and serve something less powerful than God who made them?

Therefore evil shall come upon thee; thou shalt not know
from whence it riseth: and mischief shall fall upon thee; thou shall not
be able to put it off: and desolation shall come upon thee
suddenly, which thou shall not know.
Stand now with thine enchantments and the multitude of thy sorceries,
wherein thou hast labored from your youth; if so be thou able to profit,
if so be thou mayest prevail.
Thou art wearied in the multitude of thy counsels.
Let now the astrologers, the stargazers, the monthly prognosticators,
stand up, and save thee from these things that shall come upon thee.
Behold, they shall be as stubble; the fire shall burn them;
they shall not deliver themselves from the power of the flame: there shall not be a
coal to warm it, nor fire to sit before it . . . none shall save thee.

—Isaiah 47:11-15

Here God speaks unequivocally about the impotence of astrologers and other predictors. (Such as tarot cards, yarrow sticks, astrology, Feng Shui, and the I Ching, to name a few). He also says that they will fail in the end, and in fact those who employ these practices will burn for their sins against God's word.

> *And he put down the idolatrous priests, whom the kings of Judah*
> *had ordained to burn incense in the high places in the cities of Judah,*
> *and in the places round about Jerusalem; them also that*
> *burned incense unto Baal, to the sun, and to the moon,*
> *and to the planets, and to all the host of heaven.*
> —2 Kings 23:5

Once again scripture refers to astrology and idolatry as an abomination to Him.

> *Then God turned, and gave them up to worship the host of*
> *heaven; as it is written in the book of the prophets:*
> *O ye house of Israel, have ye offered to me slain beasts and sacrifices*
> *by the space of forty years in the wilderness?*
> *Yea, you took up the tabernacle of Moloch,*
> *and the star of your god Remphan, figures which ye made to*
> *worship them; and I will carry you away beyond Babylon.*
> —Acts 7:42, 43

> *And changed the glory of the uncorruptible God into an image*
> *made like to corruptible man, and to birds, and fourfooted*
> *beasts, and creeping things.*
> —Romans 1:23

> *Who changed the truth of God into a lie, and worshiped*
> *and served the creature more than the Creator,*
> *who is blessed forever.*
> —Romans 1:25

In these prior verses, God addresses the worship of animals and birds, which are considered corruptible and therefore inferior, rather than the incorruptible God.

How art thou fallen from heaven, O Lucifer, son of the morning!
how art thou cut down to the ground, which didst weaken the nations!
For thou hast said in thine heart, I will ascend into heaven,
I will exalt my throne above the stars of God: I will sit also upon the mount
of the congregation, in the sides of the north: I will
ascend above the heights of the clouds; I will be like the most High.
Yet thou shalt be brought down to hell,
to the sides of the pit.

—Isaiah 14:12-15

Here God tells us that the root of these practices is Satan and that He will bring Satan down at the end. Interestingly, we are also told that Satan weakened the nations, implying that his influence caused the fall and perversion of what started out well.

For he built up again the high places which Hezekiah his father had destroyed;
and he reared up altars for Baal, and made a grove, as did
Ahab king of Israel; and worshiped all the host of
heaven, and served them.
And he built altars in the house
of the LORD, of which the LORD said, In Jerusalem will I put my name.
And he built altars for all the host of heaven in the two courts
of the house of the LORD.
And he made his son pass through the fire,
and observed times, and used enchantments,
and dealt with familiar spirits and wizards:
he wrought much wickedness in the sight of the LORD,
to provoke him to anger.

—2 Kings 21:3-6

Soothsayers, witchcraft, spiritists, mediums, and wooden images for worship are all mentioned as evil in the sight of God.

They provoked him to jealousy with strange gods,
with abominations provoked they him to anger.
They sacrificed unto demons, not to God; to gods they knew not,
to new gods that came newly up, whom your fathers feared not.

—Deuteronomy 32:16, 17

Using the name of, trusting in, or sacrificing to foreign gods angers God.

> *What say I then? that the idol is any thing, or that*
> *which is offered in sacrifice to idols is any thing?*
> *But I say, that the things which the Gentiles sacrifice, they*
> *sacrifice to devils and not to God: and I*
> *would not that ye should have fellowship with devils.*
> *Ye cannot drink the cup of the Lord, and the cup of devils: ye*
> *cannot be partakers of the Lord's table, and of the table of devils.*
> —1 Corinthians 10:19-21

Here scripture clearly states that we cannot place our faith, trust, and loyalty both in God and in any practice that also demands faith, trust and loyalty. We must make a choice between God's way and fellowship with demons through these other means.

> *And the rest of the men which were not killed by these plagues*
> *yet repented not of the works of their hands,*
> *that they should not worship devils, and idols of gold,*
> *and silver, and brass, and stone, and of wood:*
> *which neither can see, nor hear, nor walk.*
> —Revelation 9:20

What do these verses tell us? They are absolute and once again clearly and unequivocally warn against astrology, idolatry, soothsayers, spiritists, and mediums, thus tools such as séances, the Ouija board, diviners and divining tools such as coins, sticks, tarot cards, witchcraft, and thinking of man as all-powerful, as a god within himself.

What does scripture say about Satan? Verses throughout both the Old Testament and the New Testament warn of the activities of Satan and describe his powers. Mary had read Grandma's journal, *When God Broke Grandma's Heart* and asked if she could copy what it said about Satan. I still had the list Grandma had prepared for use in her journal, so I copied it and gave it to Mary.

When he speaketh a lie, he speaketh of his own:
for he is a liar and the father of it.

—John 8:44

Now the serpent was more subtil than any beast of the field
which the LORD God had made.

—Genesis 3:1

He was a murderer from the beginning,
and abode not in the truth,
because there is no truth in him.

—John 8:44

The serpent beguiled me, and I did eat.

—Genesis 3:13

Called the Devil, and Satan,
which deceiveth the whole world.

—Revelation 12:9

Then was Jesus led up of the Spirit into the wilderness
to be tempted of the devil . . .
and when the tempter came to him, he said . . .

—Matthew 4:1, 3

Additionally,

- Satan can move men to do his bidding: 1 Chronicles 21:1
- Satan can walk back and forth on the earth: Job 2:7
- Satan can cause illness: Job 2:7
- Satan can take God's word from men's hearts: Mark 4:15
- Satan can enter man: Luke 22:3
- Satan can blind the minds of them which believe not: 2 Corinthians 4:4
- Satan can transform himself: 2 Corinthians 11:14
- Satan can send messengers to hurt man: 2 Corinthians 12:7

- Satan can hinder people: 1 Thessalonians 2:18
- Satan can produce signs and has powers: 2 Thessalonians 2:9

> *Even him, whose coming is after the working of Satan*
> *with all power and signs and lying wonders . . .*
> —2 Thessalonians 2:9

This verse tells us that Satan is capable of producing signs and wonders. This can support a belief in certain practices, symbols, or people. To safeguard us from being misled in this manner, God warns us not to embrace the practices of astrology, divining, numerology, and other occult practices. This would include Feng Shui.

We had to admit that we are a people who are fascinated by old truths and ancient practices. We are curious and sometimes in awe of what ancient cultures were able to accomplish and what discoveries were made. We'd often ask ourselves questions about these ancient people and enjoyed watching programs that taught about them. Matt remarked that with questions about these ancient practices unanswered, we tend to doubt the word of God and trust instead our own inadequate conclusions. Our ego is such that we value the decisions of our own mind, the "facts" we ourselves have determined (that to us appear so brilliant), rather than trust God's word.

We thought it so incredible and so important to note again that God never says these ancient practices do not have validity. In fact, many do have validity. What God says is to beware the invoking of these practices if they include astrology, idolatry, numerology, witchcraft, sorcery, and other occult practices as Satan can seriously harm our spiritual lives through these practices. Like the tree of knowledge in the Garden of Eden, opening these areas can lead us down a road where danger lurks in the form of misinformation and dependency. God tells we are in spiritual danger when we invoke these powers and tells us we may lose all opportunity to enter into the kingdom of heaven if we succumb to following these gods. What gods, what powers are these? Is this why God says in His first commandment to Moses, *"I am the Lord thy God. Thou shalt have no other gods before me"*?

Throughout scripture, God tells us about Satan and about the angels that follow Satan and the power they have. Scripture explains that one-third of the angels that were in heaven accompanied Satan when he was cast out of heaven. Therefore Satan has a large workforce to do his bidding. These fallen angels work diligently to harm man. This is why we are warned to prevent these spirits from gaining a foothold in our lives. Again, God seeks to help us, not hinder us.

Then goeth he, and taketh with himself
seven other spirits more wicked than himself,
and they enter in and dwell there:
and the last state of that man is worse than the first.
Even so shall it be also unto this wicked generation.

—Matthew 12:45

Mary asked how God expects us to understand what He wants when it seems so complex. I tried to explain that when we read the Bible and listen to our ministers, we learn not only of God's plan and how He will help us, but also of Satan's plan and how he wants to harm us. I explained that as we learn, the pieces fall into place, and its seeming complexity becomes simple and understandable. God promises to "lift the veil from our eyes," and "open our understanding" when we seek His word. Mary was fascinated, saying she had never heard these things before. I located one of the scriptures that explained why so many did not understand the Bible and read it to Mary.

But their hearts were blinded:
for until this day remaineth the same vail untaken away
in the reading of the old testament; which vail is done away in Christ.
But even unto this day, when Moses is read, the vail is upon their heart.
Nevertheless when it shall turn to the Lord,
the vail shall be taken away.

—2 Corinthians 3:14-16

Then opened he their understanding,
that they might understand the scriptures.

—Luke 24:45

I told Mary that until I'd worked on Grandma's journal, I too had simply not understood the magnitude, the simplicity, and the incredible love in God's plan.

Matt said that when we turn from complete trust in God, we risk so much. He said it was as if we were offered a dish of candy but were told that a few pieces of the candy were poisoned. Would we eat any of that candy? Would we offer the dish of candy to our children? Similarly, we do not know at what point or with which practice we will fall into the hands of Satan, so God warns us simply to stay away from the practices that can give Satan even the smallest grip on our lives. God promises that as we turn to Him, He will open our understanding.

Matt said that what he felt was so dangerous is that not all parts of Feng Shui or all parts of other occult practices are areas where Satan will harm us. Some recommendations may be mathematically correct, physically sound, and psychologically helpful, and some recommendations have practical applications. Some have simply been a result of superstition where some practice once brought success, and that success stayed as a recommendation within the tenets of Feng Shui. Like the dish of candy, some candies are fine. But how can we know which parts are not, which parts would be poisonous to our spiritual life, which parts would eventually and insidiously allow Satan to gain a stronghold on our lives and a death grip on our souls?

We then entered a lively discussion of how the Chinese philosophy, culture, and religion began to lay the groundwork for Feng Shui. We thought that perhaps, using this information, we could compare some Feng Shui recommendations to those we may use throughout all design practices and could see what recommendations may have become tainted.

Grandma's trunk revealed a manuscript that explained so much about the people and the culture in that time and showed us that the ancient Chinese used ritual as a means to guide people to proper interaction with one another. It was thought that a doctrine of ritual regarding the treatment of ancestors, parents, and neighbors would teach people a noble attitude and help them define what makes one "good." This doctrine was handed down to the people, from approximately 2205 BCE by the sages of the Xia, Shang or Yin, and Zhou dynasties. This was considered the teachings of the ancients and revered by the people.

However, in time, competition for land and food caused an upheaval throughout China, and few villages were safe. The people had to prepare themselves against marauders and be ready to defend themselves, their families, and their possessions at all times. Many of the ancient teachings and rituals were lost during these times of competition.

Grandma's manuscript explained that in 551 BCE, Confucius was born in east China. Combining the old teachings of the ancients with techniques for finding peace in the existing chaos of China at that time, Confucius developed a manner of interaction between people that caused him to become an influential philosopher. Confucius instituted ethics for the people to live by. These ethics were a combination of the ancient teachings, including the I Ching, for defining when to take action and when to wait, and a new code of living that would bring harmony between the people.

There were about 124 feudal states in China when Confucius was born and, due to the warring nature of the people at that time, these states were reduced to about 70 during his lifetime. Competition for land and power resulted in murder and conflict and a great deal of suffering for the people. Confucius determined that the loss of ritual and propriety led to the loss of honor and trust between people. He sought to find a way to encourage peace between the various factions. He traveled throughout the feudal states to bring his philosophy to the people. Confucius was very popular and, as a result, acquired a great number of disciples who later developed the various "schools" of Confucianism that penetrated throughout China and into Vietnam, Korea, and Japan. Confucius went on to do a good work for his people through reestablishing the ancient rituals and adding additional teachings to establish a code of ethical behavior. Eventually the warring between the states diminished.

However, during the time that the fighting went on in all the provinces of China, the people were forced to take measures to protect themselves from the invaders from other provinces. These measures included any form of protection that they could conceive. This was one of the times that gave birth to many of the superstitions of present-day Feng Shui.

For example, wind chimes, primitively made from reeds and shells or stones, were hung in doorways. When a door opened, the occupants would be warned that someone had entered the house. Wind chimes were also hung above the second floor or loft bed to alert the occupants if anyone was on the roof. Further, cooking areas might have had a reflective item behind the area in order to alert the cook that someone was approaching behind him. Also, pieces of reflective materials (today's crystals) may have been used on a porch or at the edge of a field as a sort of gazing ball reflecting movement from other areas of the property to warn occupants of someone approaching. Did these bring good luck? Yes, they did. Certainly they would bring good luck if they did warn the occupants of impending danger. Good fortune thus rested on the occupants of the home that employed the use of these articles.

Also, during this period of time, hygiene was not as it is today, and pesticides and antibiotics were nonexistent. Thus, Feng Shui's recommendation to purchase new mattresses when moving was also of medical and practical benefit to avoid carrying vermin and germs from one house to another.

In the countryside, materials were hand hewn and limited. The people were poor, and homes often old and of inferior quality. Therefore, beams above a bed could fail and come down in a fierce storm, frightening, injuring, or perhaps killing anyone lying beneath them. Wind chimes would alert the occupants of that bed should a severe storm be brewing so they could evacuate the dangerous areas of the house. And so goes the many explanations of how these "lucky" practices may have come into being.

Feng Shui, originally available only to the ruling class, began to find its way to the general population. The "lucky" practices the people had learned to employ for their safety found their way into Feng Shui practices and may have thus perverted an otherwise meritorious study of nature and how man interacts with nature to his benefit. In addition to the superstitions of good-luck symbols, the use of astrology, idolatry, and other occult practices along with Feng Shui became a valuable tool for Satan. God knew this and warned His children through His word in scripture.

I am the LORD thy God, which have brought thee out of the
land of Egypt, out of the house of bondage.
Thou shalt have no other gods before me.
Thou shalt not make unto thee any graven image, or any likeness
of any thing that is in heaven above, or that is in the earth beneath, or
that is in the water under the earth.
Thou shalt not bow down
thyself to them, nor serve them:
for I the LORD thy God am a jealous God

—Exodus 20:2-5

Matt said that we know the mind of man cannot begin to understand the mysteries of this world. As God placed the stars in the skies for the wise men to follow, he also admonishes that there are powers there that man is not to try to understand. We may not understand how the sun stood still for Joshua as he fought, but at the same time we do know that God gives us the tools for managing our lives and staying in harmony with what he has created for us now and in the future. He also teaches us that we should cease our labor for one day each week and remember Him that day. This is why we go to church, listen for what God wants to teach us, and often have fellowship with other believers, so we can continue in conversation about Him.

> *Remember the sabbath day, to keep it holy.*
> *Six days shalt thou labour, and do all thy work:*
> *but the seventh day is the sabbath of the LORD*
> *thy God: in it thou shalt not do any work, thou, nor thy son,*
> *nor thy daughter, nor thy male servant, nor thy maidservant,*
> *nor thy cattle, nor thy stranger that is within thy gates*
> —Exodus 20:8-10

We also know that scripture, empirical studies from the discipline of psychology, and the history of Chinese culture can help us explain some of the "miracles" of various beliefs. We are also taught that Satan has power here on earth.

> *And they worshiped the dragon who gave power unto the*
> *beast: and they worshiped the beast, saying,*
> *Who is like unto the beast? who is able to make war with him?*
> —Revelation 13:4

> *And the great dragon was cast out, that old serpent, called*
> *the Devil, and Satan, which deceiveth the whole world:*
> *he was cast out into the earth, and his angels were cast out with him.*
> —Revelation 12:9

Human beings are equipped with the fight-or-flight response, which means that we can often make a split-second decision whether to stand and fight or to flee from a situation that we feel is dangerous or threatening. The changes in our body (the release of adrenaline, for instance) when reacting to this response syndrome are what allow for extraordinary strength or endurance when required in an emergency.

These observations help us understand why many Feng Shui applications are practical and psychologically sound. These then become lures, like the innocent apple in the Garden of Eden, and if we are not careful or aware, it is through these things that we can fall prey to trusting the wrong spirits. Only knowing the word of God through scripture can keep us safe.

> *Whose adorning let it not be that outward adorning of plaiting the*
> *hair, and of wearing of gold, or of putting on of apparel;*
> *But let it be the hidden man of the heart,*
> *in that which is not corruptible,*
> *even the adornment of a meek and quiet spirit,*
> *which is in the sight of God a great price.*
> —1 Peter 3:3, 4

In the Chinese culture, every form of life is believed to have its own strength or goodness that can be of benefit to mankind. This leads to a symbolism that is very important to the Chinese. Other cultures, such as the American Indian tribes and many African tribes for example, also embraced this belief. It is in fact a universal belief that was found in all tribes at one time or another.

Matt observed that just as we may carry a rabbit's foot, jump over cracks in the sidewalks, hang a medal on our rearview mirror in the car, or hang a picture of our religious leader on the walls of our home, so has Feng Shui developed symbols of those things that bring good fortune or the remembrance of a happy experience. It must be acknowledged that these articles often bring a sense of well-being to us and also helps demonstrate the power of the mind.

However, even though we may concede that good or bad "luck" can indeed come in cycles and that there are many forces in nature that we do not understand, the Christian community still advocates that we place our trust only in God. He can direct all forces, all experiences. There may be a lesson, an experience, that we may need to derive from our current situation that will allow us to develop, to learn, to help ourselves and others, and thus to become more pleasing in God's eyes. It is imperative to remember the Bible passages that indicate God's admonitions because they are for our good, meant to help us navigate through dangerous times.

However, once we are assured that we do place God above all things in our life, are faithful in our service and tithing, and consult Him in all things, there should be no harm in placing a symbol of something we admire in nature into our homes. We can also ask for guidance when contemplating this as God hears all prayers, all pleas, and is faithful to respond. God

Himself authorized the carving of angels and pomegranates and palm tress for decorations on those structures He authorized to be built. Therefore, the use of any object for decorating and beautifying purposes is okay, but not for luck, power, control, prayer, or anything even remotely connected with idolatry, demons, spirits, or gods.

> *Out of the south cometh the whirlwind: and cold out of the north.*
> *By the breath of God frost is given;*
> *and the breadth of the waters is straitened.*
> *Also by watering he wearieth the thick cloud;*
> *he scattereth his bright cloud: And it is turned round about by his counsels;*
> *that they may do whatsoever he commandeth them*
> *upon the face of the world in the earth*
>
> —Job 37:9-12

> *Where wast thou when I laid the foundations of the earth?*
> *declare, if thou hast understanding.*
> *Who hath laid the measures thereof, if thou knowest?*
> *or who hath stretched the line upon it?*
> *Whereupon are the foundations thereof fastened?*
> *or who laid the corner stone thereof?*
>
> —Job 38:4-6

I told Kevin and Mary that just as Feng Shui makes promises, so does God. He tells us how to plan our home according to His will so we can obtain His blessing. The word of God is not dangerous, is in fact a safety net for us and a road with a great reward at the end, pleasing the heart of our Heavenly Father. If we do this, the power that lives in our homes and in our hearts will be from God, and we can make our home a Bethany. Satan will be unable to invade because we will be wearing the armor of God He speaks of in scripture. We will then be on the road to planning and implementing a happy life in harmony with the word of God.

While there may be some parts of Feng Shui that carry no negative influences according to the word of God, where some of the recommendations are practical and psychologically sound, nevertheless, there are many we should not employ, as they are associated with superstition and negative to the word of God. Like the pieces of candy in the dish, can we tell which ones are poisoned and which are safe? Shouldn't we avoid them all?

Chapter Ten

THE CHALLENGE

They have turned aside quickly out of the way which I commanded them: they have made them a molten calf, and worshiped it, and have sacrificed thereunto, and said, These be thy gods, O Israel, which have brought thee up out of the land of Egypt.

—Exodus 32:8

We had been working on the house again and beginning to see how lovely it would be when we finished. Mary and Kevin came over early. Later in the morning, when the men said that they needed to run to the store for some additional materials, Mary asked if we could go across the street for a cup of tea. Matt and Kevin had long ago worked out an agreement that Kevin would be Matt's "right-hand man" on our renovation. Then, after the wedding, Matt would help Kevin build the art studio for Mary in the carriage house. Kevin and Matt were both pleased because they enjoyed one another's company so much, and this arrangement provided them with a great excuse to spend time together. Mary and I often joked with them about the male bonding process and how building materials and sports talk were surefire methods to make this happen!

Before we left, Mary and I instructed Matt and Kevin to perfect a little exercise we wanted them to try. "We want you to be able to do the exercise for us by this afternoon," I said and explained. "While sitting down, lift your right foot slightly off the floor and begin making clockwise turns with your leg and foot, keeping it close to, but not touching, the ground. Then, while doing this with your foot, raise your left arm above your waist and begin drawing the number six in the air with your left index finger. When we get back, we'll see who can do it best and maybe in the process prove who is the really the weaker sex!" As we left, the men were already trying to begin the exercise but couldn't do it unless they were sitting down, and they needed to get to the store. Mary and I grinned at one another.

When Mary asked me over for a cup of tea, I knew she wanted to finish her story. I said a quick prayer that God would instill in me the right words and correct reactions to help Mary trust me and ultimately learn to trust God. I knew that telling me was difficult for her and that it was important that I impart a response that helped her have faith in me as a friend. I'd always felt we have to earn trust and that it is a special gift that friends give one another, one to be cherished and protected, and a painful experience if that trust is broken. Realizing the importance of what Mary was to tell me and of my response, I was quite apprehensive because of an incident that occurred shortly after we all got together this morning.

As soon as we began working and talking, Mary said that when she read Grandma's journal, she related to Grandma's personality and wanted to find the peace and wisdom that Grandma found. I told her that we all long for what Grandma found, that most of us didn't know how to go about getting it. I told her we all needed love and acceptance and needed loyalty from those around us. "God understands this," I said, "and wants to help us find it, but it has to start within ourselves, with repairing our own self-esteem and learning what true goodness is." I tried to explain that when Adam and Eve ate the apple, they opened the door to the curse that made us have to learn about evil to appreciate what is good. This is our inheritance from Adam and Eve and is what is called inherited sin. Our sins and the sins of our forefathers are passed along, from generation to generation, like our DNA, and some people never escape those patterns. Only when we ask and allow God to cleanse us *and* we take on the fight to overcome it can we break free. "Why else," I asked, "would God speak over and over again about being an overcomer, fighting the good fight, watching for our enemy, praying for those who died in their sins, if it were not ongoing and important for us to do these things?"

When I said this, I was surprised to see Mary begin to cry, her chest heaving and her mouth gasping for breath and tears cascading down her face. I didn't know what had happened. She couldn't seem to stop. She sobbed so much, and even when I held her, she couldn't catch her breath and continued to cry. My heart went out to her, and I realized that this was because the rest of Mary's story, the part she hadn't told me, the part that continued to plague her, was so painful for her and what I'd said had triggered that memory.

To me, Mary was a lovely, sensitive, compassionate, striving soul who longed to be loved and accepted, longed to do the right thing. I felt that for some reason she felt that she needed forgiveness for whatever she perceived she had done wrong. I knew that only God could restore her faith in herself and help her end her pain, especially her fear, but I also felt the responsibility of doing my best to show her that path. A pure heart was what God looked for, not what mistakes we may have made or what evil may have entrapped us. Mary did have a pure and seeking heart, and I knew God was working to draw her to Him.

I told Mary that Matt and I saw her as a most wonderful woman whom we loved and that we would be her friends and stand by her no matter what. I also said that God saw her beautiful heart too and that she was very precious to Him. Slowly, Mary stopped crying, smiled at me, and made the decision to tell me the rest of her story.

As we sipped our tea, Mary began her story by throwing me an abrupt and stark sentence so unexpectedly that I immediately recognized she was testing me, watching fearfully and apprehensively for my reaction. She wanted to see if I cringed or looked upset. I could see how worried she was that I would judge her or would find her lacking somehow.

Mary had blurted out the words "I had a baby and they made me give it away." "Oh Mary," I said, "that must have been so difficult for you." Mary went on, "I can't stand the pain anymore, and sometimes I want to die from the guilt. I worry about her, where she is, how she is, who her parents are, what they are like, how do they treat her? I want her back, and I want her not to hate me." When Mary looked at me, my heart contracted. I could feel the pain she felt and silently prayed, *Please, God, help her, help me to help her too.*

Mary told me that a few weeks after the second rape, the dentist died in a car accident as he was driving to the airport to pick up his son who had finally decided to visit his father after six years away. The dentist had been drunk when he left his house. His car glanced off the side of another car, went out of control, jumped the guardrail, and, still accelerating, hit a tree without seeming to touch the ground. When the police arrived, they found the car suspended in the lower branches of the tree. The dentist apparently died instantly when his head hit the windshield on impact.

His son obtained a rental car when his father did not arrive to pick him up at the airport and drove to his father's house. A few hours later, the police arrived at the house, not knowing who would be there, and gave him the news of his father's death. The son arranged for a quick funeral, packed up some of the supplies from the dental office, put the house up for sale, and went back to his wife's family. He was never heard from again.

It was after these terrible circumstances, after the townspeople fell back into the simple complacency of their small town rituals, and eleven weeks after the rape, that Mary discovered she was pregnant. Three weeks later she told her mother, not admitting who the father was. Her parents were furious, horribly embarrassed by the shame of what Mary had done and upset to learn it was too late for Mary to have an abortion. Pressuring her to admit who the father was and angry with her for withholding this information, they decided to send Mary to a home for unwed mothers in another state and keep what had happened a secret. They demanded that Mary give the baby up for adoption. Mary was still only fourteen years old.

The baby came early, but to Mary's relief, the baby was healthy. Mary said that it tore at her heart to give the baby away and that she has relived that day, those moments, every day of her life since it happened. "She had dark hair like mine, and she was so beautiful, so soft and so sweet. She never deserved this, never deserved to be given away," Mary said. "I need to know she's okay. I want her back, I want her to live with me. I want her to forgive me." Again, Mary began to cry. Again, I held her and tried to comfort her.

"Mary, God can always work things out, especially when we think it impossible to do so. When we bring our concerns to Him, He is already working on fixing them. Most of the time we can't begin to imagine how He could possibly fix our troubles, but He will, and sometimes, most times, He fixes our problems to our utter amazement and joy. I've seen proof of this in my life, in Matt's, in Grandma's, and in my mom's. And I know I will see it in yours."

I asked Mary, "Would it be okay with you if we prayed together?" Mary, still weeping, agreed and moved her chair to sit close to me, shoulder to shoulder as if she were a little girl seeking comfort. She folded her tiny hands into her lap, waiting for my words. I wished I could take away her worries and her pain. In praying, I knew I could ask God to do this.

So I began to pray, saying,

Dearest Heavenly Father,
We thank you for loving us so much that You have already
made the perfect plan for our lives despite what Satan does to us.
Help us to trust in that and through that trust to develop a pure heart. Please
forgive us our mistakes and teach us and help us be overcomers and
worthy for the First Resurrection.
We come before You now to plead for comfort, guidance, and the restoration of our hope.
We ask for a miracle. We ask you to place into our hearts the surety of Your words
that all that happens can be for the good of those that love You.
Help Mary in her need, Father,
let her know how much You love her. Give her an experience of faith
so she will know You are with her in this time of trouble and will be forever with her.
Father, please also give her peace. Jesus Christ told us that our own peace
He leaves with us, but also that His peace He gladly gives us.
Mary needs to feel that peace now. Please bless this home, Father,
bless Mary and Kevin's love for one another, bless Mary's child, and please, Father,
continue to bless the friendship we have together and for which we thank You.
Help us learn of you every day of our lives and follow your words.
For all things, Father, we thank you from the bottom of our hearts
and ask these things in the name of our Lord Jesus Christ,
Amen.

Mary cried softly during the prayer but had stopped by the time I finished. She leaned over to hug me and said that she was so glad God had sent us to them. In a tiny gentle voice, she asked me to teach her about God, and I promised I would and that together we would grow in faith and serve God, and He would bless us and also bless our future. I told her of the promise God gave when He said,

I the LORD have called thee in righteousness,
and will hold thine hand, and will keep thee.

—Isaiah 42:6

After clearing the table of the teacups, we walked hand in hand across the street where the men were unloading their building materials from the car. Mary seemed so much happier. Kevin could see it immediately and looked at me mouthing a silent "Thank you." I smiled and gave him a secret thumbs-up. But then, to lighten the mood, I asked Matt and Kevin to demonstrate that little exercise for us. They tried, and tried again, and could not do it.

Their right foot would reverse direction to counterclockwise as soon as they began to draw the number six with their left hand. "We can do it," I said, and Mary came to sit next to me on the window seat. Mary and I began to giggle remembering our little plan to trick our "macho" men.

Sitting close to me, Mary began moving her right foot in a clockwise motion. Once Mary had her foot in motion, I moved my left hand to draw the number six in the air. "That's cheating," the guys yelled, both highly indignant. "No way," I said, "it's the superior brain of a female using teamwork to get the job done!" "You can never beat a woman," Kevin said, shaking his head while Matt laughed. Then Matt asked Kevin if he'd ever heard of the four "gives" of marriage and repeated the little joke my brother told him. "Marriage is: Give, Give in, Forgive, and . . . Give up!" And Mary playfully pulled on his ear while Matt sheepishly said, "Sorry!"

Once inside and all working again, Matt asked if any of us had ever heard the word "Vastu," and none of us had. He was excited and began telling us that he'd just learned something new. He said that while they were waiting in the lumberyard, he read a section of Grandma's manuscript that was titled "Vastu." Matt said he brought the manuscript with him to the lumberyard because last night he'd thumbed through it and noticed the Vastu heading. He was curious, never having heard that word before, and began to read, but soon he was distracted by other demands and had to put the manuscript down. This morning, his curiosity got the best of him, and on impulse, he grabbed the manuscript when they were leaving for the lumberyard thinking he could look at it while the lumber was being cut. He said it was fascinating and something he'd never heard about and commented that Grandma was a whiz at research!

Matt told us that Vastu was the Indian equivalent of Feng Shui, and entire building developments in India were built according to the tenets of Vastu. He went on to explain that Vastu is an ancient Indian science of architecture and design that seeks to align the living spaces of the home with unseen spiritual and natural laws. It is about three thousand years old, but not yet as popular worldwide as Feng Shui. It was first documented around 1200 BCE in the Hindu Vedas and closely linked to Aryurveda and Yoga. Like Feng Shui, Vastu seeks to provide harmony and well-being in the home and for its occupants by using the relationship between the environment and our state of mind and bodies.

To practice Vastu, Prana, which is likened to the Qi of Feng Shui, must be enabled to flow freely through the house. Prana is known as the "divine breath" in Hindu thinking and considered an energy that has the power to give all things health and life. According to the beliefs of Vastu, the evil gods purported to live in every home must be controlled, usually by using the electromagnetic pull of the earth and the five elements. Matt explained that by using specific open areas in a home, specific furniture placement, specific colors, and the use of statues of various Indian gods such as Shiva, Ganesh, and Purusha, to name a few, the home will be a more serene place to live. Matt said that he also found an article in Grandma's trunk about some residential developments in New Delhi that advertise the homes they built as based on Vastu principles to attract buyers.

Matt said he would try to describe Vastu briefly and simply, by explaining that for decorating purposes a square (*sakala*) is made that contains nine smaller squares around each side, with other squares filling in the center. Referring from time to time to the manuscript, Matt said that the eight compass directions are assigned to the sakala, the four sides being the cardinal directions. Sections of the sakala are assigned to the four elements of fire, water/air, earth, and ether. While a different god rules each square, eight gods are considered powerful enough to cause trouble in the home. These eight gods are called the Vedic gods, and each rules a different section of the sakala. The god Purusha governs all these gods and is drawn on the squares as an overlay of the entire sakala rather than a portion of the sakala that the other gods occupy.

Vastu also makes use of astrology, which is called Jyotish. Jyotish requires the exact time and place of birth to be accurate in its recommendations. Further, for Vastu followers, it is often recommended that there be a prayer room which would contain dishes of sweets and flower petals in water that are offered up to the god or goddess revered. Incense, chants, and the sound of clanging bells may also be used.

The part of Vastu that many people readily accept is its belief that the electromagnetic field of the earth has an important impact on the human body. Scientists have agreed that the electromagnetic field of the earth creates a subtle vibration, promoting a force or energy that impacts the body, and that the earth's atmosphere is filled with electromagnetic energy produced by negatively and positively charged ions. The human body produces its own electromagnetic field, which interacts with the earth. However, Matt said, just what this does to the human body has not been determined scientifically and empirically. Nevertheless, the premise of Vastu is that this electromagnetic field impacts the human body and that positioning oneself and one's rooms and furnishings according to this electromagnetic field will have a beneficial effect on the mind and body and will appease the gods that cause the negative influences in one's life.

Further, Vastu followers must often change the function or designation of their rooms to gain the proper magnetic flow assigned to each room. For instance, one might be told that the dining room must become the daughter's bedroom, or that the living room should become the dining room to gain the benefits of the proper magnetic pull of the earth or the specified cardinal direction. While this electromagnetic area of Vastu appears benign and is thus readily embraced by many, Matt said that it is important to note that the other more serious requirements of Vastu oppose scripture and he felt would surely open the home to satanic forces.

> *For I know this, that after my departing shall grievous*
> *wolves enter in among you, not sparing the flock.*
> *Also of your own selves shall men arise,*
> *speaking perverse things, to draw away the*
> *disciples after them.*
> *Therefore watch.*
>
> —Acts 20:29-31

Matt really had our attention now and went on to describe that in Vastu, a drawing of a god, facedown on the floor of the room to be decorated, is the basis for decorating that room. It is believed that this god was cast from heaven to cover all the earth and every thing we touch. It is because of this decorating basis that, biblically, a comparison can be made between Purusha and Satan, whose name had been Lucifer. According to scripture, when Lucifer was cast out of the heavens, he came to earth to have rule over earth.

> *And the great dragon was cast out, that old serpent,*
> *called the Devil, and Satan, which deceiveth the whole world:*
> *he was cast out into the earth,*
> *and his angels were cast out with him*
>
> —Revelation 12:9

Perhaps this event actually influenced the drawings in which Purusha (Lucifer) covers the earth and all that we touch. Matt said that while this similarity may then make Vastu more credible to the Christian religious community, we must remember that other scriptural passages stress the dangers of trying to appeal to these gods (spirits) and the need to seek protection and direction from our Heavenly Father only.

> *And whosoever shall offend one of these little ones that believe in me,*
> *it is better for him that a millstone were hanged about his neck,*
> *and he were cast into the sea.*
>
> —Mark 9:42

Matt felt that the same arguments that we used against Feng Shui can be used against Vastu. Statues of gods or of inanimate objects that we trust to have power over and to change our life's circumstances are idols in the eyes of our Heavenly Father and are not pleasing to Him.

God's ability to produce an earth that interacts with man for the benefit of man, and at God's will, is fully acknowledged by all Christians. Therefore, many of the tenets of Vastu and Feng Shui that are based on the study of nature may help us understand our world and ourselves. Suggestions for a healthy flow of air, a lack of clutter, cheerful colors, a flowing floor plan, and the balanced placement of furniture are all good things. Likewise, it is possible that the electromagnetic pull of the earth does impact man.

However, Matt said, when gods and inanimate objects and idols become the accoutrements we bring into our homes, to which we pray, pay homage, trust, chant, follow blindly, then we stumble in our efforts to be children of our Heavenly Father. We must worry when a desire to "appease" the gods allows Satan to enter our hearts to slowly, assiduously take away our faith and reliance on God.

We need to remember that God controls all things, including Qi or Prana, including the electromagnetic forces, and all other effects and forces found in, on, or surrounding the earth. According to the Bible, even greater forces than ever before seen will be loosed for the destruction prophesied to come.

> *For in that day every man shall cast away his idols of silver,*
> *and his idols of gold, which your own*
> *hands have made unto you for a sin.*
>
> —Isaiah 31:7

*The first angel sounded, and there followed hail and fire mingled
with blood, and they were cast upon the earth: and the third part of the trees
was burnt up, and all green grass was burnt up. And the second angel sounded,
and as it were a great mountain burning with fire was
cast into the sea: and the third part of the sea became blood.
And the third part of creatures which were in the sea, and had life, died;
and the third part of the ships were destroyed. And the third angel sounded,
and there fell a great star from heaven, burning as it were a lamp, and it fell
upon the third part of the rivers, and upon the fountains of waters;
And the name of the star is called Wormwood: and the third part of
the waters became wormwood; and many men died of the waters,
because they were made bitter. And the fourth angel sounded:
and the third part of the sun was smitten, and the third part of the moon,
and the third part of the stars; so as the third part of them were darkened,
and the day shone not for a third part of it, and the night likewise.*

—Revelation 8:7-12

*And the rest of the men which were not killed by these plagues
yet repented not of the works of their hands,
that they should not worship devils, and idols of gold,
and silver, and brass, and stone, and of wood, which
neither can see, nor hear, nor walk.*

—Revelation 9:20

I mentioned that as we become armed with this information, we begin to better understand that what God tells in regard to fads, fantasies, and lucky charms is vital to our spiritual well-being. Therefore to learn and heed His words is our lifeline. And more importantly we need to recognize that we have been warned, we have been told, and we have been shown the path to travel, and clearly shown how subtle Satan is as he uses even decorating as a way to trip us up.

Mary and Kevin were astounded, explaining that they had no idea, that now they could see things a little differently even though they were still confused. They felt they were being warned and wanted to learn more. Matt and I breathed a sigh of relief and silently thanked our Heavenly Father.

Later, after Kevin and Mary had left, having already obtained Mary's permission, I told Matt what Mary told me and said that we needed to help them understand their role in God's plan of salvation. Suddenly we realized that in all these months, Matt and I had never invited Kevin and Mary to come to church with us. We knew they could find any answer to any question or problem if they sought the solution through the word of God. We had. When we'd lost Matt's brother and Grandma in the same year, we'd both been distraught, but it had brought us to the challenge of seeing what God would tell us and how He would explain things to us. And He did!

Now we saw that we had been remiss, caught up with working on the house, caught up with great conversation and debate, and forgetting what really mattered for Kevin and Mary. We vowed we would do our best to tell them we found our answers both in the Bible and by sitting under the word of God at church. We'd talked about it but hadn't acted!

We decided that we needed to talk with Kevin and Mary to see where they were spiritually so we could offer timely help and support and, most of all, invite them to church. We remembered that Christ said,

Inasmuch as ye have done it unto one of the least of these my brethren,
ye have done it unto me.
—Matthew 25:40

I also had an idea I wanted to pursue for Mary and told Matt about it, but he suggested I do not mention it to Kevin and Mary yet. It had come into my mind that Mary's child would be about fourteen or fifteen years old now and that when the child was eighteen, she could have her adoption records opened. Mary could prepare for that possibility and perhaps could finally find the peace she longed for. But now wasn't the time to bring this up. Many other emotions and fears had to be dealt with first, and a faith in God begun that would enable them both to find the right path to take and to be the right example to their child.

The key to everything would begin with their trust in us. I tried to examine my conduct and my message to see if I would trust the person producing these recommendations and realized that Matt and I had really not talked emotionally about our relationship with God and should have. Love, or true love anyway, begins with how much we love God, and we can only love Him because He first showed us how by loving us first, and unconditionally. Sometimes it's a struggle to demonstrate our love by our striving to learn His word and then to live those words. If I wasn't an example of this, how could Mary believe that I could be trusted, or could love her, and accept what she saw as failure?

Sometimes it's so hard to tell one another that we really want to be a good friend and love and help properly, and that we mean to stick by them through good and bad times. We wanted to be good friends and the kind of neighbors Christ spoke of when He said we should love one another and forgive one another, even lay down our life for one another as He did for us.

Friends cheer the good things that happen, helping you celebrate without jealousy, and friends stand shoulder to shoulder with you, never leaving you when bad things happen. We wondered if Kevin and Mary felt we had this capacity.

Women seem to need things said out loud, and many times, before they are able to process, believe, and internalize this knowledge, they need to see and experience *and hear!* Men on the other hand seem to be okay with just a simple one-time grunt of "good job, buddy." They don't seem to test or need repetition the way women do. I was a psychologist and still didn't have all these answers, but I was determined to do a better job of being an example to Kevin and Mary. Matt said that he had the same goal.

We would invite Kevin and Mary to attend church with us, but we wanted to explain why we had chosen to attend church services twice a week, why we felt it important. Millions of people choose not to go to church and believe it is not necessary to being a good person, or even being a spiritual person who believes in God. Could these multitudes be right, or were they in jeopardy?

We decided to ask God for help by again going to the Bible to look for answers. We thought that examining the words of Christ's apostles as they spoke to the churches they established might lead us to these answers. For us, going to church covered four major areas we felt important for our life. The first was to let God know that because we loved Him, we set aside some specific time for Him. The second was to let God know we believed He spoke to us through the men of God He ordained to lead and guide us to the First Resurrection. The third was to appreciate the Holy Spirit that opens our understanding, and brings us together in the fellowship and breaking of bread with other believers that the apostles of old spoke about. The fourth was to avail ourselves the wonderful gift of Holy Communion, which is the remembrance of Christ's sacrifice, His suffering, death, and ascension, allowing us the forgiveness of sin and the strengthening of our resolve not to repeat those sins. As we searched the Bible, we found these:

And they continued stedfastly in the apostles' doctrine and fellowship,
and in breaking of bread, and in prayers.
—Acts 2:42

And the Lord added to the church daily such as should be saved.
—Acts 2:47

Howbeit many of them which heard the word believed.
—Acts 4:4

But we will give ourselves continually to prayer,
and to the ministry of the word.
—Acts 6:4

And he commanded us to preach unto the people,
and to testify that it is he which was ordained of God.
—Acts 10:42

Take heed therefore unto yourselves, and to all the flock,
over the which the Holy Ghost hath made you overseers,
to feed the church of God, which he hath purchased with his own blood.
—Acts 20:28

And he gave some, apostles; and some, prophets; and some, evangelists;
and some pastors and teachers; For the perfecting of the saints,
for the work of the ministry, for the edifying of the body of Christ.
—Ephesians 4:11, 12

He that hath an ear,
let him hear what the Spirit saith unto the churches
—Revelation 2:7

He that hath an ear,
let him hear what the Spirit saith unto the churches.
—Revelation 2:11

And he that overcometh, and keepeth my works unto the end,
to him will I give power over the nations.
—Revelation 2:26

He that hath an ear,
let him hear what the Spirit saith unto the churches.
—Revelation 2:29

He that hath an ear,
let him hear what the Spirit saith unto the churches
—Revelation 3:13

So then because thou art lukewarm,
and neither cold nor hot, I will spue thee out of my mouth.
—Revelation 3:16

He that hath an ear,
let him hear what the Spirit saith unto the churches
—Revelation 3:22

And the Spirit and the bride say, Come.
And let him that heareth say, Come.
And let him that is athirst come.
And whosoever will, let him take the water of life freely.
—Revelation 22:17

Howbeit when he, the Spirit of truth, is come,
he will guide you into all truth.
—John 16:13

Thy words were found, and I did eat them;
and thy word was unto me the joy and rejoicing of mine heart.
—Jeremiah 15:16

He that heareth you heareth me.
—Luke 10:16

Kevin lay in bed unable to sleep. All the things that Matt and Sarah told him that day about God, church, scripture, commitment felt so right to him. He listened as Matt grouped together all those verses that used the same words about "he that hath an ear, let him hear," and it had amazed him. He knew these statements must be very important to be repeated so many times and in so many places in the Bible. And it made sense that God would love those who demonstrated they loved Him. "Even in a friendship," Kevin thought, "I'd rather pick the guy who seemed to really like me and want to be with me rather than one who appeared to be indifferent."

Kevin wanted God in his life. He wanted Feng Shui out of his life. He wanted fear out of Mary's life. He wanted them both to be bonded in faith like Matt and Sarah were. He wanted someone like Matt to talk to when he was perplexed or worried. He wanted Matt to pray for him, and he wanted to pray for Matt. He wanted to be a good husband and eventually a good father who taught his children what was right. He felt inadequate because he hadn't accomplished these things in all the years that he and Mary had been together. He longed for Mary to want these things too and believed that she did. "If it wasn't for her fear," he thought, "everything would be different."

So for the first time since he was a child, Kevin folded his hands to pray. He knelt beside the sleeping Mary, admiring her beauty and her innocence, and spoke to God from his heart. He stumbled at first, but he persevered. He began by pouring out his love for Mary and his concern for her fears, and how much he wanted to find the right path for them to walk, be a responsible husband. He asked God to help them, told Him that he was sorry to be so lost. He promised to do better if God would just help him understand what he was supposed to do. He told God how much it hurt him to fight with Mary and explained that he didn't want to hurt her and felt that only God could show him how to make the changes they needed without having to fight. He asked that God draw their hearts to Him, open their understanding of the scriptures, and fill them with the wisdom they needed. He asked for forgiveness for not looking after Mary spiritually in the past and asked God to help him learn how to do this in the future.

And for the first time in a long time, Kevin sobbed. The emotion he felt welled into his throat. His tears released the terrible lump his felt in his throat and relieved the pain. He had to stop praying. But suddenly he knew that what he was asking for was the right thing, that what he wanted in his life was what he'd always wanted and just hadn't known. He recognized that despite the pain, it was a good kind of emotion, one that seemed to release all his pent-up worries and all his indecisiveness. He felt somehow free in his heart, and he hadn't felt this in a long time. He was filled with the hope that He and Mary had finally found what had been missing in their life, and for the first time he truly believed that Mary would be whole again. He continued his prayer long enough to thank God for sending Matt and Sarah into their lives, for helping him in so many ways, and for what He would provide for them in the future. Then Kevin crawled into bed beside Mary and with a thankful, hopeful heart, finally slept through the night without worry.

Chapter Eleven

HOW GRANDMA CHASED THE SPIRITS

It was my birthday, and Mary and Kevin had planned a dinner at their house as a surprise for me. Matt knew about it, but I had no idea! Mary lowered the dimmer on her chandelier to create a special mood in the room and set the table beautifully with candles and all the accoutrements for a very special dinner. A beautifully folded, brightly colored cloth napkin was encased in an ornate napkin ring which lay angled across the plates. There were tall crystal wineglasses next to matching crystal water goblets placed above and off center to the plates. These lent an elegant formality to the setting, and the soft light from the chandelier shimmered off the crystal. The floral arrangement in the center of the table matched the colors in the napkins and tablecloth, and the silverware gleamed in their place beside the dishes. To my surprise, my favorite CD of church songs, sung by the youth who had gathered for a weekend together in Denver, Colorado, was playing in the background. I turned to Matt and smiled, telling him that through the music, I recognized his hand in this surprise as well!

Mary and Kevin had gone to a lot of trouble for me, and I was deeply touched. The gift of oneself is truly precious and not something everyone is willing to give! We sat down, and to our joy, Kevin asked Matt to bless the food before we ate together, and we all bent our heads and folded our hands in prayer. And Matt prayed.

Dear Heavenly Father,
we come before Thee in humble thankfulness for all You have provided for us.
We thank You even for the troubles we have encountered in our lives
because we know you will use them to make us better children of God
and create in us a pure and understanding heart.
We thank You for this food, Father,
and ask that You bless it and the hands that prepared this wonderful dinner
and beautiful table out of love. Please bless this house
and all who live here that they may come into the fullness of Your glory.
Lay into this evening and this food what we need to sustain us in body,
mind, soul, and spirit and help us too to be found worthy
on that great day that You send Your son to take us home.
All these things, Father, we ask in Jesus' name.
Amen.

Mary served a delicious pork roast flavored with rosemary and onions, creamy scalloped potatoes, steaming snow peas with butter, a wonderful and colorful salad tossed with Italian balsamic dressing, and topped it off with hot golden biscuits. We had a feast! Of course, we ate too much but loved every minute of it.

When we cleared the table of the dinner dishes, Mary brought out a pot of coffee and a beautiful birthday cake. Mary said that she made the cake herself. She'd placed a dozen candles on it and lit every one so I could make a wish and blow them out. When we finished our dessert and were just as full as could be, Mary brought me a lovely gift, beautifully wrapped and held together with exquisite gold ribbons tied in a huge bow. I opened the gift at the table. It was a statue of a delicate, graceful angel with arms outstretched and face looking toward heaven. I just loved it and said I would place it in a special spot in our new home. I was so touched by Mary and Kevin's thoughtfulness and expression of love.

As the evening drew to a close, Mary stood to toast our friendship and told us that she and Kevin felt gifted by God in our friendship and that they had decided to attend church with us the next morning . . . just to give it a try . . . no promises . . . just try it on for size.

Matt and I were so pleased that Kevin and Mary wanted to come to church with us. Earlier we'd reviewed some of the Bible verses that reminded us why we felt it important to go to church, and now we shared these verses with Kevin and Mary, explaining how the words we heard strengthened our faith, taught us about God's plan, and reminded us of His great and everlasting love for us. All these things worked together to help us retain our trust in Him through good times and bad.

We tried to express the incredible sense of joy we felt as we heard the choir sing and as we prayed before the service. Matt said that most people did not realize that without receiving the forgiveness of sin, they always carried the burden of their sin. Even something one might think of as a simple or less important sin such as gossiping or road anger carried a weight which, over time, made one sad and tired, maybe even ill. He said that we did not recognize how often we sinned, even when we thought we were not sinning, and felt it was arrogant to think we were not sinning every day by what we did or did not do or by what we sometimes thought. Matt felt that it was so wonderful to be free of sin and receive Holy Communion worthily at every service.

We were thrilled that Kevin and Mary would come to church with us and knew we would pray later asking God to touch their hearts in a very special way so they would know that He knew they were there and His word was especially for them.

We arranged to pick them up Sunday morning, explaining that Kevin and I sang in the choir so we could not sit with them and would need to arrive about a half hour before the service started. On the drive to the church, we explained the simple procedure for Holy Communion so they would feel comfortable. We settled them in seats right across the aisle from where we sat in choir and gave them hymnbooks to use for the opening hymn and for the communion hymn. Mary, as usual, looked wonderful in a black velvet skirt, silky red blouse, and a black-and-white checkerboard velvet poncho. Kevin looked terrific in a black blazer with brass buttons and gray slacks. He had even worn a red tie.

After service we decided to go to brunch together. We wanted to hear their reaction to the service and were thrilled when they said they liked it, learned so much, and wanted to come again next week. We invited Kevin and Mary to come to my apartment after we ate so they could get a feel for our (and Grandma's) decorating choices. They loved the idea, and when we had given them the grand tour of the apartment, they said they could see why we had chosen our traditional house and its wonderful old-world setting. They felt the ambiance of our new house was reflected in the setting of my apartment with its tall arched windows, high ceilings, beautiful dark woodwork, and hardwood floors.

They loved Grandma's antiques and remarked on some of her unique accessories. They noticed the clocks right away. I'd written about the clocks in the journal that Matt and I compiled after Matt's brother and Grandma died. When I'd later reread what I wrote, I could see that my love of clocks and their unique chimes matched Grandma's love of clocks. I was lucky that Matt felt the same way and enjoyed their chiming too. When the quarter hour came and all the clocks in the apartment began to chime, slightly apart in timing, Kevin and Mary smiled and said that this was so fitting. They loved all the chiming and couldn't wait to see and hear the clocks when they were finally in place in our new home.

As we sat in the living room to talk for a while, Kevin said he collected hand-carved decoy ducks similar to those used for hunting. He asked Matt to describe how one could recognize the line between loving and collecting something, whether it was clocks or any other collectible, and making these thing idols in a home. We tried to explain the difference. Matt ran to get our concordance and Bible, showing Kevin how to use the concordance to find specific subjects. Kevin had never seen a concordance before and marveled at the size and weight of ours.

Matt and Kevin searched for the word *idol* and found many references, but then Matt saw the word *idolatry* and said this word might give them more immediate insight since what they were really concerned about at the moment was what constituted the practice of idolatry. Finally, though, they decided to look at a number of words in the concordance such as *witchcraft*, *sorcery*, and *astrology* to locate the scriptures that applied. This made sense, and we agreed that maybe we should look at a few under each heading. Matt wanted to show Kevin how to use the concordance along with the Bible, and together they skimmed the brief description the concordance gave of the first few verses that used the word they sought. Kevin began to look them up in the Bible, using the index to find the proper chapter.

> *Wherefore, my dearly beloved, flee from idolatry.*
> —1 Corinthians 10:14

> *And I would not that ye should have fellowship with devils.*
> —1 Corinthians 10:20

Ye cannot drink the cup of the Lord, and the cup of devils:
ye cannot be partakers of the Lord's table, and of the table of devils.
—1 Corinthians 10:21

Ye cannot do the things that ye would . . .
Now the works of the flesh are manifest, which are these; . . . idolatry,
witchcraft, . . . they which
do such things shall not inherit the kingdom of God
—Galatians 5:17, 19-21

And the king . . . made a covenant before the LORD . . . to keep his
commandments and his testimonies and his statutes with all their
heart and all their soul.
—2 Kings 23:3

And he put down the idolatrous priests . . . burned incense . . .
to the sun, and to the moon, and to the planets, and to all the host of heaven.
—2 Kings 23:5

Moreover the workers with familiar spirits,
and the wizards, and the images, and the idols,
and all the abominations . . . did Josiah put away
that he might perform the words of the law
. . . found in the house of the LORD.
—2 Kings 23:24

And he did very abominably in following idols, according to all things.
—1 Kings 21:26

And wrought wicked things to provoke the LORD to anger:
For they served idols whereof the LORD said unto them,
Ye shall not do this thing.
—2 Kings 17:11, 12

And worshipped all the host of heaven . . . ,
and used divination and enchantments . . .
to do evil in the sight of the LORD, to provoke him to anger.
—2 Kings 17:16, 17

And the LORD rejected all . . . and afflicted them.
—2 Kings 17:20

Kevin asked if Matt knew the exact meaning of the word *divination,* and Matt said he would look it up in the dictionary. They found that *Webster's Dictionary* said *divination* was *"the art or practice that seeks to foresee or foretell future events or discover hidden knowledge usually by the interpretation of omens or by the aid of supernatural powers."* They began a discussion about how the promises of Feng Shui, gained through the use of symbolism, astrology, numerology, or offsetting and enhancing situations by using the I Ching, fit Webster's definition of *divination.*

Kevin wanted to push on and continue to amass definitive answers to the questions he had about Feng Shui. He respected Matt and said he wanted to have the kind of faith we had. He wanted Mary to find peace. He asked Matt for a verse that would apply to them if they stopped using Feng Shui. They tossed some words back and forth, knowing that the word *sin* was too broad a topic, when Matt suddenly remembered the scripture that used the word *overcomer* and found this:

To him that overcometh will I grant to sit with me in my throne.
—Revelation 3:21

Matt tried to explain to Kevin that God often described an overcomer as someone who had put on a clean robe, or washed his robe and what God promised those who did this:

What are these which are arrayed in white robes? . . .
These are they which came out of great tribulation,
and have washed their robes,
and made them white in the blood of the Lamb.
—Revelation 7:13, 14

And God shall wipe away all tears from their eyes.
—Revelation 7:17

We saw that Mary had tears in her eyes, and when Kevin went to her and took her in his arms, Matt signaled to Kevin that we would go into the kitchen and make some tea while he comforted her. We could hear him telling her how much he loved her and that we all wanted her to be happy and find peace. He said if they would decide to serve God, Mary could find what she needed. Matt and I found ourselves with tears in our eyes too, and we hoped that this was a turning point for Mary to find her way to God so He could truly wipe away her fears and give her His assurances. When the tea was ready and we could hear Mary talking once again to Kevin, we carried the tea tray into the living room.

Mary came to sit between Matt and me and took our hands. She said that she was blessed to have such good friends. She told us that she wanted to learn about God and wanted to leave Feng Shui. She said that she was still afraid and asked if we would continue to help her until she felt stronger, and of course we gladly agreed. She looked at Kevin and told him that she had told me most of her story and why she had so much fear. She explained to Kevin that she told me I could tell Matt her story. Now, she said, she wanted to finish her story because then there would be no more secrets.

Mary told us she had nightmares, sometimes of falling into an abyss from which she would never escape and other times about her child, wondering where she was, if she was safe and happy, or if something terrible had happened to her. She told us of her guilt about not standing up to her parents and trying to keep her child. She told us that although she'd never wanted to give up her child, she felt it was her only recourse and had finally signed the adoption papers. She said she constantly relived the day they came to take her child and could hardly bear the pain of remembering. The memory ate at her, wore her out, kept her from sleeping, kept her at a high-pitched level of anxiety, filled her with guilt and worry, and made her distrustful of everyone. It also made her feel dirty and ashamed and different. Sometimes she even felt hatred for her mother for making her give up her child. She said she struggled with the terrible thought of being glad the dentist died in the car accident and could make no claims on her child, then felt even more guilt because she had such a thought.

Mary told us that after signing the papers, she went back home and was expected to finish school as if nothing happened. She met Kevin a few months after she came home. She was fifteen when she slowly came to trust Kevin as a friend. He never acted like a boyfriend, just someone who seemed to stand near her and look after her. She felt safe with Kevin. He never asked her questions, never commented on how quiet she was, always seemed at ease with the quiet of just being together without talking, yet always able to fill in with chatter when needed. Together, against the rest of the world, they helped one another with their studies, reports, homework, after-school activities, and with the major chore of examining the offers from various colleges they thought they might attend. They didn't need anyone else. Eventually Mary told him her story, and when he simply accepted it telling her not to worry, it would all work out in the end, she felt her heart melt with appreciation for his calm, strength, and support. For the first time since the rape, after telling Kevin she thought that maybe someday she could have a normal life.

Mary let go of Matt's and Sarah's hands and went to sit next to Kevin. Looking at Matt and Sarah, she said, "I've never told Kevin that someday I need to find my child just to know she is okay, and I worry that Kevin will not want me to do this. My nightmares sometimes include pictures in my mind of my child's rejection of me, even her hatred."

Kevin told Mary he had always known she would want to find her child and that she would not do it alone; he would be right beside her. He said that her child, who would *never* reject her, would be his child too. He added that he had always known that God would make this whole circumstance all right someday. Mary sighed with relief, so glad she had no more secrets, had such a wonderful support system, and best of all had acceptance and love despite the circumstances. We all had lumps in our throats and tears ready to spill from our eyes in thankfulness. We knew we sat in a ring of love and felt in this moment that we also sat under the protection of a loving God who would see this situation through . . . and we were humbled . . . and we were grateful.

We told Mary that we too would stand beside her, and that together as brothers and sisters in faith, we would meet all challenges. Mary would never be alone. *"Isn't that what Jesus did with His friends,"* I asked. With Matt and Sarah and Kevin and God all rooting for her and right next to her, Mary felt there was a wonderful future ahead of them all. And I added, "After all, what child could resist loving this incredible, fantastic foursome!"

Matt suggested we all pray about this matter, every morning and every night, and reminded us that there was incredible power in prayer and in establishing a relationship with God. When we have a relationship with God, He gives so much to us because we become His children. Some of the things God promises are these:

Blessed and holy is he that hath part in the first resurrection.
—Revelation 20:6

And God shall wipe away all tears from their eyes;
and there shall be no more death, neither sorrow, nor crying,
neither shall there be any more pain: for the former things are passed away.
—Revelation 21:4

Matt smiled and said we have another promise:

He that overcometh shall inherit all things;
and I will be his God, and he shall be my son.
But the fearful, and unbelieving, and the abominable,
and murderers, and whoremongers, and sorcerers,
and idolaters, and all liars, shall have their part in the lake
which burneth with fire and brimstone: which is the second death.
—Revelation 21:7, 8

Mary asked how we ever came to know all these things, and simultaneously Matt and I answered, "Grandma!" We smiled at one another, and then I remembered the manuscripts and journals I'd wanted to show Kevin. First I showed Kevin and Mary a picture of Grandma, and I reiterated how she asked me to help her write her journal, which I called "When God Broke Grandma's Heart." I explained that through this experience I had come to know God by knowing Grandma. She'd taught me how God carried her through every one of her trials and tribulations and how, when it was time, He brought her out of a terrible relationship in which she had been unequally yoked and into His word so she could begin a new life. She'd taught me that through these tragedies, she finally listened to God and came to understand what was most important in life and how to change her circumstances.

I explained that a year or so after we wrote this journal, Matt lost his brother and we both had to fight for our faith because we couldn't seem to accept that God should or would allow such a tragedy to happen in his brother's life. We were angry with God and needed to understand why He allowed certain things to transpire that seemed so unfair. Remembering Grandma's ways, we decided to study the Bible to find our answers. We did find our answers and ended up writing another journal, which we called "When God Took Grandma Home."

We laughingly told Kevin and Mary about how Grandma chased the spirits by yelling "NO!" every time a thought came to her that she recognized as either from the spirit of fear or another spirit that she knew was not from God. Grandma told us that she yelled "NO!" loud and clear fifty times a day at first, but then eventually those spirits decided to leave her alone. Over time she needed to yell "NO!" a lot less frequently.

We told them that we too yelled "NO" and we'd each laugh when we heard the other yell "NO!" from another room or even when we were walking hand in hand down the street together. We didn't always tell one another what we'd been thinking, but we knew we'd just waged another war and won.

We reminded Kevin and Mary of the story we'd told them about how surprised we were that we so easily fell prey to the spirits of this world when we'd first lost our house. We thought we had our faith down pat and knew right from wrong and would easily stay on the right path, but didn't. Instead, we lost our faith and became angry when we didn't get what we wanted, when we wanted it.

We'd learned that living our faith was a daily ongoing battle because Satan would always want to get us back, break us, so God would lose that one extra person that might have meant He'd reached the number he longed for and could then send His son for them. Mary and Kevin didn't quite understand, so Matt went to the last journal we'd written, *When God Took Grandma Home*, and found the passage that explained God's plan of salvation to show them and started to tell them, in his own words, what it said.

"In the beginning God longed to fill His kingdom with souls who would truly love one another and love His Son and Him as well. He wanted these souls to understand the value of love, trust, and loyalty, and to choose to practice these attributes voluntarily. God began His plan by creating the earth in its limited universe. Then He created Adam and Eve to live happily in the Garden of Eden, walking and talking with Him.

But the angel Lucifer, later known as Satan, rebelled against God because he was jealous of Christ and of the new being, man, that God wanted to bring to fruition. As a result of his rebellion, Satan was thrown to earth with the angels who had followed Satan and disobeyed God. These numbered one-third of all the angels. Satan knew God's plan and that, when it was completed and God had obtained all the faithful loving souls He longed for, Satan would be thrown into hell for what he had done. To prevent God's plan from moving forward and thus forestall his own destruction, Lucifer destroyed God's relationship of trust and loyalty with Adam and Eve by enticing them to sin through disobedience. God then banished Adam and Eve as he had banished Satan.

But God, knowing what Satan would do, provided a way for Adam and Eve, and the generations to follow, to escape the captivity Satan proposed for them and return to God. Christ offered Himself as the perfect sacrifice by which the sins of man could be forgiven.

At every turn, Satan interfered with God's plan, trying to break those who would follow God. But many were strengthened and tested through these attacks, becoming like gold in the fires of Satan. From these God is building what the Bible calls the Bride of Christ.

God even provided for those who died in their sins by creating a means of testimony in eternity while grace is still available on earth. Christ entered hell after His death to give testimony of His triumph to those who had died in their sins before He came so they too could find forgiveness. Since then God asks his faithful to help both those who live and those who died.

God has allotted a certain amount of time for His chosen ones to be made ready, and when that time is up, His son will return to earth for the First Resurrection to take to heaven those from eternity who have obtained forgiveness and those alive who are faithful. When they are gone, grace will also be gone, and the destruction will begin. This will be Armageddon, where Satan will make his last stand against God.

One-third of all the people on earth will die, and when the destruction ends, God will send His son back to earth with those He had taken up before the destruction. They will have resurrected (perfect) bodies and will reign as kings and priests for one thousand years of peace to bring testimony to everyone who ever lived. Satan will be bound during this time, unable to influence mankind.

But after the one thousand years of peace, Satan will be loosed again for a little while so those who have just accepted God can be tried. Satan will wreak havoc on those not firm in their faith. Then will come the Day of Judgment when everyone, except those taken by Christ for the First Resurrection, will be judged. Some, which the Bible calls the "goats," will be cast into hell with Satan forever, while others, called the "lambs," will inhabit God's new kingdom where there will be no sorrow and no tears. Those taken for the First Resurrection will continue to reign as kings and priests in the new kingdom."

Matt reiterated our desire to work toward the completion of God's work here on earth and wait patiently for the return of His son. We pray that those we love will be together again.

> *But if we hope for that we see not,*
> *then do we with patience wait for it.*
>
> —Romans 8:25

Our hearts were filled with contentment and thankfulness. We had worked hard to learn what God wanted to tell us, and now we hoped we knew how to live our life even though we would always be in a battle with the spirits of this world. We wanted to share what we had learned with as many as would listen. Matt laid aside the journal and leaned back on the couch with a sigh, and we all could sense that we had been especially blessed. We were so thankful for what God had shown us during this time together.

"How many people know about the wonderful gifts God gives us, how many understand God's plan for our future, how many know of His unlimited kindness? I wish we could tell everyone, I wish we could help all those who are sad," I said. Matt thought about what I said for a while and then added, "We *will* tell others, maybe not a lot at once, but over time, we will tell everyone we meet, and soon more will know than we thought possible. We'll tell someone, and they will tell someone, and it will blossom!"

For a moment, there was silence in the room. Kevin and Mary didn't speak, and we wondered what they were thinking. Matt and I sat in silence too, waiting for them to speak. Finally, after what seemed such a long time to us, Kevin cleared his throat and quietly said, "Thank you. Without your simple explanation, it would have taken us a lifetime to understand, and here, as you have laid it out, it is so simple, so . . . right."

Then Mary said quietly, "I never knew, I just never understood before. Thank you."

When the awe of the moment and the tug of spiritual understanding we had just experienced sunk in, Matt grabbed my hand, and we kneeled in front of Mary and Kevin and Matt prayed,

Dear Heavenly Father,
Thank you for providing this special moment.
Thank you for this miracle of faith and for letting us share it together.
Thank you for giving us such a special legacy from Grandma that could reach out to so many. Thank you for removing the veil from our eyes that the Bible speaks of.
Thank you for Your incredible love and provision.
Help us to keep this moment ever in our hearts and in our prayers.
And Thank you Father for giving us such wonderful friends with whom we can share our faith.
In Jesus' name we pray.
Amen.

Chapter Twelve

AN EXPERIENCE OF FAITH

Peace
When I asked for help and guidance, God helped me to find
A way to walk and plan my life. He was loving, just and kind.
If I'd continued following the original path I chose,
I know I would have had to walk with even greater woes.
Today my steps are measured and my path is filled with light,
My heart's no longer empty, and my days are sunshine bright.
I work and labor honestly, still seem to have no time,
Yet have a peace within me that is heavenly and sublime.
So stay with me now, Father, keep my footsteps firm,
Help me each and every day to seek your words and learn.
Help me in my own soul and help those I love so much,
Help me share with others your perfect loving touch.

Helen Gumienny Glowacki

Our wedding was fast approaching, and the renovations to the house were moving quickly. The bedrooms, living room, dining room, porch, and hallways were completed. Their woodwork gleamed from a good scrubbing, some light sanding, then staining, and finally three coats of varnish. We'd refinished the beautiful panel doors throughout the house, and Matt and Kevin built closets in the bedrooms after we'd found the right doors for them. We'd gone hunting in a few salvage stores to look for closet doors that would match those in the rest of the house. We hunted high and low and finally found what we wanted, although most of them had been painted. We sent the painted doors out to a professional paint-stripping shop and then stained and varnished them ourselves to match the other woodwork. Matt and Kevin had framed the closet door openings to fit these doors. Thus, the closets looked as if they had always been there, had been built when the house was built.

The three bathrooms and the kitchen had been gutted, the walls spackled and painted, the windows repaired, and the new plumbing was in place. We had already ordered our bathroom and kitchen fixtures, cabinets, and appliances. This had taken a huge chunk out of our budget. Now all we needed to choose were the counter tops. We wanted granite, but first we wanted to see the kitchen progress so we could get a better idea about which color and pattern to choose for the counters.

The remaining walls in the house had been repaired and painted, and we were now ready to have the floors refinished. This was going to be a messy job, and while we realized we'd have some touch-up painting to do after the floors were finished, we felt that getting the basic paint on the walls and the high places needing ladders would be best done first. Matt and Kevin removed all the doors and put them in the garage. Mary and I moved the rest of the items we had accumulated and put these into the garage as well. Matt decided to build some shelves on one of the garage walls and a large workbench while the floors were being refinished and amazed me by completing this project in just one day. Now he felt more organized and could find tools with less effort.

The floor refinishers would take a full week to complete all the floors, so Matt and I had a week off from working on the house until we could enter the house and walk on the finished floors. We planned to devote this time to wedding plans since the wedding was now less than two months away. We needed to reassure our family that we were on target with what we needed to get done. Mary and Kevin agreed to be in our wedding party. We were thrilled about that. They'd already met most of our family members and seemed to fit in perfectly. We felt so blessed to have met them.

Kevin and Mary were coming to church regularly, and it touched our hearts every time we saw them bow their heads in prayer and each time they went up for Holy Communion. We loved our conversations about God and the wonder of His plan for us. Often we joked when Mary would tell us how many times a day she was yelling "NO" out loud "to send those horrid little fear spirits away." We were proud of her for the effort she was making to please God and change her life around.

She and Kevin told us they were praying regularly for their "little" girl and asking God to bring about a meeting between them as soon as she was eighteen. They asked us to pray for this miracle too, and we gladly did. Kevin and Mary were happy; their lives were filled with hope instead of fear and anxiety. One evening, with grins across their faces, they sheepishly told us they were trying to have a baby. Their joy with this decision was evident, and we were happy for them and marveled at the change in their life in such a short time. We were so glad that God gave us such loving friends, ones with whom we could share our faith.

The wind chimes were gone from Mary's entry hall; the bright red front door was refinished and stained a rich dark walnut. The box of coins had been removed from Kevin's desk and the bed placed on another wall, not on the awkward angle recommended by the Feng Shui master. A few other things were removed from the house that had been directly related to Feng Shui, and those that remained were simply items they liked but now attached no special attributes to. One of these items was a lovely fountain in the yard that could be enjoyed from the living-room window. And Mary had proudly shown us how lovely the exquisite trunk Kevin's sister had refinished for them looked in their living room. Kevin simply beamed!

Mary's panic attacks still tried to rear their ugly head, but Mary continued to yell "NO!" in a loud and clear voice, and they would subside for a while. She knew it might take time to rid herself of these attacks, but she knew eventually she would win this battle and beat the spirits that wanted to keep her sad and fearful. Now, because Mary understood what they were and why they did not want to leave her and that God would help her overcome them, her bouts of anxiety no longer took the kind of toll on her health that they had in the past. With the help and advice of her physician, she'd been cutting back on the medications she'd been taking for anxiety and depression and was almost fully weaned now. She felt so much better. Kevin and Mary were even taking the same powdered vitamins three times a day that we took, and this too had a positive impact on how she felt.

We were fully aware, and even discussed the fact, that life would eventually send us another blow and that it would hurt, but now we understood why and who would be the instigator of our pain. We also knew that by putting on the armor of God and trusting Him, we would weather the storms and come out better than we had been when we first began our journey of faith. Together we would remain faithful, support one another in prayer and in fellowship, and come through okay. Once in awhile we would remind ourselves of what that armor was that God spoke about, and we would pull out the Bible and read,

> *Put on the whole armour of God, that ye may be able*
> *to stand against the wiles of the devil.*
>
> —Ephesians 6:11

> *Wherefore take unto you the whole armour of God,*
> *that ye may be able to withstand in the evil day,*
> *and having done all, to stand.*
>
> —Ephesians 6:13

> *The night is far spent, the day is at hand:*
> *let us therefore cast off the works of darkness,*
> *and let us put on the armour of light.*
>
> —Romans 13:12

Mary and Kevin grew in faith and soon understood that this armor came to us through the sacraments of Holy Baptism, Holy Sealing, and Holy Communion that God provided and through the prayer, tithing, fellowship, and trust we contributed. The armor protected the children of God so well that even Satan could not penetrate it unless God allowed Satan this access so God could work it to our benefit! We were so incredibly blessed!

One Sunday after church we made plans to go to our local pancake house then back to my apartment to spend some time together. While we were eating our pancakes (my favorite is called a German pancake which was as big as a plate, curled up on the sides, and served with lemon, butter, and powdered sugar), Mary began to tell us about a thought that kept popping into her head over and over again. She'd tried to stop the thought, she explained, but it kept coming back. She asked if we felt that the reason the thought kept coming was because she was supposed to do something about it. Matt laughed, saying, "Mary, how can we answer that question if we don't know what your thought is"? We were excited and waited to hear what she would tell us.

"Whether I am washing dishes, doing laundry, making the bed, or driving to work," Mary said, "the same thought will pop into my head, and before

I know it I'm daydreaming about the possibilities this thought has opened before me." "What thought?" we asked almost simultaneously. Mary went on to explain that she would envision her little girl, now fourteen years old, smiling and walking toward her with her arms outstretched, as if she wanted to give Mary a hug.

Mary said the exact same picture flashed into her head so many times that she wondered if it had any significance or if it were merely wishful thinking. She explained that at first she'd tried to push away the thought, believing that the timing for such thoughts would be in about four more years when the adoption records could be opened. To think of it now might only bring her disappointment. She said she'd used the "NO!" trick many times for this thought, but it had persisted. Surprisingly, the thought did not make her sad or anxious; it just seemed to be a fact somehow. She said she'd even seen her little girl's face and that she had Mary's coal black hair and blue eyes, but was a little taller than Mary.

Kevin said he was worried about Mary's thoughts, believing that this could be harmful to them and that perhaps it would be better not to think this way. He worried that Mary would develop false hopes and that the disappointment this could bring might inhibit Mary's progress in moving away from her sadness and anxiety.

Matt and I didn't know what to say except that it was important for us to pray about it and ask God to remove the thought if it would be detrimental to them and, conversely, to help them understand the thought if it was something they needed to explore. We also suggested that Kevin and Mary put something extra into the offering box at the back of the church as a thank-you to God for taking care of this problem, but Mary was one step ahead of us and already started to do this. We decided that Mary's thought was something that would have to play itself out over the next few weeks.

We talked of the many new songs the choir had been rehearsing and were now incorporating into their repertoire. Each of us mentioned our favorite songs, and when Kevin tried to hum one of them, Matt laughed and told him that he definitely needed some training and that he himself would help Kevin if he joined the choir. Kevin didn't think he'd be allowed in with his terrible voice, and Matt teased him, telling him not to quit his day job for a singing career. But Mary said, "No, Kevin, with a little training, you can do it. I like your voice and you'd get the hang of it in no time. In fact, let's both join the choir." Kevin was incredulous at first, surprised by Mary's words, then pleased by them. We continued to encourage him, and he began to think that maybe they would enjoy it after all. Matt explained that they need only to attend three Wednesday night rehearsals and then could begin singing with the choir. He added that they could attend even more rehearsals if they felt they needed more before actually singing.

Mary told us she loved so many of the songs and their inspiring words and melodies. "They move my heart," she said. We spoke for a few minutes about how much the songs that the choir presented before service helped us let go of the troubles we had and allowed us to concentrate on the power and love of God. Matt explained that he'd often have a lump in his throat from emotion or tap his foot with joy as we sang because the music and the words reached so deeply into his heart.

The following Wednesday, both Kevin and Mary stayed after service to attend the choir rehearsal and thoroughly enjoyed the bantering, the silly mistakes, and the wonderful triumphs of the group. They were surprised by how much fun we had. The choir director determined that Mary was a soprano and Kevin a tenor. On the way home, we sang in falsetto voices pretending to be opera singers, yet rejoicing in how close the sharing of this experience had brought us and how it supported our faith.

A week and a half later, after the Sunday morning service, Mary met us on the sidewalk after shaking hands with the ministers, and we could see that something had happened. She was white and her hands shook, yet when she smiled, we could see her immense joy. "What happened?" we asked. Mary suggested we go to the pancake house so we could take time to talk, and there she would tell us her story. We couldn't wait to get to the pancake house so we could hear what Mary would say. As soon as we'd ordered, we turned to Mary expectantly, and she began.

"During the past week," she said, "I recalled something about a Bible verse Sarah quoted to me a few months ago, and it was something to the effect that God said we could test Him. I searched for the piece of paper upon which Sarah had written the verses, and when I found it, I was able to locate the particular verse I remembered. It was where God says,

And prove me now herewith,
saith the LORD of hosts, if I will not open you the windows of heaven,
and pour you out for you a blessing that there shall not be room enough to receive it.
—Malachi 3:10

Mary went on to say that she had also seen another verse I'd given her that said,

Call unto me, and I will answer thee,
and show thee great and mighty things.

—Jeremiah 33:3

She told us she read these verses over and over again and began to pray that God would show her what to do, how to find her answers, and what path she was to walk. She reminded Him that He had shown Matt and me what we needed to know after Grandma and Matt's brother died. Matt and I had written in our journal about that experience. Mary asked God to help her that way too. She told us that she'd been not only praying her "regular" prayers but also tried (as we'd told her) to have a real conversation with God about her feelings and hopes and concerns. She explained that she asked God to speak to her somehow and that perhaps, if she would listen carefully to each sermon, she would hear something that could be applied to her circumstance.

Mary and Kevin had been surprised by the fact that the ministers never wrote out their sermon or made an attempt to memorize something to say but prayed that God would speak spontaneously through them and would therefore address the individual and immediate needs the congregants brought to each service. This was why the ministers were always nervous before each service. They didn't know ahead of time what they would say except that it would probably be related to the scripture they read, studied, and prayed over. The ministers often told us they prayed more fervently than we could ever imagine that God would provide what was needed during the service! The Bible told these men of God not to worry about what they would say because God himself would speak through them and they wanted to follow this, knowing it was God's words that had the substance the children of God required, not their own.

Take no thought how or what ye shall speak;
for it shall be given you in that same hour what ye shall speak.
For it is not ye that speak,
but the Spirit of your Father which speaketh in you.

—Matthew 10:19, 20

So Mary prayed her prayer and believed it. When Sunday morning came and the service began, as Mary listened, she felt her heart leap. The scripture that was the basis for the service was

> *For the eyes of the Lord are over the righteous,*
> *and his ears are open unto their prayers.*
>
> —1 Peter 3:12

Mary wondered if this could possibly be God's direct word to her, His way of letting her know he was personally answering her prayers.

There were four ministers in attendance that day, and the first to speak was the district evangelist, who had the responsibility to look after many congregations in the district. He wasn't always at this particular church because he traveled between the various congregations.

He began to speak about the scripture he had read aloud, but after a few minutes, he said that a story about a family from another country kept moving across his heart for some reason. He said that he felt he should tell the story. Mary said she felt her heart leap, for hadn't she just heard Matt and Sarah explain that the ministers should "take no thought" what to speak for, "it is the Spirit of your Father which speaketh in you"?

The minister began to relate the story of a family in Uganda, Africa. He heard the story from another minister who had recently visited that country. "Uganda," he said, "was a country in great turmoil, and politics was a dangerous game to play. Some parts of the country faced great tribulation as supporters of rebel political groups roamed the area seeking those who opposed them. These rebels burned homes and displaced the population of entire villages, killing many.

"There was a little congregation in one of these villages. When a group of rebels came through the village looking for those who disagreed with the politics they supported, they burned the church and many homes and looked for young men who might be dissidents to take as hostages. But the young men were away from the village either hunting, working, or in the fields. The rebels did not take time to look for them and decided to move on to the next village. But they did take a mother and her teenage daughter with them so they would have someone to cook for them while they were traveling from village to village.

"The husband of this woman and their two sons had been working in the fields and did not arrive back in the village until after the band of rebels had left. They were devastated to learn that the mother and daughter had been taken. They gathered the congregation together and began to pray for the mother and the teenage daughter. The father and his two sons were faithful children of God, and as they prayed, God moved their hearts to follow the trail the rebels had taken in the hope of finding their loved ones. They knew that they could rely on the prayers of the entire congregation and that God would bless their success and safe return.

"For days they followed, hot, tired, hungry, and hurting from the concern they had for their loved ones. They continued to pray and trusted God for the outcome. The next day, as they followed the trail the rebels left, they began to trek across an open field and heard a noise. Looking further into the field they saw the mother, lying in a small clearing, unable to walk because of a broken ankle. She had been left to die by the rebels because she was no longer of any use to them. But the rebels had taken the little girl, and the mother's heart was breaking from the cruel separation.

"The sons took the mother home, making a litter of branches and palm leaves with which to carry her. The father continued to follow the rebels. The following day the father caught up to the rebels and watched them from the trees. As the rebels made camp for the night and set up their tents, they also built a fire. The father watched carefully to see if he could locate his daughter. Soon he saw her carrying an armload of kindling to the campfire and beginning to place roots and vegetables into a great pot that had been set above the fire.

"He watched and waited for what seemed an eternity. When the camp was asleep and he'd located the tent his daughter was in, he crept to the rear of the tent and lifted the edge of the canvas opposite to the entrance. Miraculously, where he lifted the edge of the canvas lay his daughter. He touched her hand, laid his finger next to his lips to silence her, and led her from the tent. All night they ran, and by day they rested and gave thanks to God for His help. Finally, they reached their own village. The family was reunited, and they recognized that their success and their reunion was a gift from God."

The minister then said, "I don't know why I told that story, but maybe God was delivering a message to someone here." Then he went on to speak of things pertaining to the day's scripture and the spiritual needs of the congregation. Mary was stunned. She'd asked God for a sign, an experience of faith, a word, a way to keep her hope alive, and He had just given it to her. *Twice!* Her Heavenly Father had first caught her attention by the Bible verse chosen for that day. Mary had felt something move inside her heart when she heard those words. But then the story! God wanted her to be sure that He was speaking to her! That was amazing! Mary knew it was meant for her, meant to tell her she too would be reunited with the daughter who had been taken away from her.

Mary had prayed, asked, tithed, and trusted. God kept His word and provided everything she needed and more. He had given her a miracle, an experience of faith, and Mary couldn't wait to share her experience with us.

We too had heard the Bible verse with which the service began, and we too listened to the story. But we hadn't known that Mary asked God for this word, tithed for it, prayed over it, and believed, so we hadn't made the connection. When Mary told us her story and described how the minister's words related to her request, we were overjoyed to see her trust rewarded, her prayers answered, and her hope renewed, made fresh and strong. Now that we could see the significance of the opening scripture and the story, we were enthralled to be a part of Mary's experience of faith.

We hadn't recognized that the story of the little girl in Uganda related to Mary's daughter at first, but now it was as clear as could be. We marveled. Mary knew she would have to wait, that the adoption papers could not be made public until her little girl was eighteen, but felt that now she would wait with the hope, trust, and calm that only God could have given her.

But Mary's story wasn't yet over. God's bountiful gifts had just begun.

Two weeks later, Mary received a phone call from the adoption agency asking her to come in to talk with them. When Kevin and Mary sat down with the counselor, they learned that their little girl was named Rebecca. She was a happy and wonderfully accomplished young woman who had been raised by loving, caring parents and had remained an only child. Miracle of miracles, Mary's daughter now lived only a thirty-minute drive from Kevin and Mary.

The counselor told them that Rebecca's adoptive father had died two years ago after a yearlong struggle with cancer, and while it had devastated both mother and daughter, they continued on, caring for one another and making plans for Rebecca's future. They moved into what had been their vacation home after the father died and sold their larger home back in the state where Mary had given birth to Rebecca. As the counselor spoke, Mary marveled at the extent and complexity of God's plan to bring Mary in such close proximity to her daughter.

Rebecca had good grades and planned to become a doctor. She desired to give to others the same loving and compassionate care she had seen her father receive during his illness. Rebecca had just finished her sophomore year in high school and had already been accepted by two colleges for premed studies. The counselor told them that both Rebecca's adoptive parents had been a wonderful influence on her and loved her as they would have loved their own natural child. They had faithfully put money aside for Rebecca's education and had been proud of her grades and her many special achievements. To Kevin and Mary's surprise, they also learned that Rebecca, like Mary, liked to paint and was already a wonderful and accomplished artist, winning some awards. A local art gallery had just begun exhibiting and selling her work.

Mary and Kevin asked why the counselor called them to the adoption agency when Rebecca was still only fourteen, as they thought contact could only be made after Rebecca was eighteen. The counselor explained that he did so at the request of Rebecca and her mother and that this meeting was to determine whether or not Mary and Kevin wanted to make contact as well. Mary and Kevin were overjoyed and told the counselor they'd been praying for this and welcomed it with all their heart. When he heard their reaction, the counselor went on to tell them the rest of the story.

Rebecca's mother had recently been diagnosed with a neurological disease called Lou Gehrig's disease or ALS. After many weeks of discussion between mother, daughter, and doctors, and determining the likely progression of the illness, Rebecca and her mother agreed that Rebecca should try to find her birth mother and learn whether or not she could ever have a loving relationship with her. Rebecca's mother hoped her birth mother would be longing to find Rebecca, because when her illness became more difficult, she could rest assured that Rebecca would have a family she could count on.

Mary and Kevin were distressed to think about such a terrible illness. Rebecca and her adoptive mother had to endure not only the loss of a father and husband but now also had the worry of the mother's illness. Mary and Kevin recognized and admired the unselfish act of Rebecca's adoptive mother to allow them this opportunity to know Rebecca and begin a relationship. They decided to always include Rebecca's adoptive mother in all that they did and discussed and make her a part of their family if she would allow it.

Meanwhile, throughout their discussion with the counselor, Mary kept saying to herself, "Thank you, my precious, loving Heavenly Father. Thank you, Father. Thank you, Father." Her heart was bursting with the recognition that God had worked on this problem for years, long before Mary even came into knowing Him. Her eyes filled with grateful tears of joy and thankfulness as she marveled at the wonder of His plan for them, at the wonder of the incredible engineering that had gone into making this moment in time possible!

Mary and Kevin made arrangements to visit Rebecca and her mother the next day. It was a day of joy and thankfulness for all of them. Mary babbled about her prayers and how God had brought them together. Rebecca's mother happily agreed with Mary, saying God works miracles in our lives. She was so happy that Mary and Kevin had that special kind of relationship with God since she raised Rebecca with a strong faith as well. There wasn't a dry eye in the room.

When they were about to leave, Rebecca's mother asked Kevin to pray. Kevin wasn't yet used to doing this, especially in public, but when he met Mary's eyes and saw them shining with love and admiration, he rose to the challenge and surprised himself by not stumbling too badly over his words. Kevin felt good about it too and knew their newly found faith was right for them, that God had led them to everything they needed and more. As he looked at Rebecca, he felt pride to think he was privileged to have such a lovely daughter. Mary's face beamed with joy.

They made arrangements for both Rebecca and her mother to visit them the following week and talked for a few minutes about Matt and Sarah and how wonderful their friendship was, and how much they too looked forward to meeting Rebecca and her mother. Kevin's and Mary's hearts were full. They felt that God had given them all they could ever ask for and much more.

When Mary arrived home that afternoon, she and Kevin prayed in thanksgiving for what God brought them. Later over a cup of tea, Kevin asked Mary what she thought of the idea that they begin plans to renovate the carriage house in the back of the property and create an apartment on the lower level and put Mary's long-awaited art studio on the top level.

Rebecca and her mother could stay in the apartment whenever they visited and could even move in permanently, when Rebecca graduated from high school. "This way," he said, "we could look after Rebecca's mom, and whenever Rebecca could come home from college, she would be with all of us and would know her mom was being well cared for. When our baby arrives, we'd have a ready-made family for him between us, our carriage house occupants, and our wonderful friends and neighbors."

Mary's eyes got bigger and bigger as Kevin spoke. *Had he said "him" when referring to the baby? . . . a family,* she thought, *a real family . . . and an art studio too, for Mary and Rebecca . . . and church . . . they could all go to church together!* Mary knew that only God could have wrought such miracles. She ran to Kevin, threw her arms around him, and rejoiced.

Then as Matt and Sarah taught them, they went to their Bible, and Mary opened it, and the pages fell to Psalm 91. She closed her eyes and pointed to an area on the page and found verse 15 and 16 under her index finger. It read:

> *He shall call upon me, and I will answer him:*
> *I will be with him in trouble; I will deliver him, and honour him.*
> *With long life will I satisfy him, and shew him my salvation.*
> —Psalm 91:15, 16

That week, on Thursday evening, Mary and Kevin were busy with final plans for their weekend guests. Rebecca and her mother were due to arrive in the late afternoon on Friday, and Mary had done everything she could think of to make the guest rooms as inviting as possible. Kevin told her she was like a fluttering little bird checking everything in the house to make sure it would be perfect for their guests! She was so happy that Rebecca and her mother would be coming and spending the entire weekend with them.

Mary was also excited by the prospect that Matt and Sarah would also get to spend some time with Rebecca and her mother. On Saturday, Matt and Sarah would be joining the four of them for an elegant dinner party Mary had painstakingly planned. She'd called Rebecca to learn what everyone's favorite dish was and had prepared everything Rebecca had mentioned! Mary felt as if she had won the lottery. She had so much to look forward to, so much to be grateful for.

Gone were her fears, gone were the Feng Shui symbols of luck, replaced by a growing faith in God and a certainty that He would bring her through all things, good or bad. Her Heavenly Father had become the best friend she'd always longed for. Kevin was happier than she ever remembered him to be. He was so proud of his sister's trunk displayed in the living room and was just thrilled about the new baby . . . a boy, they thought.

And miracle of miracles, Mary had her daughter back and a wonderful new friend in Rebecca's mother. Mary and Rebecca could paint together, shop together, and plan the carriage house apartment and studio together, and they were both so pleased with having found one another after all these years. Rebecca's mother was one of those very special people who loved everyone and gave of herself unselfishly to everyone. She was easily loved in return. She, too, was looking forward to the new baby and had asked Mary if she and Rebecca could shop with them when they began to choose their baby's furnishings. Mary was so excited to think that possibly within two years Rebecca and her mom could be moving into the carriage house and they would be able to share so much.

Kevin and Mary felt that Sarah and Matt had become like a brother and sister to them. They were so grateful for their warm, loving, supportive, and godly friendship. Even more, they were thankful for the example that Sarah and Matt had been to them. What a blessing that they had met someone who cared enough to share their faith with them. Through that, Mary had learned to trust God and to have the wonderful experiences of faith that God had given her. None of this would have happened if Matt and Sarah had not bought the house across the street. Mary marveled at God's wisdom and love.

Now, their lives were so full. They had their faith to develop further and share with others. They could look forward to Matt and Sarah's wedding. They would soon plan the carriage-house renovations. They would watch Sarah and Matt decorate their house with Grandma's wonderful furnishings . . . especially the clocks. They would experience life with a new baby, surrounded by the love of so many wonderful people! Best of all, Mary's fear was gone and so were her nightmares!

Bibliography

The Holy Bible, King James Version, published by The New Apostolic Church, Canada, Thomas Nelson, Inc., Camden, NJ, 1972

James Strong, LLD, STD, *Strong's Exhaustive Concordance of the Bible*, Abington, Nashville, thirty fourth printing 1996, copyright 1890

CIBA Review, *Textiles in Biblical Times*, Basle, Switzerland: CIBA-GEIGY, 1968/2

Henry H. Halley, *Halley's Bible Handbook*, Zondervan Publishing House, Grand Rapids, Michigan, 24 Th edition, Copyright 1965

Henry M. Morris, *Many Infallible Proofs*, Moody Press, Chicago, 3rd printing 1977

Henry M. Morris, *The Bible and Modern Science*, Moody Press, Chicago, 1951, 1968

Donald Grey Barnhouse, *The Invisible War*, Zondervan Publishing House, Grand Rapids, Michigan, 12 Th printing 1976 copyright 1965

Juliet Pegrum, *The Vastu Home*, Ulysses Press, 2002, Berkeley CA, Ducan Baird Publishers London

Kathleen Cox, *Vastu Living, Creating a Home for the Soul*, Marlowe & Company, New York, 2000

Suzanne White, *The New Chinese Astrology*, St. Martin's Press, New York, 1993

Kwan Lau, *The Secrets of Chinese Astrology*, Tengu Books, Trumbull, Connecticut, 4 Th printing, 2001

Carol K. Anthony and Hanna Moog, *I Ching, The Oracle of the Cosmic Way*, I Ching Books, Anthony Publishing Company, Stow, Massachusetts, 2002

Ralph D. Sawyer and Mei-Chun Lee Sawyer, *Ling Ch'i Ching, A Classic Chinese Oracle*, Shambhala Publications, Inc., Boston, Massachusetts, 1995

Wang Bi, translated by Richard John Lynn, *The Classic of Changes, a new translation of the I Ching*, Columbia University Press, New York, 1994

Huston Smith and Phillip Novak, *Buddhism, A Concise Introduction,* HarperCollins, New York, 2003

Kulananda, *Thorsons Principles of Buddhism,* Harper Collins Publishers, 1996

Eva Wong, *Feng Shui, The Ancient Wisdom of Harmonious Living for Modern Times,* Shambhala Publications, Inc., Boston, Massachusetts, 1996

JohnDennis Govert, *Feng Shui, Art and Harmony of Place,* Daikakuji Publications, Phoenix, Arizona, 1993

Websters Dictionary

Scriptural Index

The scriptures used throughout this book have been grouped into the following categories to assist the reader in further study. The first index is to assist the reader in locating these verses by their content, and the second index assists the reader in locating the scriptures by chapter and verse.

- the *Commitment* God asks of us,

- the *Design* and Harmony of God's creation,

- the *Devil,* Satan: his power and influence,

- the *Forgiveness* we need to obtain,

- the *Idolatry* and Divination God hates,

- the *Instruction* God gives to help us,

- the *Power* that is God's alone,

- the *Promises* God makes to us,

- the *Protection* God freely offers,

- the *Refining* process we must endure,

- the *Sinful* nature of all men,

- the *Warnings* God issues to help us.

The *Commitment* God asks of us

As For me and my house	Joshua 24:5	Chapter 3, page 53
For the hearts . . . have grown dull	Acts 28:27	Page 62
For there is no fear of God	Romans 3:18	Page 62
You are stiff necked, resisting Holy Spirit	Acts 7:51	Chapter 8, page 127
Whatever ye do, ye do to me	Matthew 25:40	Chapter 10, page 153
Continue stedfastly in doctrine, fellowship	Acts 2:42	Page 155
Give to prayer, to the ministry of the word	Acts 6:4	Page 204
Preach to the people, testify	Acts 10:42	Page 155
Thy word was unto me rejoicing	Jeremiah 15:16	Page 157

The *Design* and Harmony of God's Creation

Cedar carved with flowers	1 Kings 6:18	Message, page 20
Cherubims of olive tree	1 Kings 6:23	Message, page 20
Cherubims with gold	1 Kings 6:28	Message, page 20
Pomegranates of bronze	Jeremiah 52:22	Message, page 20
Ram skins dyed red	Exodus 26:14, 15	Message, page 20
Lampstand of gold	Exodus 25:31	Message, page 20
Curtains of blue linen	Exodus 20:1	Chapter 3, page 56

The *Devil,* Satan: his powers and influence

Seven other spirits enter and dwell	Matthew 12:45	Chapter 5, 82 & 136
Jesus was tempted, all this I give you	Luke 4:1, 2, 5, 6	Chapter 6, page 95
Lord said Do not lay a hand on his person	Job 1:11, 12	Page 95
You who weakened the nations	Isaiah 14:12-15	Chapter 9, page 132
He is a liar and the father of it	John 8:44	Page 134
The serpent was more cunning	Genesis 3:1	Page 134
There is no truth in him	John 8:44	Page 134
The serpent deceived me	Genesis 3:13	Page 134
Satan deceives the whole world	Revelation 12:9	Page 134
To be tempted by the devil	Matthew 4:1, 3	Page 134
Can move men to do his bidding	1 Chronicles 21:1	Page 134
Walks back and forth on the earth	Job 1:7	Page 134
Can cause illness	Job 2:7	Page 134
Takes God's words from men's hearts	Mark 4:15	Page 134
Enters man	Luke 22:3 & John 13:27	Page 134
Blinds the mind of nonbelievers	2 Corinthians 11:14	Page 134

The *Forgiveness* we need to obtain

The *Idolatry* and Divination, God hates

The *Instruction* God gives to help us

The *Power* that is God's alone

The *Promises* God willingly makes to us

Therefore will not in fear	Psalm 46:1	Message, Page 18
Whatsoever he doeth shall prosper	Psalm 1:1-3	Message, page 18
I will never leave you or forsake you	Hebrews 13:5	Chapter 7, page 100
When you pass through, I will be with you	Isaiah 43:2	Page 100
He will be a refuge and a shelter	Isaiah 32:2	Page 101
I will cover you with My hand	Exodus 33:22	Page 100
Take courage, I have overcome	John 16:33	Page 101
Call to Me and I will answer	Jeremiah 33:3	Page 101
Blessed they that hunger for righteousness	Matthew 5:6	Page 101
Test Me, I will pour out a blessing	Malachi 3:10	Page 102
The days of your mourning will finish	Isaiah 60:20	Page 103
Nothing is too difficult for Thee	Jeremiah 32:17	Page 104
All things for good, those who love God	Romans 8:28	Page 104
Let not your heart be troubled . . . fearful	John 14:27	Page 104
Pour out your heart, God is a refuge	Psalm 62:8	Chapter 8, page 127
Walk with me in white, they are worthy	Revelation 3:4	Chapter 9, page 129
Understand scripture by removing the veil	2 Corinthians 3:14-16	Page 136
Open your understanding of the scriptures	Luke 24:45	Page 136
A gentle, quiet spirit is precious	1 Peter 3:3, 4	Page 141
I will hold thine hand	Isaiah 42:6	Chapter 10, page 147
He that keepeth my words, will I give	Revelation 2:26	Page 156
To him that overcometh, sit in my throne	Revelation 3:21	Chapter 11, page 164
God shall wipe away all tears	Revelation 7:17	Page 165
Blessed and Holy He in the first resurrection	Revelation 20:6	Page 167
God shall wipe away tears, death, sorrow	Revelation 21:4	Page 167

The *Protection* God freely offers

Who put trust in you, You defend	Psalm 5:11	Chapter 5, page 84
The angel encamps . . . and rescues	Psalm 34:7	Chapter 7, page 103
A defense for the helpless, a refuge	Isaiah 25:4	Page 104
Lord is my salvation, whom shall I fear	Psalm 27:1	Page 105
Put on the armour, stand against the devil	Ephesians 6:11	Chapter 12, page 175
Take up the armour, withstand evil	Ephesians 6:13	Page 175
Cast off darkness, put on armour	Romans 13:12	Page 175

The *Refining* process we must endure

The *Sinful* nature of all men

The *Warnings* God issues to help us

Scriptural Index by Chapter and Verse

Matthew 18:14 (he that humbleth himself), *76*

Matthew 6:12 (forgive us our debts, as we forgive), *76*

The idolatry and divination, God hates

1 Corinthians 10:14 (my dearly beloved, flee from idolatry), *162*

1 Corinthians 10:20 (ye should not have fellowships with devils), *162*

1 Kings 21:26 (he did very abominably in following idols), *163*

2 Kings 17:11, 12 (they served idols . . . the LORD said, Ye shall not), *163*

2 Kings 17:16, 17 (worshipped host of heaven . . . used divination), *164*

2 Kings 21:36 (used enchantments, and dealt with familiar spirits and wizards), *132*

2 Kings 23:24 (wizards . . .images . . . idols), *163*

2 Kings 23:5 (he put down the idolatrous priests), *131*

2 Kings 23:5 (put down the idolatrous priests . . . sun . . . moon . . . planets), *163*

Acts 19:19 (Many of them also . . . used curious arts), *61*

Galatians 5:1721 (idolatry . . . shall not inherit the kingdom of God), *163*

Isaiah 47:1114 (evil shall come upon . . . thy sorceries), *130*

Micah 5:12, 13 (I will cut off witchcrafts), *62*

Romans 1:23 (image made like to corruptible man), *131*

Acts 8:11 (he had bewitched them with sorceries), *114*

Revelation 21:7, 8 (sorcerers . . . idolaters . . . liars shall . . . burneth), *167*

The instruction God gives to help us

1 Corinthians 10:1921 (I would not that ye have fellowship with devils), *133*

Acts 2:47 (added to the church . . . as . . . saved), *155*

Acts 20:28 (Take heed . . . to feed the church), *155*

Deuteronomy 8:11 (Beware . . . not keeping his commandments), *113*

Ephesians 4:11, 12 (he gave . . . apostles, . . . prophets, . . . evangelists), *155*

Exodus 20:25 (Thou shalt not bow down . . . nor serve them), *139*

Exodus 20:810 (Remember the Sabbath day), *140*

Galatians 3:5 (doeth he it by the . . . law, or by . . . faith), *97*

John 16:13 (the Spirit . . . will guide you into all truth), *156*

Luke 10:16 (He that heareth you heareth me), *157*

Luke 10:19(what ye speak . . . your Father . . . speaketh), *178*

Micah 4:2 (Come . . . he will teach us of his ways), *104*

Proverbs 24:3 (Through wisdom is an house builded), *124*

Psalm 18:28 (the LORD . . . will enlighten my darkness), *113*

Psalm 25:4, 5 (teach me . . . lead me . . . thou art my salvation), *109*

Revelation 2:11 (let him hear what the Spirit saith), *156*

Revelation 2:29 (He that hath an ear), *156*

Revelation 2:7 (He that hath an ear, let him hear), *155*

Revelation 22:17 (let him that heareth say, Come . . . take), *156*

Excerpt From Book Four

THE GRANDDAUGHTER AND THE MONKEY SWING

It was a few weeks before the wedding, and we'd been scrambling to get the last of the furniture moved from our storage unit to the house and, of course, to finish the last few things that needed to be done on the house. We'd gone over budget in the renovation . . . everyone had told us we would go over budget . . . so we decided to wait until fall to do the landscaping and outside painting.

We were almost finished installing the new kitchen cabinets and knew that the counters were going to be another last-minute rush to get done on time. But at least this was a job for the contractor, not one that we had to complete ourselves. The windows in the eating area had taken us a long time to fix. The kitchen windows had been in bad shape and needed lots of tender loving care to restore, but it had been worth the work. They looked wonderful now, and we hadn't had to go to the tremendous expense of replacing them. We'd had to replace the ropes and pulleys by removing the windows, and we also had to carefully and painstakingly repair and refinish the wood. We also replaced all the window hardware.

In the kitchen work area, we chose to install wide base cabinets with three large full extension drawers rather than the conventional single or double doors most base cabinets have, and they were excellent for storage! No more reaching into the bottom back of a dark recess hoping to find the lost item we needed; just open and there in plain view was everything that we had placed into the drawer. We'd seen these cabinets in a home show and also found them in the kitchen showroom where we purchased our cabinets. We loved how convenient they were for pots and pans, for corning ware and even for small appliances. They required little bending or effort to reach whatever they held.

The cabinets were stained a dark cherry with a slight antiquing effect. We chose traditional cathedral-door top cabinets and with their dark cherry stain, they looked rich and elegant and fit well with the old architecture of the house, the thick dark moldings and hardwood floors. We'd purchased matching cherry stained crown moldings and four beautifully carved corbels for each end of the two beams across the kitchen ceiling. We also purchased two four-drawer sets of little spice drawers that we planned to use to store tea, our stevia and Splenda sugar substitutes, and other "packet" supplies. These were the crowning touch for the kitchen and, while they were expensive, we were thrilled with the way they looked.

We'd already brought some of Grandma's furniture from our storage unit to the house, and with every addition, every delivery, we were amazed at how well each item fit a particular wall or seemed so right for a particular room. There was so much joy attached to every thing we'd kept of Grandma's and my only wish was that she could be here to share in that joy and be a part of our wedding day.

Once in a while, I still felt sad remembering Grandma and my mom and Matt's brother and realized anew that they would not be here to see our home, attend our wedding, or know the children we hoped to have one day. This was heartrending. I'd have to remind myself that God never makes a mistake and that He'd given me an incredible gift in the legacy of their love and their faith, and in His promise that we would see them again someday. But I still needed Matt to reassure me, to remind me that God knew best, and hold me when the tears came.

Our wedding plans seemed under control, although there were lots of last-minute jitters about the bridesmaids' gowns and tuxedo colors since the trim on the gowns were to match the vests of the tuxedos and the tuxedo cummerbunds were to match the waist ribbons on the gowns, and these had somehow been switched. But my sister-in-law was a gem with what I termed the "girly stuff," and I knew she'd have it perfect before the wedding. She was always patient and efficient, willing to make phone calls and follow-up on what was needed to make everything come out the way we'd planned. Barbara was one of the most thoughtful people I'd ever met.

Barbara and Rebecca's mother became inseparable and worked well together on the wedding plans. I was so pleased to see Elizabeth become such an integral part of the family and we were all so proud of her courage and willingness to love everyone. Mary was pleased too.

I was so blessed in my family . . . and in Matt's. My brothers were great guys not only to me, but to Matt as well, and they all got along well. Matt's sister and I felt like real sisters, and she had welcomed me into the family with open arms. I genuinely liked Matt's entire family.

Everyone had taken on a chore or two for the wedding, and this had allowed Matt and me to keep our attention focused on the renovation of our house. We were incredibly busy but felt incredibly cared for!

Matt's sister never missed sending me a nice "mushy" birthday card, which I *loved*, and never missed calling or visiting on a regular basis. She had been a real blessing during this wildly busy period of our lives and pitched in with any chore where we needed help. Her husband, Matt's brother-in-law Jim, was the family comedian, and we all loved to listen to his political banter and his observations about each of us when we seemed too engrossed in mundane matters. He loved to play devil's advocate, and we often found ourselves in hot political debate. He could be sarcastic but never seemed to cross the line from funny to offensive.

My two brothers loved Matt and often told me that I'd made a great choice! Whenever I'd get mad at Matt, and this seldom happened *of course,* they'd come to me and tell me to make up with him because he was such a gem. And I usually agreed with them! I was glad that everyone truly liked one another. It made me feel good and gave all of us the incentive to spend time with one another. We were all hard workers, we all loved having "family," and we all had similar values, which made for a perfect friendship even outside of the family ties.

Our new neighbors, Kevin and Mary, were also just the greatest people. We teased one another about becoming good friends amidst pieces of wood lath, old plaster mixed with horsehair, plaster dust, Sheetrock, Dagwood sandwiches, and old oak moldings. They too were to be in our wedding party, bringing the number of bridesmaids and groomsmen to four couples.

Mary's gown had to be adjusted a few times to accommodate the new baby scheduled to arrive a month after our wedding.

Fourteen-year-old Rebecca, Mary and Kevin's daughter, would be our flower girl. She was thrilled with the prospect of being in the wedding and so happy to have, as she put it, "discovered a whole new family" when she and Mary met after so many years apart. We were glad that Elizabeth, Rebecca's adoptive mother, (a truly remarkable woman), would also be at the wedding to help Barbara with last minute problems, and planned to stay at Kevin and Mary's house for the entire wedding weekend. We were thrilled to have met her and gotten to know what a special and brave and unselfish woman she is. Her illness had shown us what true courage and faith can do.

My younger brother who was not yet married would also be in the wedding party. He was the actor in our family, always ready to imitate a rock star, a famous dancer, a comedian, or even a female runway model. He really made us laugh. We called him the "chameleon" because he could change into any personality we called for! He was a hard worker, almost compulsive in wanting to get things done and in keeping things neat and organized. We could all learn from him, but he could also be a slave driver! The best part of his personality is that he was always cheerful.

He had recently become engaged to a very pretty girl, and she was doing her best to get used to our rambunctious, religious, close-knit family. But the relationship was not going as well as we had hoped, and only time would tell what would happen. The wedding plans were made, and my brother's fiancé was also to be in the wedding party. So far, we had been keeping our to-do lists under control.

The wedding party would consist of (1) my older brother Caleb, who would be Matt's best man, and his wife, (2) Matt's sister Barbara who would be my maid of honor, and her husband, (3) Our new neighbors, Kevin and Mary, (4) My younger brother Joshua and his fiance Debbie, and (5) Mary's daughter Rebecca would be our flower girl. Elizabeth would act as my surrogate mother since my mom and Grandma could not be at the wedding. Everything seemed ready and on schedule, and while it was a large wedding party, it was made up of special people we loved. We looked forward to receiving the special blessing attached to the marriage sacrament. We were very excited to imagine that day, and it was almost here!

But as the days moved closer to the actual wedding day and all kinds of last-minute decisions had to be made, strange things began to happen. Things that made no sense and made us wonder what or who was instigating all this trouble. We began a quest to solve the mystery of why these odd occurrences had begun. We wanted answers before the wedding. We wanted everything to be perfect, and right now they were not. Something was afoot.

As we tried to unravel what was happening, in time we began to focus on my younger brother and his fiancé. Through Elizabeth's friend John we discovered that they were both struggling with a serious heartache that they were not sharing with us, nor with one another, and we wanted to help.

About The Author

Helen Gumienny Glowacki is an interior designer, writer, teacher, and motivational speaker. She was the host, writer, and producer of the television series *The Contemporary Woman*, broadcast by UA-Columbia Cablevision, which addressed interior design and the health, relationship, parenting, and life issues of interest to women.

Helen also co-hosted a number of twenty-four-hour telethons featuring celebrity guests to raise funds for various community projects and was a guest co-host for a cable television game show.

Helen's writing credentials include an extensive background as a freelance feature writer and a staff writer for four newspapers; author of newsletter articles; developer of marketing manuals, most notably for the INOVA Hospital System; and designer and editor of a newsletter for the Martin/St. Lucie Chapter of the United States Amateur Ballroom Dancers Association.

A graduate of William Paterson University, Helen received her Bachelor of Arts degree in communications, magna cum laude. Helen also has an associate of science degree with honors and is a registered nurse. She has served on the boards of directors for two associations and taught interior design for adult school programs. Some of her larger design projects include Avon Headquarters in Morton Grove, Illinois, and Chilton Hospital in Pequannock, New Jersey and was listed in *Who's Who of American Women* and *Who's Who of Women Executives* in 1992.

As a popular speaker at ease with an audience, Helen addresses aspects of interior design and addresses the work of God and His word through scripture. Her venues have included women's groups, church groups, community service and religious organizations, high schools and colleges, libraries, cruise ships, and large adult—and assisted-living condominium complexes.

Helen appeared as a guest on a radio show and performed dance routines for theater groups, television, army camps, and veteran's hospitals. She held the title Mrs. Packanack Lake for five years and has received a number of community service awards.

Helen has donated her *"Grandmother Series"* novels and her *"Why God Why Series"* of non-fiction books to cancer centers, drug and alcohol rehabilitation centers, prisons and mission schools, most notably to *The Henwood Foundation* in Zambia, Africa to bring testimony. She also posts articles on her Facebook wall which address our relationship with God,

Helens greatest joys are her husband, two children, and four grandchildren, and singing in the choir of the New Apostolic Church. She and her husband enjoy ballroom dancing and have performed for various charitable functions. Her heart's desire is to help others find the love and comforting presence of God through her writing.

To learn more about Helen's novels and her non-fiction books, visit her website at www.helenglowacki.com.

To become a distributor or to purchase in quantity for a fund raising project or to provide testimony, please send an email to helen@helenglowacki.com.

Helen's readers can also visit the author on Face Book at http://www.facebook.com/pages/The-Grandmother-Series/155300907853909?ref=ts.

Novels (Book Size 6 x 9)

by Helen Glowacki

When God Broke Grandma's Heart: (208 pages) Rising from sorrow to become a beacon of faith   Grandma struggles in an abusive marriage until God moves her from unequally yoked and broken to the healing of His love and forgiveness. Her granddaughter Sarah learns where to find answers to her problems and carries that legacy to those she loves.   **Paperback: ISBN 978-1-9847-2110-8**

When God Took Grandma Home: (268 pages) About the heartache of drug addiction, of the enemy who destroys children through drugs, why God allows righteous anger, why we should pray for those in eternity and a description an incredible experience of faith for Matt and Sarah about why God allowed such heartache to occur.
Paperback: ISBN 978-1-9847-2111-5

When Grandma Chased the Spirits: (216 Pages) The magnetism of idolatry, it's invisible power, and the heartache of bearing a child out of wedlock brings debilitating panic attacks to Mary and affects her husband Kevin. When Matt and Sarah tell them about their faith, God engineers a miracle to solve what that they thought impossible to resolve. **Paperback: ISBN 978-1-0847-2112-2**

The Granddaughter and the Monkey Swing: (292 pages) A wedding, a broken engagement, renovating and decorating a home through Divine Proportion, the truth about Halloween, and the gift of role models create a tender story of friendship. Helping through the planning and problems of a wedding culminates in the unveiling of a secret. **Paperback: ISBN 978-1-9847-211309**

Grandma's Little Book of Poetry: The Story of God's Plan of Salvation: (285 pages) This beautiful whimsical story for all ages, begins when Sarah finds a manuscript in Grandma's desk and recognizes the story Grandma read to her and Josh and Caleb when they were children. Angels watch the inhabitants below them struggle to find God. **Paperback: ISBN 978-1-9847-2114-6**

Abiding Faith, Hidden Treasure: (270 pages) Serving in Iraq, Jim loses his faith to see a loving God allow so much heartache. Barbara invites him to dinner where Grandma shows him why creation and evolution co-exist and God's enemy creates the injustices Jim blames on God. Letters from the grave bring an incredible experience of faith. **Paperback: ISBN 978-1-9847-2115-3**

And Then They Asked God: (295 Pages) When Rebecca and Jayden arrive at their college campus they are overwhelmed by betrayal. Losing the values Rebecca once cherished fills her with guilt so monumental that she cannot forgive herself. Chaldeth the evil angel is defeated when God's grace frees Jayden and brings Rebecca's recovery. **Paperback: ISBN 978-1-9847-2116-0**

Non-Fiction Books (5 ½ x 8)

by Helen Glowacki

A Politically Incorrect Bible Study: The Get Some Gumption Handbook when Enough is Enough: (297 pages) Fifty timely and controversial issues are examined under the politically correct approach along with a description of what scripture says is the approach that He wants his children to take. **Paperback: ISBN 978-1-4507-9074-1**

The Many Faces o Depression: How To Be Happy: (220 pages) We all face heartache, and all feel sad from time to time. But depression comes from a satanic attack that robs us of hope and our relationship with God. Thus our Heavenly Father tells us through scripture how we can tap into His blessing and find joy even in tribulation. **Paperback: ISBN 978-1-4507-9077-2**

What No One Tells You About Addictions: (220 Pages) Discussing the merits of tough love, the selfish co-dependency of the enabler, what scripture tells us about spiritual warfare and invasion, and generational sin, make this book a must read. **Paperback: ISBN 978-1- 4507--9075-8**

To What Purpose?: (126 pages) The first book of the *Why God Why* series is written to provide answers to questions about why we are here and what we need to learn. It is

written in an easy to read and easy to understand manner and one you will want to share.
Paperback: ISBN 978-1-4507-7580-9

Why God, Why?: (126 pages) This second book in the *Why God Why* Series describes why we experience heartache, its purpose, and how to face it. It answers questions about God's plan for us and what we need to do to be found worthy. **Paperback: ISBN 978-1-4507-7581-6**

Why Trust Scripture?: (126 pages) This third book in the *Why God, Why* Series addresses the challenges against scripture, who wrote the Bible, the importance of the sacraments, what role Satan plays, and how health and the Bible are related. **Paperback: ISBN 978-1-4507-7582-3**

What Should I Know about Life after Death and the Coming Tribulation?: (126 pages) What occurs following death, what will happen during the tribulation, and what the seven seals could mean to us are explained in this fourth book of the series. **Paperback: ISBN 978-1-4507-7583-0**

What Does God Want Me to do Right Now?: (126 pages) A concise explanation of what God asks of us, how we can live up to His expectations what is required to become a part of the Bride of Christ, and what God plans for the future with or without us. **Paperback: ISBN 978-1 4507-9076-5**

Do The Little Sins REALLY Count?: (126 pages) Most of us believe that the little sins we commit each day are not important on the grander scale, but what does scripture tell us? And interesting look at the Bride of Christ. **Paperback: ISBN 978-9847-2117-7**

Book Reviews

Rev. Richard C. Freund, President, New Apostolic Church USA, Sea Cliff, New York: Magnificent writer, a story that makes the reader become emotionally involved, a joy to read, strong Christian values. *"When God Broke Grandma's Heart",* best seller quality.

Rev. Fred Krueger, (Ret.) Lutheran Minister 12 yrs and Clinical Social Worker 26 yrs, Dallas, Texas: "Inspiring, grabs the heart, author headed to the bestseller list, a pleasure to read, masterful. *"When God Took Grandma Home"* filled with insight into God's plan!

Rev. Richard C. Freund, President, New Apostolic Church USA, Sea Cliff, New York: *"When God Took Grandma Home"* "Delights, brings comfort to those who grieve. Inspires, gives insight into the after-life, masterful portrayal.

Priest Derryck Beukes, Montana-De Aar Congregation, Northern Cape, South Africa: Dear Helen, I personally often use your articles in my soul care visits, especially where youth are involved. I can assure you that your articles made a difference to my way of thinking, and I am busy encouraging fellow priests to read your works, as they are so factual and insightful! Thank you for your hard work. II thank God for you, and the wisdom He gave you! Please continue with the excellent work.

Deacon Shadreck Wilima, Overspill Congregation, Ndola, Zambia: Your articles prompt realistic examples which New Apostolic Christians need for their everyday living.

<u>Youth Chairperson, Sunday School teacher, Mulenga Ernest, Lusaka Central Congregation, Lusaka, Zambia</u>: Through your writing I am constantly reminded of what to be aware of. I pray that God keeps you in the hollow of His hand, guards you and guides you to reach your brethren as you do me. Thanks for caring for the souls of many.

<u>Priest Aurelio Cerullo, Atripalda Congregation, Campania, Southern Italy:</u> Your books and articles, and even your social networking are a means to bring brothers and sisters the words of our faith and to touch the hearts of those who do not know our faith. Our goal can still be found through the grace of the apostolate and in this sense, the word's from 1 Corinthians 15:58 assumes an important meaning: *"Therefore, my beloved brethren, be steadfast, immovable, always abounding in the work of the Lord, Knowing That your labor is not in vain in the Lord".* Now that I am a minister of God for about a year I too am grateful to our beloved Father in Heaven for having opened the eyes of my soul, for having removed the plugs from my ears of my heart to hear and listen to His will in connection and communion with those who precede us, guided by the light of the Holy Spirit. God's work always evolves and adapts to the times and even via computers, cell phones and smart phones. I Thank God for having been able to know you, you're a very valuable pearl. God bless you richly.

<u>NOTE:</u> The articles which are referred to in these reviews are excerpts from Helen Glowacki's non-fiction books. Not shown are reviews by the ministers who oversee *The Henwood Foundation*'s New Apostolic Mission Schools in Zambia and review all reading materials prior to distribution.

Priest Andrew Muliokela, Alexandria Virginia congregation: *The Granddaughter and the Monkey Swing* and this series of books is awesome! A journey unlike another, read a great novel, learn about confidence, love and support but also learning Bible verses at the same time! Helen Glowacki teaches through her books and I recommend them 100%. You'll enjoy the journey!

Priest Kevin Speranza, Palm Beach Gardens Congregation, Florida: *And Then They Asked God* so happy I read this, weaves and documents biblical precepts, addresses political correctness, moral & political corruption, biased teaching, the insidious growth of socialism renamed progressivism, self-importance, guilt and its debilitating power. WELL DONE! Identifies danger, artfully shows Biblically how to address them.

Frederick Rothe, Retired NAC Minister, Fort Pierce, Florida: Retired minister spending 48 years serving God another 30 in the congregation. These books contain an accurate account of what God wants of us, why we suffer. The application of scripture and the people in the stories stand for the principles God wants in all of us.

Patricia Robinson, wife of a Ret. Rector, Indiana 5 star rating: *When God Broke Grandma's Heart*: WONDERFUL INSPIRATIONAL NOVEL, enjoyed this book, well written, Bible references , how to achieve peace of mind and soul .

Colette van Loggerenberg, wife of a Priest, Scottsville Congregation of Pietermaritzberg, South Africa: *Grandma's Little Book of Poetry: The Story of God's Plan of Salvation:* This has to be one of the BEST EVER books that I have read....If you ever get the chance to get one of Helen's novels...READ IT. It's like a fairytale but a TRUE fairytale.....Close your eyes and picture this: Grandma with her hair in a bun, glasses perched delicately on her nose, sitting delicately on her nose, sitting in a rockying chair with her grandchildren sitting on the floor with BIG eyes hanging onto her every word.....but with a twist!!!!! If you have doubts about PRAYERS...read this book. I LOVED IT...thank you Helen Glowacki in a rocking chair and her grandchildren sitting on the floor with BIG eyes hanging onto her every word.....but with a twist!!!!! If you have doubts about PRAYER...read this book. I LOVED IT...thank you!

Debbie Espeland, wife of a Rector, Palm Beach Gardens Congregation, Florida: 5 star rating: **When God Took Grandma Home** is so HEARTWARMING! This book touched my heart. It is both heartwarming and very spiritual.

Aletta Venter, wife of a Deacon, Scottsville Congregation, Pietermaritzburg, South Africa: *"Grandma's Little Book of Poetry: The Story of God's Plan of Salvation".* What a learning process for me. Oooh I just **love** the way the angels are telling the story, **very original!** When is mankind ever going to learn? The inhabitant's lesson was to learn of good and evil. And they failed miserably each time. The devil has his agenda, and the inhabitants are the target. They call upon God for help, the angels rejoiced. Great....!!!

Priest Luke Jansen, Sr. V. P., Medical Connections, Boca Raton, Florida: "To Ms. Glowacki, author of **The Grandma Series**: grateful for your books, refreshing to find a Christian author who sees the *difference* between religion and spirituality AND that the two can and should be used in the same sentence."

Aletta Venter, wife of a Deacon, Pietermaritzburg, South Africa: *"Abiding Faith, Hidden Treasure"* is the deepest and most rewarding novel I have ever read, touched my soul, made me cry, author's understanding of God's work is astounding, opens the mysteries

Katharina Leipp, Schopfheim, Germany: This is the first time I have ever heard of a female New Apostolic author and I am very impressed by your articles. I have sent your link to my Shepherd and German friends and would like you to consider advertising in our German *Our Family Magazine.*

Rosemarie Schaal, wife of a retired Evangelist, Palm City, Florida: *Abiding Faith, Hidden Treasure:* Reader develops empathy, feels emotion, hears a battle between scientific and spiritual knowledge. Skillful, detailed, brilliant, vivid, teaches nothing happens that is not planned by Him.

Claudine Visagie, South Africa: I'm trying to think of a way to introduce Helen's books and articles to others... especially to our youth. They are life changing!

Rabecca Mukuta Mukato, Lusaka, Zambia, Africa: Speaking on behalf of my Dad, District Elder Mulako, your articles are brilliant because they have changed me! Because of your articles my Dad has less headaches!

Edith Stier, 32 Years as the wife of a Minister, (Ret. Dist. Ev), Clifton, New Jersey: *The Grandma Series* helps those in need, inspirational, heartwarming, ends with a beautiful example of how God explains our pain, renews hope, shows us the way, creates miracles. I love this series.

Tammera Shelton, M.S. Psychology, Odenton, Maryland: I find *"When God Broke Grandma's Heart"* inspirational, beautifully portrays need to let go of negative events and that despite injustice, no pain is for naught.

Robert W. Rothe, USMC 1970-1976, Nevada: 5 star rating: *When God Broke Grandma's Heart:* Outstanding writer, kept me riveted, an angel sent to help through trying days. Thank you for helping me find peace.

Frank Geores, from Port St. Lucie, Florida: *"When Grandma Chased The Spirits:* beautiful spiritual experience, can see caring nature and loving heart of author, eloquently reveals her love for God and search for truth. Worthy of the Star of Bethlehem rating. Thank you for sharing your magnificent gift.

Ben Lodwick, Avid Reader., from Brookfield, Wisconsin: Wow! An eye opener about God's plan of salvation, and why bad things happen to good people. Reminds me of Jim LaHaye and Jerry B. Jenkins "Left Behind Series". MUST READ!"

Dr. Walter Forman From North Palm Beach, Florida: *Grandma's Little Book of Poetry: The Story of God's Plan of Salvation:* a "wonderful book about success and failure in life. All Helen's novels are wonderful, a balm for the soul and an education to the seeker."

Susan Day, From Jupiter, Florida: *Abiding Faith, Hidden Treasure* : I hated to put it down, couldn't wait to pick it up, read all Helen's books, proves every point, shows what to do through God's words. I am 90 and Helen's books have helped me call on God.

Georgette Rothe, From Fort Piece, Florida: *Abiding Faith, Hidden Treasure* was more than I expected, like a Biblical course making you re-evaluate your beliefs, enjoyed the journey very much.

Fred D'Alauro, from Palm Beach Shores, Florida: Internet 5 star rating: **When God Took Grandma Home:** Remarkable! Inspirational and moving. A fascinating storyteller with a real message.

Debra Forman, Chester, New York. Internet 5 star rating: *When God Broke Grandma's Heart:* Written from the heart, shares the strong beliefs that shelters us in times of need, courage captivates the reader. Thank you.

Anonymous: Internet 5 star rating: *When God Broke Grandma's Heart:* WHEN LIFE GETS YOU DOWN, PICK THIS BOOK UP, it wrapped its arms around me. A wonderful read. Congratulations on an inspiring work.

A reviewer, a reader in Kentucky: Internet 5 star rating: *When God Broke Grandma's Heart:* Well written, heartwarming, overcoming heartbreak through God, touches your heart. A worthwhile read for all generations.

A reader: Internet 5 star rating: *When God Broke Grandma's Heart:* a must read for all generations. FANTASTIC!

A reviewer Internet 5 star rating: *When God Took Grandma Home:* Moves you, captivating.

A reviewer, a Kentucky reader: Internet 5 star rating: *When God Took Grandma Home:* MUST READ! Touching story of life's tragedies and how lessons learned from these heartbreaking events can turn into blessings.

Novel Characters

Grandma: Grandma's life was filled with sibling betrayal and marital abuse. Her love of God, home remedies and famous boxing stance touches the heart.

Sarah: Sarah helps Grandma write her journal, learns about God's plan of salvation and the enemy who wants to harm her. She carries on Grandma's legacy of faith.

Matt: Matt, Sarah's husband, has a rock-like faith but when he loses a loved one, struggles with his anger with God, until he has a miraculous experience of faith.

Paul: Paul is Matt's older brother who earned a Captain's license for a seagoing tugboat. His faith sustains him despite enduring terrible circumstances.

Mary and Kevin: Mary and Kevin become Matt and Sarah's neighbors and friends. Mary's panic attacks end when God brings a miracle they never thought possible.

Elizabeth: Elizabeth adopts Rebecca, loses her husband twelve years later, is confronted with a potentially deadly illness and searches for Rebecca's birth mother.

Rebecca: Rebecca is Elizabeth daughter and Jayden's friend. Her father's death, the illness her mother faces, and a series of challenges at college almost destroy her.

John: John, a deacon, lost his wife to a debilitating disease, becomes Elizabeth's friend, and helps his daughter and grandson through a difficult divorce.

Jayden: Jayden is John's grandson and becomes Rebecca's friend. He has learned that prayer helps solve problems and he and Rebecca begin to share their faith.

Wade and Ruth: Wade is Jim's boss and friend who adopts two children from Iraq. Ruth is Jayden's mother and John's daughter who struggles to let go of the past.

Joshua and Debbie: Joshua, Sarah's younger brother, was demanding and judgmental until Caleb stepped in. Debbie looks to Joshua's family to be her role models.

Caleb and Ann: Caleb is Sarah and Josh's older brother and the family looks to him as they once looked to Grandma. Ann, Caleb's wife harbors a secret sadness.

Barbara and Jim: Barbara, Matt's sister is also Sarah's close friend. Her husband Jim plays devil's advocate in family debates, and matchmaker for his friend Wade.

Heza and Bara: Heza and Bara endured a suicide bomber attack when Bara was one and one half years old and Heza as she was born. They are adopted by Wade.

Chaldeth: Chaldeth is a fallen angel sent to destroy Grandma's family. He plots to bring great heartache to Rebecca and Jayden and their family to break their faith.

Durk: Durk, abused by a cruel father, is a sophomore at the college Rebecca and Jayden attend. He brings great harm to Rebecca and Jayden but Jim gives him a second chance and Jayden and Rebecca offer him forgiveness.

Professsor T. Nagorra, and Emils, and Dean Peerca: These tenured professors befriend Durk and engage in activities which brings harm to the students and the campus.

Professors Doog and Sendnik, and President Legna: These three share a faith in God, a love for their country, and desire to be role models. They help save the campus.

www.ingramcontent.com/pod-product-compliance
Lightning Source LLC
Chambersburg PA
CBHW031109260626
47172CB00001B/286